Sush

32 stories about Hunger

To Susan

With love

Roly

Published by
Freight
49–53 Virginia Street
Glasgow
G1 1TS

ISBN 978-0-9544024-6-4
First published 2010

A CIP catalogue record for this book is available from The British Library

Typeset in Garamond. Printed by Lewis Printers, Ceredigion, Wales.

Sushirexia

32 stories about Hunger

Edited by Gordon Jenkins, Robert Smith
and John Dingwall

Published by Freight, Glasgow

Contents

Sushirexia

Preface

So this is the preface. This is where we're supposed to give you an insight into the editing process that shaped this anthology, together with a couple of well chosen anecdotes. Ideally, these should highlight our grit and determination in the face of editorial adversity but, above all, they must be amusing.

Unfortunately for you, dear reader, nothing particularly amusing occurred. This was a terrible shame because a year is a long time without at least a bit of a laugh. As for editorial adversity, the process was straightforward. Of course, our main aim was to define and publish a clear editorial process to ensure we maintained the Glasgow University tradition of excellence: you must decide if we succeeded in this or not.

With a tentative process in place, we racked our brains for an inspiring theme (not as much fun as it sounds, even when parrying feints and thrusts from the mysterious Cyrano.) Hunger emerged in a flash of inspiration from John's fevered mind: the poor man's never been the same since.

We sweated for two months over the lack of submissions, which, in true student style, all arrived on the closing date. We developed a fiendishly complicated review process based on a blind distribution and scoring system (worth a Masters in Combinatorial Mathematics but not in Creative Writing we fear.) After much toil and deliberation, and more months than we originally planned, we accepted these thirty two stories which we hope you will enjoy reading.

Presumably, all the fun stuff will come later. Mind you Adrian Searle, our publisher from Freight, has warned us that this is where the hard work starts. Oh, well…

Our tutors - Michael Schmidt, Elizabeth Reeder, Zoe Strachan, Laura Marney and Kei Miller deserve a special vote of thanks for their nurturing and encouragement in workshops and classes throughout the year. Joyce

Ito and Sarah Ward deserve particular praise for taking time from their own project to join us in making the selection and editorial decisions. Wendy Burt and Nikki Axford, the Departmental Administrators, helped enormously in assisting with the submission process. We are grateful too to Jackie Copleton for allowing us to borrow the title of her story for the collection as a whole, and to Nick Brooks for supplying words of encouragement. We would not have got this far without Adrian at Freight and we thank him for all his efforts.

This anthology represents the efforts of a diverse set of writers registered for the M.Litt in Creative Writing at the University of Glasgow during the academic session 2008-2009: both full time and part time students. Many originate from Scotland or other parts of the UK. Due to the international reputation of its teachers and successes of past graduates, the course also attracts many from overseas who endure the physical grief of a Glasgow winter and damp of summer to experience the warmth and inspiration the course affords. This session we were joined for the first time by Distance Learners as far afield as the Caribbean and their input is appreciated. We thank all who contributed work and trust you enjoy the fruits of their labours.

John Dingwall
Gordon Jenkins
Rob Smith

Foreword

Nick Brooks

It has been eight years since I graduated from Glasgow University's Creative Writing MLitt. Eight years since I became – for better or worse – an occasional professional author. I say 'professional' but one of the things I learned on that course, along with much besides, was that you're only really a professional so long as there is money coming in for your work. Otherwise, like it or not, you are an amateur. I don't mean this as a dismissal of any penniless scribes out there (or in here), far from it. I include myself among that happy race. Publication and money aren't the only reasons to write. In most cases, they aren't even that. It's just that many writers value their success purely in terms of publication and its rewards - or otherwise.

At the turn of the millennium, as a beginning writer and recent university graduate, publication wasn't even on my horizon, and money had to be begged and borrowed just to take a place on the course. But I genuinely felt that there was no other place in the world for me right at that moment. If I hadn't been offered a place I might have continued and found my own way. It would have taken a great deal longer however, than it did for me, I have no doubt at all. It was through my time as a student on the course that I felt my own work began to reach a kind of simmer, and I had to struggle hard to keep it bubbling – and to prevent it from boiling over. But this is a constant struggle for any writer. Where the course really helped was in allowing me to enter a busy kitchen full of talented amateurs, all of them trying to keep their own pots bubbling. There was a sense of shared urgency and competition that spurred myself and others on to try harder, to write better. Because there is nothing better in the world, no better place to be than the beginning of something you have found that you love. And I loved writing and wanted to be good at it. That's still my main aim: to be good at writing and to get better at it.

Yet, critics of creative writing courses are wont to forget the importance of the crucible such courses provide: writers are attempting to forge their own identities as authors and are themselves forged in the doing. The academic and creative demands of the course itself ensure this process in a way that solitary authors rarely experience: there is no one standing over the lone writer demanding a tighter sentence structure, a workable metaphor, a lucid opening, a joke that's funny. Both peer review and one-to-one close reading with a tutor always ensure that an aspiring writer knows where he or she stands: a beginning writer has to trust solely in their own judgement, and that is not always guaranteed to be wholly reliable. Critical processes, like creative ones, are honed over time and with practice, but a creative writing course can, at best, offer an understanding of what good practice is. Work that is written is not simply sent to a single editor to censure or praise: there are no editors for a beginner. Only professionals have editors. There is, in the first instance, only the writing. There is no audience either: but the context of a creative writing course provides one for the writer who seeks that sort of challenge. On a creative writing course, writing can be 'pressure tested' in front of not-always-sympathetic peers. This is a process I found invaluable. The opportunity to face regular, often harsh and uncomfortable criticism of the kind offered by peer readings cannot be understated. My own first experience of reading my work aloud was terrifying, but revelatory. What worked and what didn't; what engaged and what fell flat... live reading in front of other writers allowed me to pressure-test my writing, to gauge its effect, to give what was intended primarily for the page the chance to prove itself to someone other than just myself. It moulded the way I thought about writing, particularly writing for an audience. I don't mean simply for performance: that's a discipline that makes its own very specific demands. What I mean is to understand what people will and will not respond to in a piece of writing, whether reading privately or listening to someone else perform extracts from their own works. Of course, writers are always telling you that they only write for themselves. But I've yet to meet one. And you won't either. JD Salinger has sadly passed away now, and he was the only one I've heard of. All writers who seek publication are seeking an audience, however small. It's that simple. Writers of poetry may exclude themselves from this summation by default.

None of us beginners are born: we are made. The crucible of Glasgow's MLitt is where it all began for me. I am certain that if it hadn't been for my tutorials with punmeister general Prof Willy Maley, as well as all the conversations, arguments, drunken evenings and shaky afternoon seminars with everyone who studied on the course at the same time as myself, then I would be a poorer writer and a poorer person for the lack. Much of the company that year went on to bigger and better things. Many of us still keep in touch and get together to talk about writing over a drink. A few of us became occasional professionals, and others still found fame, prizes, glory, and money. Though not so many of the latter: it's a precarious business, writing. It is always a challenge to keep going with time, work, families, and of course the ever present pressure of finance.

Around about this time of year, some eight years back, Freight produced the first anthology of students' writing, 'The Knuckle End': I was lucky enough to have a short story included. I can't claim that it was my first published story, but it was the first one in which I felt I began to show any inkling of how my identity as a 'voice' might evolve; even if it is clearly the writing of a beginner enjoying himself. Yet, for all its failings, I'm still proud of it: in those days, that someone might want to publish something you had written was a marvellous thing. It remains so. Out with the old and in with the new. This year's anthology, entitled 'Sushirexia' and celebrating the course's fifteenth year with work by its most recent graduates is awaiting you, the reader, to begin. I won't say anything about its contents or about names to watch out for: that is the role of the critic. In an anthology of beginning writers' work we should at least open play on a level pitch. From a fellow beginner, welcome. Put your best foot forward.

Sushirexia

Marianas Trench

Neil Mackay

The Sumerians invented the second, and the hour and the minute, the sixty within sixty formula, and divided the world into twelve hours of light and dark.

The second is supposedly next to nothing. Look down from the page, breathe, and look up again, and it's gone. It's been the same for nearly five thousand years, since the terraces of the Ziggurat of Ur were first built. It's the tiniest fraction of existence we have to measure out our lives.

Don't think too much about time. More raindrops fell today than the number of people who have lived on the earth or ever will live here.

Time is an error. The actual infinite can not be measured. At best, time is a container; a cup made to hold what we remember putting in it or leaving out.

We feel we hold sway over it too – that we can break it down, chop it up, freeze-frame it – until it decides to move on.

My only example: a sunny summer day at an open air theatre, the seats and stage carved into the bowl of a cliff, hundreds of feet above a beach. A rock staircase, also fashioned from the cliff, leads down to the sand and the sea. At the end of the play, with our children pleading to get to the beach, my wife calls to me. I turn from my younger child and look at my wife in a new red summer dress and a white hat.

Which memory would you keep? The wife, lifting herself on her toes and twirling around, her skirt belling out; her tanned legs? The child walking away?

In 1901, before anyone I've ever known was born, two English academics visited the Palace of Versailles. Charlotte-Anne Moberly and Eleanor Jourdain broke off from their tour party and wandered alone to Marie Antoinette's Petit Trianon, the little chateau in the gardens where the Queen would play at being a shepherdess in Arcadia with her friends and lovers. The two lady authors met the grounds men who tended the place for Marie-Antoinette, and nodded to her friends, and even spoke to the Queen herself.

Their experience of time ruined them. Who's going to listen to an Oxford professor who says her mind and body travelled back nearly two hundred years in the space of an afternoon to meet the Queen of France?

You must wish they were right, though – that they did visit the past and talk to the dead.

My wife knelt to pack up a picnic hamper, putting an empty bottle of wine and paper cups and plates back into the wicker basket. She looked up at me, smiling.

I'd broken down time; chopped it up, froze it. I was conscious that I'd, for a second, mastered time with a bit of happiness.

Those Oxford academics bring a whole lot of lost schoolboy phrases to mind. *Mutatis mutandis. Nunc pro tunc.*

My wife's eyes moved from my face to something I couldn't see behind me. She stood up and shouted, pointing.

Our youngest daughter, Suzanne, was running straight for the stairs carved into the rock face. There were 400 steps. From the edge of the theatre, at the top of the cliff, the staircase turned sharply to the right and dropped steeply to the beach below. There was no handrail; nothing to stop you falling into space. We knew that Suzanne was not going to turn right. She didn't even know that the stairs did turn right. She only saw the sign 'Steps to Beach'. She was going to keep on running, straight into the air and down through the hundreds of feet to the sand below.

I shouted her name, but the crowd of holidaymakers leaving the theatre was too noisy for her to hear me. Our older daughter, who was only six herself but could see what was happening, called out as well.

We keep a mathematical counting machine in our heads. Mine told me that I couldn't catch her. Ten yards takes about a second. Too much time had passed between the interstices: the moment I turned away from my wife, and the following second when I realised I should run.

I did run, though, and my nails scraped along the back of Suzanne's legs as she fell off the edge and through my hands. I could see the rake marks left by my fingers above her sandshoes as she dropped from the ledge down to the beach below, screaming in her bathing suit, a rotating star of arms and legs, pulled across a moment and away from me forever.

Those old Latin quotes keep coming back. '*Lente, lente, currite noctis equi*'. Run slowly, slowly, horses of the night. I would have happily kept her there like that forever – gravity arrested, Suzanne in space, a few feet above the ground, screaming but not dead, for the rest of her life.

I can feel the impact in my chest as I land on her – if I'd caught up with her. The tumble would have winded us both. Maybe it would have broken one of her bones. I was running to rugby tackle her. I couldn't worry about hurting her. I'd have caught her at the lip of the cliff and dragged her to the ground, my hands on her swimming costume and both our faces dangling off the edge, safely, looking down at the drop. I'd have picked her up and slapped her across the legs and hit her hard until her mother stopped me, and we'd have hugged her, and it would have become a story we told every time Suzanne did something stupid: 'The day Suzanne nearly killed herself'.

Time doesn't fly by in fast-forward. After I watched her fall and hit the ground, there was no double-time whirl of people shouting and pointing, and no speeded-up howl of police and ambulance sirens. Time just disappears. It eats up and marches on through space leaving all of us behind.

Whatever way you calculate it, the distance from one side of that event to the other can not be gauged using time alone. How can you just leave it to time to measure the fissure stepped over? A fissure no wider than a human hair, but as deep as the Marianas Trench.

Sushirexia

Feeding

Kirsty Logan

—•—

Before moving to the Outback, I had no concept of darkness. I thought I did, sure: weekends spent in Shoalhaven were pitch-black and silent compared to the eternal neon of Sydney. But Shoalhaven had street-lights, house security lights, the odd car on a midnight errand.

Out here, we're the only lights for miles.

We're in bed by 10pm. We don't have jobs and can go to bed whenever we like; but it makes more sense to get up with the light.

I reach out for Shelly. The room is so dark that white spots dance in front of my eyes. All I can feel is a mass of fabric. She used to sleep in just my boxer shorts, her breasts soft and heavy against my chest. Now it's flannel pyjamas in all weather. I wiggle my hand between the layers of fabric, trying to find flesh. I haven't even located a button when she elbows me in the chest.

I wake suddenly; feeling like something has just gone down my throat. In a lifetime, the average person swallows eight spiders in their sleep. At that thought, I'm fumbling for the lamp, blinking in the glare. Shelly's side of the bed is empty, the sheets crumpled back. Her pyjamas lie in a heap on the floor.

I try to shout, but my throat is sleep-dry. I cough, choke.

'Shelly!'

My voice echoes in the empty room. Aside from a bed and lamp, we haven't furnished this room yet.

'Shelly!'

I hear a tapping outside the window. In the spotlight of the lamp, everything looks like a movie set. I take the stairs three at a time, the rough wood splintering my soles. I flip on the kitchen light. The back door is wide open, hanging motionless in the heavy night. I feel stupid, standing by the kitchen table in nothing but my underwear. I scrabble through a drawer, my hand searching for the biggest kitchen knife. I grip the handle in my sweaty fist, square my shoulders, and walk outside.

Shelly is crouched in the vegetable garden. Her skin glows white against the naked stumps of tomato plants.

'Shelly.' It comes out as a whisper. She doesn't react. I take a step closer, dropping the knife onto the doorstep.

'Shelly.' She turns. She's wearing her green gardening gloves, a trowel in one hand.

'Peter.' She smiles. 'Could you pass me the compost bag?'

'It's the middle of the night! What the hell are you doing? I thought you'd been... I thought something had happened.'

She shrugs. I can't help noticing the way the movement makes her breasts bounce.

'I just thought the tomatoes would be hungry.' She stands, leans, and grabs the bag of compost. She thrusts a glove into the bag and throws a dark handful over the tomato plants.

'But why now?'

'The plants needed it.' Shelly pulls off her gloves and straightens, her body spread out under the sky. She stretches her arms up above her head and I can see the hollows of her armpits, the ridges of her ribs, the skin tight across her hip-bones. She pushes me to the ground and straddles my hips. The ground is dry, the cracks in the mud large enough to fit a fingertip.

'We need it,' she says.

We make love in the glow from the open kitchen door. The sky is flat, a vast nothing above us. I dig my fingers into the cracked earth so I don't fall up into the empty sky. Shelly tries to pull me on top, but I stop her. I don't want her to touch the starving ground.

I spend the next fortnight in the second bedroom. If we'd moved here a year ago, this would have been Jeremy's room. Shelly and I call this room the study, the library, the guest bedroom: everything except the nursery.

Even so, I've painted the walls butter-yellow so that they'll work for a boy or a girl.

Shelly spends every minute of daylight in the garden. Grass has not grown. Dandelions have not grown. She has planted carrots, cucumber, peas, lettuce, courgettes: they have not grown. In our month here, it has rained once. I stay in the second bedroom, painting the walls with sunlight.

Soon my stomach informs me that it's past lunchtime.

I put my paintbrush in the turpentine jar, wipe my hands on newspaper. I slide the window up, wedging it open with an old jam-jar. I lean out of the window and my hand slips off the sill.

There's a small child in the garden. She wears her mother's sunhat and a white dress three sizes too big. I open my mouth to shout, and realise the little girl is Shelly. Barefoot among the naked trees, she looks like Thumbelina.

I go downstairs and into the kitchen. From the doorway Shelly looks human-sized. She feels my gaze and looks up. The sunhat casts shadows under her cheekbones.

'Hungry?'

She shakes her head, rams her trowel into the ground.

I crack ice from the freezer, pour milk into mugs. The heat outside is choking. I shield my eyes with one arm, trying to hold the mugs steady. Ice cubes clunk against the thick china. I stand next to Shelly, making sure my shadow covers her exposed skin.

I hand her the only mug that still has the handle attached. She stands, looks up at me.

'Thanks,' she says. We grip our mugs and survey the graveyard of twigs.

'What are you planting?'

'Whatever will grow.'

I think: nothing will grow.

I say: 'Something will. When it rains, all this will sprout up.'

I gulp my milk. The ice cubes leave a drop at the tip of my nose. Shelly laughs and dabs it with the hem of her voluminous dress. With a jolt I realise it's one of her maternity dresses. The white lace hem is dusted brown where she's been kneeling on it.

'I love you.' She stands on tiptoe and presses her mouth to mine.

'I love you, too.'

I finish my milk, kiss her freckled shoulder, and go upstairs to start sanding the window frame. With the window up I can hear the earth outside cracking in the heat. I hear Shelly muttering something about the sun, saying that everything would be okay if not for the sun, it's all the sun's fault.

Later, I go out to the garden. The only mug with a handle sits on the doorstep. The ice has melted, the milk turned yellow and curdled in the sun. I tip it into the sink. It's only then that I realise my misunderstanding. Not sun. Son.

I lie in bed, listening to the crunch of trowel against hard earth. The light faded hours ago, and the room's edges are barely visible. I ball up the bed sheets and kick them to the floor. I fumble to the window and lean out.

Shelly,' I whisper into the black.

The crunch of a trowel, then –

'Yes.'

'Are you coming to bed?'

'Yes.' The steady crunch.

'Can't you do that tomorrow? You've been in that garden all day.'

'The plants need it.'

She digs; I wait.

'Shelly. Please.'

She stops. The clatter of a trowel thrown aside.

'You're right, Peter. I'll come up to bed now.'

I crawl back into bed and drag the sheets over my legs. In the pitch-black silence, sleep comes quickly. In my dreams, the crunch of a trowel.

I make dinner: defrosted chicken, carrots, peas. If I make the food plain, maybe Shelly will manage to eat some.

She prods at her carrots, piling them up at the side of her plate until the stack falls and scatters her peas. She cuts her chicken into thumb-sized bits, then carefully shreds it with the tines of her fork. After twenty minutes, I get sick of looking at my empty plate.

'Is the chook undercooked?'

'No.'

'So why aren't you eating it?'

She shrugs. Her fingers look as hard and thin as the cutlery. I look at her until she meets my eyes. She picks up a pea between forefinger and thumb, and places it on her tongue. She swallows.

'Happy?'

Her cheeks are so sunken that I can see the pea where she's tucked it. I wonder how long she can keep it there before spitting it out. She stands, catching her chair legs on the torn linoleum.

'I'll wash up.' She puts her full plate on my empty one and takes them to the sink. I leave the room before she goes outside to spit out the pea.

The house is so quiet that I can hear myself breathing. I gave up on painting hours ago to stand, breathing paint fumes and looking at the window. The sun is falling behind the back of the world, dyeing the ground. It looks like a battlefield, red and scattered with the bones of trees.

The crunch of Shelly's trowel had become so constant, like a ticking clock, that I don't immediately notice its absence. I lean out of the window, paint flakes digging into my palms, and scan the garden. Naked plants cower in the bloody soil, Shelly's trowel and gloves sit neatly on the doorstep. In the sun's last light, a pale glow among the roots.

I tiptoe downstairs, unaware I'm holding my breath. The dinner plates sit by the sink, bone-dry. I step over the gardening gloves and into the garden. I can feel the cracks in the soil with my soles. The tomato plants seem to bend towards me as I approach, their twigs rubbing together like insect legs. I blink hard, watching the inside of my lids: the sun's afterglow leaves fat orange tomatoes on the empty vines.

The light has gone. I rub my hands in the soil, feeling for the pale glow. I feel gristle and snatch my hands back.

Chicken bones.

I'm onto my last useable paintbrush and Shelly has snapped the handle off her trowel. We've run out of milk, bread and toilet paper.

It's time for a trip into town.

This is a larger undertaking than it sounds. The nearest grocery store is 100 kilometres away, the nearest hardware store is 200. Our jeep has no air-con, and if driven for more than an hour solid, thick white steam leaks out from the bonnet.

Shelly hasn't worn shoes for a month, and complains when she has to squeeze her dusty toes into her sneakers. Shoes don't bother me, but the jeep does. It has been sitting in the sun all morning, and the red vinyl seats are almost bubbling. We sit on folded towels, but the heat still seeps through. I try to hold the steering wheel with my fingertips.

Once we build up some speed, the heat isn't so bad. The driver's window only opens halfway, but we still get a good breeze. Shelly presses the radio buttons. The music is full of static, but it is music. She taps her fingers on her knees, ochre with ingrained dirt. I haven't seen her wear those cut-off shorts since we were teenagers; I didn't know she still had them. Her bare legs look like daisy stems, the same width from ankle to thigh. She starts to sway in her seat. From the corner of my eye I see her mouth sneer up at one corner. Then –

'It's a nice day for a' – she cocks a finger at me – 'white wedding.'

She pushes her ponytail so that the front of her hair raises up into a quiff.

'It's a nice day to –'

'Start again.' We draw out the syllables, wailing in chorus. I turn to look at Shelly – her hair quiffed up, her lip in an Idol sneer. Laughing, I look back at the windscreen.

There is a rabbit in the road.

I slam on the brakes, the seatbelt pressing out my shout. Shelly's hands grip her knees, her knuckles tight. The car is still. A ticking noise comes from the bonnet.

'Is it ?'

I shake my head: it was too close. I thunk open the door and walk around to the fender. The rabbit lies between the front and back wheels. Its head is perfect: brown and fluffy, with long ears and limpid eyes. The rest of its body is a flat red oval, leaking onto the tarmac.

'Stay in the car, Shelly.'

I hear her door open, then click shut. She stares at me through the windscreen, her face expressionless. She leans forward and switches off the radio.

From the boot I pull out bin-bags and a shovel. I wrap the bundle in plastic and put it in the boot. I spend five minutes rubbing my hands on the towel from my seat.

We say nothing for the rest of the drive.

I pull up in front of the grocery store and switch off the engine.

'I'll put it in the big bins behind the shop.'

'No.' Shelly's voice is too loud in the suffocating car. 'I want to bury her.'

'Shelly, we –'

'In the garden.'

We buy bread, milk, toilet paper. We buy paintbrushes and a trowel. We buy a small metal box.

Back home, I bury the rabbit while Shelly is in the shower. I don't want her to see it.

We fall asleep as close as ears of wheat: chest to back, fingers entwined. I kiss the skin at the nape of her neck, soft like rabbit fur. I dream of nothing.

When I wake my hands are empty and I can hear the crunch of a trowel. I stumble across to the window. In the black night all I can see is Shelly's white back as she crouches over.

I feel my way downstairs and run my hand over the kitchen wall. I find the light switch, but my finger won't move. The crunch of metal against soil seems deafening. I close my eyes and switch on the light. I only open them when the crunch stops.

'Peter.' Shelly stands in the open doorway, the metal box in her hands. I know without looking that it is empty. I step back, scraping my heels against the wall.

'Why?' It comes out as a croak.

'The plants needed it.'

I lie in bed, listening to the metronome of Shelly's trowel.

I lift the pillow off my face. 'Come to bed!'

Her voice floats up through the night. 'Yeah.' It's barely a word, more of a grunt.

She's been in the garden since dawn. She doesn't even bother dressing any more, just kneels in the dirt until it coats her skin. Her palms are so rough that the calluses form ridges like the cracks in the earth. She doesn't wash, so our bed is full of the grit of ochre dirt, tiny dried-up leaves, flakes of skin from her sunburned back.

I clench my fists under the sheet. 'Shelly! Now!'

She doesn't grunt, doesn't break her rhythm.

In the months we've been here, nothing has grown. Shelly has planted every seed we could afford, and they sit motionless under the topsoil, sleeping or dead. The nursery is finished, pristine and smelling of paint.

Last week Shelly threw away her maternity clothes. They swamp her, so heavy with fabric that she can hardly lift her arms. I haven't looked at her nakedness in days. When I go into the garden, I keep my eyes fixed firmly on the top of her head. I can't even look at her eyes, can't bear to see the bones and shadows around them.

I think I shout for her again, but it might only be in my dream.

I wake to a tapping above my head, and think: that's not the trowel. The taps grow louder, banging on the tin roof like an out-of-tune orchestra. I look at the window, at the sky's odd motion, and realise. Rain.

I rub my dreams out of my eyes, cough up the words I tried to shout. Shelly's side of the bed is unwrinkled. Her pillow sits on the floor where I threw it. I know what I should do: look out of the window, then leap down the stairs three at a time while screaming her name. I stand up, neaten the sheets, step carefully on the edges of the stairs so I don't get splinters. I walk into the kitchen with my eyes on the torn linoleum. I go to the sink, turn on the tap, drink a glass of water. The rain deafens me against the windows. I take a deep breath and open the back door.

The world outside is green.

Grass carpets the earth, pea-pods shiver as raindrops hit, courgettes sit heavily like sleeping animals. The air smells like greenhouses and wet dirt. Everything is so clean. I walk through the garden, the grass spotting my feet with mud, leaves wiping my bare arms. The rain wets my hair and cools the night-sweat on my back. I raise my hands to feel the falling water, the rubbery leaves, the bright firm fruit.

Shelly lies among the tomato plants. Each tomato is as fat and red as an overfed belly. Her cheeks are concave, her collarbones so sharp they seem about to pierce her chest. Her belly is famine-swollen, tight and round between the jut of her ribs and the cup of her hip-bones. The rain falls into her eyes.

I pull a handful of grapes from the vine and jam them into my mouth, the juice running down my chin. I tip my head to the sky and let the fat raindrops wash everything away.

Sushirexia

The Crabman and the Fishwife

Duncan Muir

Every day Archie was the same, anytime Irene told him to do something his knuckles and teeth would clench. Stubborn old bastard. It was usually over him taking off his trousers at the back door. I don't want my house reeking like a crab creel, she'd tell him. He faced away from her as he stood on the step and peeled off his sodden jeans one leg at a time. Cast outside, rough and crusted by a layer of salt, the denims would hold their memory of his shape, a knee, a calf, the bulge of his groin. Irene looked on with a hand on the worktop and a fist on her hip as he stumbled by her sideways on pale stubby legs; she always took it as an opportunity to check his underwear for pee stains. She could hardly believe how a grown man could make such a mess in his pants or how long he tried to keep them on for, soiled to a second skin. He was the same about washing his hands; he wanted them filthy, fingertips black. It was as if he liked to wallow in the flavour of his own filth and fluids.

The day that everything changed Archie arrived home holding his hands curled close to his chest, his face stuck in surprise; eyes out on stalks. The first thing Irene noticed was how pathetic he looked. She was instantly repulsed. Then she noticed the blood, he was covered in it. She was hardly surprised, she'd become used to her husband's clumsiness, his wake of disorder. He was covered in scars, bait hook holes in his neck and ears and torn fingers from banding lobster claws. There was a curved scar on the left side of his back just under the ribs, from the time he backed onto a knife Irene was chopping carrots with. Glaikit fool. He didn't just make a mess of himself, he smashed crockery, dropped food everywhere and as for his aim well... Archie was all thumbs, no fingers.

She sat him down on the step and wrapped each hand in a tea towel. Then she pulled off his wellies and his coarse, stinking jeans, leaving them outside before bringing him into the house bare-legged. His pants were in a right state, worse than usual. She told him he needed to go to the hospital in Oban, but he just shook his head and stared, empty-eyed, mute. He never could face up to anything. Soft old bugger. Irene cleaned and bandaged his hands as best she could before heading down to the slip by the house. Archie never berthed at the pier in Scalasaig with the rest of the island's fishermen. He couldn't even enjoy the company of his own kind. He was that type of loner.

There, she found in and around the engine all eight of Archie's fingers. They were cold and lifeless, the skin as hard as the nails. One was just a little stub bent to the side. It reminded Irene of Archie's penis, his little pinkie prick. She smiled as she threw it overboard followed by the rest, one after the other. The gulls gathered and fought over her husband's flesh. She saved his ring finger till last; a black-headed gull caught it as it hit the water and flew off with a glint of gold in its beak.

Back at the house, she told him she couldn't find his fingers, said the birds got there before her. Staring out at the sea, his eyes flashing, reflecting the slow beam of the lighthouse, he let out a slow sigh and pulled his shorn hands, bandaged to mittens, close to his chest.

After a few days that felt like a week she took his bandages off to stop him chewing on them. She had tried telling him to stop it, telling him he looked like an imbecile, an eedyit, but he just kept chewing, kept staring with blank unseeing eyes. Beneath the white fabric she found that her husband's knuckles had healed into thick pumice-grey scabs that were overgrowing the wounds themselves and spreading up the backs and calloused palms of his hands.

Each day his wounds claimed another part of Archie. His wrists and forearms followed his hands; swallowed under smooth welts. His fleshiness was slowly cast beneath hardness. At least it wasn't as unsightly as him sitting there, chewing on his dressings like some decrepit cretin. She watched him half expecting him to move or twitch and stop his usual moody charade. He had never done crabbit right. They did argue, or rather Irene would shout. He would scuttle out the house and sit mending creels at the back of the garden where the grass faded to pebble shore. He always ran away, always to the sea. If she followed him, still screaming, he kept walking and headed out in the fishing boat. She said he never buried his head in the sand; always his whole body. All that time at sea, just Archie and the waves, had made him simple she said, a shell of the man she married. He told her that was her problem – she only saw the surface, never the depths. His moods never lasted though, he always cracked first. He couldn't keep it up. Well, that and a lot of other things. He didn't look it, but Irene knew her husband was soft.

Archie's welts spread further each day. First up his arms making them stiff like old lobster claws, the joints fused, elbows set at angles. His fingerless hands did not quite meet in front of his chest, palms and thumbs open, solidified in two lopsided forks. Two days after his arms were engulfed to the shoulder, the left and the right welts joined seamlessly in the middle of his chest and back forming one big shellac rash that spread downwards, encasing his torso in a solid Romanesque breastplate.

Irene wasn't used to having her husband in the house, in her house. He seemed to suck up space, demanding attention like a bad smell. He hadn't spoken or acknowledged her or even really moved at all since she told him about the fingers and she felt a slight pang of guilt. Maybe she should have brought them back; maybe they could have been sewn back on? Maybe she should have forced him to go to the hospital? She could have made him go. She got her own way with Archie every time. Something had stopped her pushing it though, somehow at the time it served him right.

As she was considering this an acrid smell assaulted her nose. Her guilt was short lived: he had pissed himself again. Archie's urine always had a strange salty tang, Irene put it down to his job, his proximity to the sea. She noticed it going to the bathroom after him and washing his underwear, sometimes his bed sheets.

The last time they had been in the same bed was one of their anniversaries. He lay on top of her, sweating. She was waiting for him to catch his breath, to get back on his side. At first she thought it was sweat seeping between her thighs until the smell caught her throat and threw her into a rage. 'Why don't you just shit on me too?' She screamed and pushed him onto his back. He lay in a spreading puddle and watched his wife's naked hips and arse wobble into the hall for the last time.

Archie pissed himself roughly three times a day until his waist, hips and buttocks were devoured by shades of grey. His genitals receded to a Ken doll bulge; his orifices sealed. It took four whole days, the pale pinkish skin disappearing like a slipping stocking, before he lost his legs and feet. Head and face were last to go, solidifying like a leaden hood being drawn up from the back of his neck until all that remained were two watery eyes staring out from a sombre mask. Unwilling to close, even to blink, his veined whites, blue irises and black pupils faded to a steely grisaille.

For weeks Archie sat statuesque encased in the opalescence of polished oyster shell. Irene had stripped him of his clothes. He looked like a piece of modern art solidified in front of her. When she stood directly in front of him he looked frozen as if ready to leap into the air and wrap his hands, what was left of them, around her throat. Yet no matter where she stood, he never seemed to look at her, he was always looking away. She spent ages walking around him considering what to do, considering the practicalities of disposing of a spouse who is encased in shell. He looked heavy, immovable. If she broke him into bits with a sledge hammer, would this still count as mutilation? Would he be solid all the way through or would his insides still be soft?

Soft. He remembered being soft, or did he? Was it softness he remembered or just a lack of definition, the numbing complexity of softness? Archie was unsure. He felt another existence, that other world just out of his reach. If he could explain it, he'd liken it to being underwater: things felt fluid, unclear – his mind like a silted sea. Images once seen with a different set of eyes flash untranslatable in his mind. Blood spattered shellfish. Severed digits. Fingerless palms. Bleeding machinery.

Since they glazed over like marbles, his eyes had been useless, he was in darkness. A new picture was forming of his surroundings though, informed not through reflections of light but through smell and taste. He was experiencing a host of new sensations. He began to feel everything, changes in air temperature to mere fractions of degrees, the dust rippling in Irene's wake, he tasted his chair with his hardened buttocks, its fibres and dyes, the biscuit crumbs, the tea stains, the urine from when he pissed himself a couple of minutes before his genitals started sealing into a sexless lump. Through his shell he smelt cigarette ash and smoke, and the sea outside, kelp rotting on the shore. The carpet was a dusty tasting aura spreading out beneath his feet. He felt each footstep made by his wife as she paced the floor. She tasted of smoke and sweat, of nicotine and meaty brine. She was soft and porous, seeping fluids and heat as she passed him by. He was aware of her exterior and what it concealed, that hardness inside and the hot flay of her tongue. When she came close he felt her breath and the malice of words he could no longer understand. He felt her seethe in front of him, a boiling brink that he mentally scrabbled sideways to avoid.

There was something quite freeing for Archie about his new form though. He felt hard, buff and, strangely, not totally cut off, not desensitised. He was surrounded by thin sensation, wispy flavours and scents that licked his shell with no definite contact. He longed for something of substance though, something he could sink into and be enveloped by. He fantasised of sinking low and deep and being swallowed by an unconditional, simple security, a liquid shroud to cover every surface, his back, his belly, and fill the crevice of each joint with a salty safeness.

Slowly he became aware of muscles, of his own muscles, stretching, flexing. He felt his arms and their power, the strong clench of his fists. He could feel legs and legs and legs and legs – more than just his own. He was robust, solid like the hull of a boat. He felt masculine, armoured, fierce and for the first time, defined. He was comfortable in his shell in a way he never knew of his skin. Archie was formed, the wide curve of his back, its serrated piecrust edges. He knew the scoop of his forearms, the points of his feet and his slow mechanical movements. Simple. He became familiar with himself, experienced his compactness and was intimate with his denseness.

With all his new sensation, his new awareness, he knew he was locked

inside himself. Inside the husk of who he once was. He felt its casing surround him, could tap it with his inner shell. He had to get out. Archie
found his strength, he felt it pushing against his shell in rushes, in waves. It
was time for them to break, for him to escape. Time for him to.....

Crack.

Crunch. Irene never had claw-crackers. She fumbled on her plate with a
nutcracker and a black-tipped claw sounding a satisfying *crack*. All that
time living with a lobsterman and she had never tasted lobster, all those
years married to a crabman and the closest thing she'd had to it was the
crabsticks from the Co-op in Oban. He'd told her a creelman can't afford
to eat crab, never mind lobster.

It surprised her that the flesh inside didn't completely fill the shell, not
tightly, there was a hollow space around the meat. Instead of the butch
muscles of the claw arms she found the inner meat loose and flaccid, the
tips of each claw tapering to a thin wobbling point. She ripped the flesh
out with her hands making sure she got every bit, savouring the taste of every morsel of meat. It was moist and sweet and delicate. She emptied both
claws and all eight legs one after the other. Snapping a leg segment with her
hands she got hit in the face by a fishy squirt of juices that dribbled down
her cheek. She ate it hot and could still hear the squeal it made in the pot
ringing in her ears. She took it out after the noise had fallen from piercing
to a long slow sigh and then faded to the simple bubble of boiling water.

After the legs she moved on to the crab's body. She turned it onto its
back and with her fingers around the piecrust edges and her thumbs between where the legs used to be she pushed the belly plate off with a flick
of her wrists. Inside was a mess of brown and yellow and a lot of empty
space, like something was missing. She licked a scoop of brown body meat
off her finger; it was thick and pasty and spread like a layer of fishy putty
in her mouth. She wasn't keen on the aftertaste, the way it lingered like
Archie, a stain on her tongue. She gave the rest a miss. In front of her was
a midden of guts, orange, brown, yellow, and fragments of shell scattered
on the plate like shale: dismembered claw tips, hairy bits of leg and so
many knees, small and tight like fused knuckles. She could see little grey-
ish organs and the hard internal shell of the crab's sack. The carapace was

opened, exposed and empty.

She picked up the plate and walked out the back door picking Archie's jeans up from the gloomy dusk of the step on her way. They were wet with rain from weeks outside. The grass's wet swish under her feet turned to the crunching of pebbles then shale. When she reached the slip the boat was gone. The coxswain of the Oban Lifeboat had called that morning. They'd found it wrecked on black rocks near Port Uisken on the Ross of Mull. He told her there was no one aboard. Irene had sounded surprised. She was surprised. She thought it might run aground at the lighthouse, Dubh Artach, or carried on out west and slipped off the horizon into the Atlantic's endless green sways.

Irene threw the denims in first. They hit the water with a dull slap then hung on the tide as it took them out to sea. In the dim sweep of the lighthouse they looked like they were swimming the breaststroke, each leg swaying separately on the waves. Next she tipped the plate of shell fragments and crab offal into the water. The shards of legs and claw sunk slowly disappearing into the green murk. The carapace floated on its back, bobbing west into the Atlantic. The current must have pulled Archie's boat back inland, into the firth and would do the same with his shell if it didn't sink first. It didn't matter. Boat or no boat Archie was lost at sea.

Sushirexia

First Taste

Linda Duncan McLaughlin

➤

the moonlight on her face is a scattered geometry
 changing constantly
  in the shadow of the leaves

like the bright kaleidoscope of dresses
 splintering and shivering
  in the music's sway

he likes to sit beside them for a while
 afterwards
  feels no particular regret

some things have to be broken
 to find out what's real
  and what's not-real

not something he feels the need to think about
 not something he wants
  to think about

he will go back there soon
 he will find a real one soon

It's Mary's first time at the Locarno Ballroom, and she is trying very hard not to look too hopeful as she sits by her watchful sister. There were conditions to this privilege: she had to promise not to say anything stupid to her sister's friends, not to talk to any man her sister danced with.....

—An mind an smile, you, her sister had said, ah don't want you sittin there wi yer face trippin ye, showin me up. But if anyb'dy dis ask ye up, ye check wi me first, right? Or wi Anne or Maggie if ah'm up. There's some right funny buggers in here.

It doesn't matter. Mary would have promised anything for this chance, and she doesn't mind the rules – she doesn't even really mind if she doesn't get lifted for a dance. Just being here is enough, and her excitement is visible in the trembling frill of her borrowed dress.

—Sit still, for God's sake!

Her sister's hiss suppresses her wriggling for a moment, but the music, the lights, the kick of stiletto heel under a froth of petticoat – they spark a delight in her that she hardly knows how to contain. The sweetie-jar blues and pinks of the dresses make her mouth water, and she leans forward in her seat, her eyes fixed on the dancers' candied swirl. She does not see the tired and stained plush of the seats, the rubbed sores in the carpet, the grubby-jacketed indifference of the dance band. She does not see the desperation in some of the faces, the tightrope of lust and wanting that they walk. But she can taste the hunger in the air, and feels the faint answering ache in her own belly.

She doesn't know quite how wonderful she is. She is pretty enough, certainly, but she shines a little too brightly in these shabby surroundings, and the thin-shouldered boys slouching at the walls are reluctant to approach her – her freshness makes them uneasy, somehow – and she sits on, alone.

and the sweet-salt tang of her
arrows through the staleness
to pierce him with hope

—Excuse me, are you dancing?

Mary is scared to look in case the question's not being directed at her, but the light touch on her shoulder confirms it: she's being asked up. She casts around for her sister, but she's still dancing with the guy with the plaid jacket. Anne and Maggie are both on the floor, too, and there is no-one to ask permission of or, more importantly, to withhold it from her. She lifts her head. He's older, but nice-looking, she thinks, and nicely dressed, polite – but she would say yes even if he were none of these things. She smiles at him, and gives him her hand to let him lead her onto the floor.

His own hand is light in the small of her back as he steers her through the dance, but she feels the touch of every fingertip. He's a good dancer, and she finds it easy to fit her steps to his. He doesn't say anything, and Mary doesn't know how to start a conversation, but she doesn't mind – nothing he could say could make this moment better. The coloured lights and the other dancers blur to a fairground whirl, but she has practised long for this and her steps are sure. She can feel the muscles in his shoulder move under her hand, and she enjoys the unfamiliar maleness of his body against hers, hard and strong. His smell is clean and sharp, and the texture of his jacket is rough against the tender skin of her inner arm. Their moving together begins to feel fluid, light, exactly right: she wants to press herself harder against him, move through him, into him. She feels a sudden urge to bite. She throws back her head, eyes closed, and gives herself up to the flood of her feeling.

the flash of her excitement
   finds an answering
       fire

She opens her eyes to find he's smiling at her, and she's horrified to feel a blush rising. Abruptly, she's back in her own body, small, unsure. In her confusion she stumbles, almost falls. His face changes and he tightens his hold, almost to the point of hurting her, and she thinks he is angry, that she has ruined the dance, spoiled his perfect execution of the steps. A final mocking cymbal-crash underlines her error. She is humiliated, comes to a stop, and stands, miserable, waiting for her dismissal.

—Mary! Her sister is suddenly beside her, her hand snaking to grab Mary's wrist, the coral slash of her mouth twisting to a snarl. Right, pal, thanks for the dance, but ah think she's a bit young fer you, is she no? She's sittin down now.

She pulls Mary away, back to their seats, scolding her for getting up to dance with someone on her own, but Mary isn't listening. She's looking back at the man, standing where she left him, as the carousel of the dance floor cranks once more into life. She nods, once. She knows he'll find her again.

he nods, once
he knows he'll find her again.

The Sin Eater

Nikki Cameron

The best cardboard for spending ten hours sitting on your backside is that thick stuff, the sort they use for the heavy-duty boxes that hold whisky or wine. Get a whole box; pull it apart carefully so that it's in one piece and then fold it flat. If you stop the water getting in, it'll last a couple of days. I'd found a really good box in the recycling bin behind the offy at the end of the main road, and went to my doorway. It's a good spot my doorway. Tam had passed it on to me when he left to go back up North. It's good because it's a doorway that no one uses anymore, just another closed up shop. But all around are loads of wee shops, the newsagents, the sandwich place, a chemist. The sort of places that people come out of with a few bits of loose change in their hands that they – well some of them anyway – don't mind throwing into the cup. Lots of people passing by on their way to the offices and the station, in and out all day long, all of them busy running somewhere, busy going nowhere. But you have to look after your spot and that's not easy, there's plenty out there who'll just jump in and grab it.

It was a bugger of a day. Rain pouring, real sideways stuff. The board was wet, no one was hanging around and I'd run out of matches to light my tab. I checked the cup, 75p, fan-bloody-tastic. I tucked the change away in my trousers and scrunched myself tight into the corner of the doorway. Some days you just have to sleep through. I'd got myself all cosy when a set of legs stopped right in front of me. Smart legs in the sort of fabric that always hangs just right and shoes polished so bright the raindrops didn't dare hang around on them. The voice that came from the legs matched.

'You're Billy McKenzie.'

That was a surprise. Generally if legs stop and speak, the conversation goes one of only a few ways. Firstly, you can get the 'You must be awful cold on a day like this, here, take it and get a hot meal.' Then you get anything from a fiver to a twenty pushed in your hand, and as you're saying your grateful thanks, they walk away pleased as punch with themselves. Happens more than you'd think but never when the sun is shining. Then of course, you get the pompous prick who tells you that they've been up since six in the morning, making money that the government takes off them just to give to lazy scroungers like you. They're always angry and you never take them on. One of them pushed Tam too far and that's why he's up North. Or you'll get the worst of the lot – the religious fucker – who thinks that being in a doorway sitting on cardboard means that you're next to being a saint and that you're guaranteed eternal life on the right hand of the Lord with the bloody lambs. They're a real pain in the neck; they never give you any money because they assume you'll spend it on drink or drugs and no one else gives you money while they're there because it looks like someone is helping you. God save me from them.

So to get legs in smart, expensive trousers, stopping and calling you by your name is a rarity.

'You're Billy McKenzie,' the voice said again.

'Aye. Bugger off,' I said. 'You're spoiling my view.' The legs didn't move.

'Billy, it's me – John.'

The rain bounced off my cheeks as I squinted up above the legs. Couldn't see a bloody thing.

The legs bent and a face came into focus right in front of me. 'Can you see me pal? It's John. John Wallace, from home, the village. You must be freezing on a day like this, let me get you a decent meal.'

John Wallace. John Wallace. Nope, couldn't remember him at all. His clean, shiny face and finely shaped fingernails didn't mean a thing. Could have been the Pope for all I recognised of him. But food sounded good and by the looks of him, it'd be proper stuff not a cheap sandwich from the shop. 'OK,' I said, 'for old time's sake.'

'Great.' He smiled at me as both of us straightened up. 'Come on, I'm just across the road.' He herded me towards the bank, my trainers slapping in the rain, the puddles parting down the middle for his leather brogues.

The door to his building opened as we reached the top of the flight of marble stairs.

'Sir.' A man in a uniform nodded but his hand balled into a fist when he saw me. 'Are you alright, Mr Wallace? Can I help with you anything?'

'No, it's fine,' John said, pulling me into a lift with him, 'my friend is just going upstairs with me, nothing to worry about.' He started to laugh once the door closed behind us. 'He's going to have a lot of fun spreading that around the building.'

His office was huge. Bigger than the space under the motorway ramp where you could find twenty of us sleeping any night of the week. I went over to the window and checked my spot. No-one there yet, but best not to leave it too long.

'So, er, John was it, how about that food you mentioned?' I was shivering now. Strange how you feel the cold more once you're inside.

He looked at me for a second then walked across to a door on the other side of the room, disappeared into it and came out with two towels. He threw one across at me and while he was drying his hair with the other one, spoke into an intercom on his desk. 'Mrs Johnston, I want you to ring the restaurant, order some soup and two steaks. Tell the manager it's urgent.'

He dropped the towel on the chair behind the desk and went over to a huge glass fronted cabinet. He got out a couple of glasses and a bottle of 20 year old McCallan's. The room was like an Aladdin's cave. Perhaps I'd have a magic lamp by the time I got out of there.

He pointed at a leather sofa by the window. 'Go on, sit down. Make yourself comfortable. The food won't be long. This'll warm you up.' He poured out the scotch. Bloody hell, it smelt good. And, see the weight of the glass when I held it. It was a long time since anything that heavy had been in my hands.

I swallowed it down in a oner. He did the same. He filled the glasses again and sat down next to me.

'You don't remember me, do you?'

'Nope.' I said. I could feel the whisky warming the toes in my left foot. 'But I'll remember anything you want me to while you're hugging that bottle mate.' He laughed and refilled the glasses.

'I saw you in that doorway a couple of days ago, there was something about you, but I couldn't place you.' He swallowed more Scotch. 'Then yesterday I heard you shout at someone and it suddenly clicked: Billy McKenzie. It's must be almost thirty years.'

I sipped a little more slowly, something was beginning to register in a place that I hadn't been to in a long time. He poured more whisky for himself.

'I lived in the village for a couple of years. We sat next to each other in school. We were best pals, did everything together. Remember the last summer? I always think of it as a kind of perfect time – fishing, football on the beach. We camped in every dune round the bay. Do you remember when we put the tent up in the back garden, the cigarettes and beer – God we were sick as dogs all night.'

He stared deep into the heart of the whisky he was swirling round the glass. I recognised that look, there's a whole lifetime in that look. 'I hated it when we moved,' he said, 'I loved that house.'

John Wallace, Johnny. I'd never forgotten that house either and I could remember a whole lot more than the taste of a first fag.

He was waiting for me to say something. But you learn a lot when you're living on the street. You learn patience. You learn to wait to see what's coming next because there's always something coming next. I sipped the whisky. The silence got him. He started to talk again.

'How are your family, Billy, they all well? Didn't you live with your gran and sister?' He paused, desperate to ask the question, not knowing if it was the done thing or not. Then, knocking back another shot, he threw himself in. 'How did you get into this mess Billy? What happened, did you lose your job?'

I looked him square on now. 'I ended up in this mess just the same way everyone else ends up in the shit. I lost my job, so I lost my wife, my kids, my house. I drank too much, took too many drugs, and met the wrong people. Whoever you knew back home isn't the same me now. I don't play football much anymore and I don't do the past. Thanks for the drink. I'm off.' I got up, heading for the door.

'No wait, there's something I've got to ask you. Don't go yet, Billy. He jumped up from the sofa, staggered and fell back down. One thing about smart trouser legs that can walk on water, they can never hold their whisky.

As I went to leave, the door opened and in walked a couple of guys carrying trays. They went past me and started to lay out plates of food on the table. Now, I can drink anything and it takes a bucket of booze to get me unsteady but the smell of really good hot food can have me tripping over my feet like a toddler. John nodded the waiters out.

I could feel his eyes at my back. He'd got me. 'Billy, you're starving, just eat the bloody food. There's no catch, I just want to ask you something.'

I walked over to the table and sat down. 'Go on then, ask.' I said and started on the soup.

He came across to the table, ignored the food and opened the bottle of red wine. He filled two glasses.

'You know how bad things are these days Billy,' he started, 'Christ; it's a mess at the bank. I've just barely hung onto my job. My Dad worked here as well but he was cleared out in January. It's hit him hard; he's gone into the worst depression I've ever seen in anyone.'

I pushed away the soup bowl and reached for the steak. 'Well, John, if you want my advice, you shouldn't invest in anything that's less than 40% proof. Always sure to bring a guaranteed result.' I laughed at my own observation and piled chips onto the plate.

'It's too late for him, Billy. His heart's going. The doctors don't think he'll last the month out. He's turned his face to the wall and given up. He looks haunted, you wouldn't recognise him now.'

I might not have recognised John, but I was bloody certain I'd recognise his old man anywhere. The food tasted sweeter by the moment. The day was going to go down as a definite winner.

John took more wine. He was going to suffer later. 'When I told Dad last night that I thought I'd recognised you on the street, he started to cry. We ended up talking for hours about that old house, about you, and your grandmother.'

'Don't tell me, your father wants to make a death bed declaration of love for my old Nana,' I said once I'd swallowed a mouthful of the tenderist bit of steak I'd ever tasted and a good gulp of wine.

'Dad had remembered her stories about the Sin Eater, Billy.' John suddenly looked as if he'd sobered up.

I pushed the plate away and stared at him. 'The Sin Eater? Are you kidding me on?' But now I could see what was happening and probably better than Johnny could.

'Billy, he's desperate to see you.' He was talking quickly, wanting to explain, obviously getting to where he'd been going the whole time.

'He was so excited when we were talking last night about living in the village, how happy we all were back then. How much he could remember you and your Gran. It was like it was the most important, the best time of his life. He's dying, Billy. I think he wants you to do the ritual for him. He wants to die peacefully.'

I stared at him. The food had turned sour in my stomach. Too many other images, other sensations were grabbing at me now. Johnny was still talking.

'You could do it for him. I'd give you as much money as you want, whatever you want, just ask. You remember my Dad. He's a good man; he was always nice to you. Please help him.' Tears were running down John's face, he'd splashed wine on the damp shirt, the stain spreading over his chest.

I felt as if I was suffocating. The smell of the food was mixing in my head with summer heat of thirty years ago, the stench of old canvas and tobacco. I could hear oystercatchers calling across the bay. Johnny had gone back into the house to clean himself up after being sick from the beer. His father staggered into the tent, drunk, crawling in beside me to say sorry for waking me up, just thought he'd check I was OK. Fine, smooth fingernails. You spend enough time sitting in a doorway; you can remember every little detail, every grope, every bit of pain in your life.

'OK' I said, 'I'll come and see him. But I don't want anything. The whisky's enough, that and a good meal!'

It was a small village we lived in. My sister and me living with my old Nana. We were right on the edge of the place. No one ever came near us, except when they needed her. But then Johnny and his parents arrived. He was the only friend I had there. He spent hours at our cottage. He loved the stories that Nana told us; the old ways, the rhythm of the sea weaving through them. He'd heard whispers about the Sin Eater. I told him what was generally known. Why the others avoided us. Nana knew too much about them all, but they would send for her anyway, near the end. She would listen to their confessions, say the words, sprinkle the salt and water on the bread, pass it over them three times, then eat it and take their sins from them. She took away their evil and pawned her soul for the sake of their eternal peace. I knew what it meant to her to do that. But she knew all kinds of magic.

It was years after John left the village that Nana told me the rest. How the sins had to be cast off into the sea. If they were still carried by the living then the dead hadn't been truly cleansed and their souls would wander crying in their grief until the end of days. The ritual was secret and a deeper magic that cast runes around the sins before they could enter the waves. I saw her do it once. I followed her and hid in the dunes, watching her say the words. I saw the burden lift from her as she stood in the shallows, the water lapping round her legs.

So I went with John to the fancy big house. And I stared into his dad's eyes. I wouldn't take his hand, even when he reached out. I leant close and heard every word. I salted the bread, passed it three times over his heart, drank the water and ate up all he'd done. After, I held John as he wept.

He never came to my doorway again, but every so often I get a pair of legs who say that Mr Wallace has recommended me for a special job; whisky and food in payment. So I complete the ritual and say the words. But I never go to the sea.

Sushirexia

Remembrance

Elinor Brown

There was only one place left to look. Armand had lost count of the weeks he had been searching, of the faceless doors he had opened into inns, churches, market halls, of the crowds he had scanned for that one, recognisable smile.

The merchant city disintegrated into a web of narrow streets, lanterns muted with red glass. He was near. The street led into a small square. A dog barked in the distance. In the far corner was a house, boarded-up, with an apothecary's sign hanging on loose hinges; exactly as Thibaud described. Armand could still hear his voice.

If you can't find me when this is over, you can always try the sanctuary.

Their last night. At dawn they had crossed enemy lines.

Armand stroked the scab across his cheek. He could peel it off, dig his nails into the raw centre and feel something.

The door was open, the passageway bare. Armand walked towards the light, an archway curtained with silk threads, strung with pearl cocoons.

'Hello?'

A shadow moved inside.

'May I come in?'

Silence.

He parted the threads, which clung to his fingers.

Inside, the room was lit with candles and a woman stood poised, her mouth open in a half-smile, lips shining around teeth. A lace dress started at her throat and clung to her breasts.

'It is late to be visiting?'

'I'm sorry. I was looking for someone. I shouldn't have disturbed you.'

He turned to leave and she slipped in front of the doorway, blocking the exit. He could see the pattern of her skin.

'It would be polite to introduce yourself.'

Thibaud's voice laughed in his head.

If your wit was as quick as your sword, you might stand a chance.

He would have had the perfect response.

'My name is Thibaud St Paul.'

He watched for her reaction, a twitch of recognition, but she held his gaze.

'They call me Clémence. Why don't you stay? You won't find anyone at this hour.'

He was tired. She stroked the wound on his cheek, trailing her smooth hand down his neck to his chest. He tensed and she stopped. She was still blocking the exit.

'You'll stay for a drink at least.'

'It seems I must.'

'Nothing is as it seems here.'

Clémence motioned him to a chair and glided over to the table, where she filled a cup from a pewter jug. She brought the cup to him. He tipped it to his lips, its sweetness masked bitter almonds. He put the cup on the arm of the chair and tried not to lick the moisture hanging on his mouth. Clémence stood over him, smiling. Her face blurred.

'You are tired. I have the perfect room for you, a bed made to measure.'

'Thank you, but I should go.'

He stood unsteadily. She took his arm.

'You will not find who you are looking for here, but you can forget.'

'Sometimes it's not possible.'

'There is always a way.'

Armand shook his head, but he let Clémence steer him into a long corridor. The floor lifted with the soles of his shoes, each step heavier than the last. They wound through the building in a tightening spiral, passing shrouded doorways.

The passage narrowed and Clémence stepped ahead. She picked her way in the gloom, untroubled by the sticky floor. Armand lumbered behind her. How Thibaud would have ridiculed him. He exhaled a laugh.

She turned.

'Something amusing, Thibaud?'

Thibaud's name in her mouth, she flayed the letters, dissecting the lie.

If you can't find me, don't worry...

Clémence scuttled ahead, laughing and stopped at an open doorway. The room was filled by a four poster bed. She leant against it, arching her eyebrows, lips glistening. Armand rested his head against the doorframe, wanting to weep.

... I'll be lying quiet in the dirt.

Clémence's long fingers held aside the canopy.

'Come, I understand. I have lost loves too.'

Close enough to touch her, he stumbled onto the bed, which sank beneath him, a hammock. Thibaud had known they would not meet again. Clémence crawled on top of him. Thibaud had known he was nothing without him. She stretched his arms above his head, her breast brushed his mouth as she wove his wrists together with silken ties. Thibaud had given him a way out.

There was no air.

Clémence sealed his lips with a stroke of her finger. Her head was shrinking, her eyes mercury. As he struggled, the cords on his wrist pulled tighter, the soft mesh beneath him held him immobile. Clémence lifted her dress up over her face, eight eyes glinting between the lace. She let her webbed skirt fall over him. His eyes met her silver-white belly, round abdomen rocking, pressing against him while her limbs pinned the web around him. He retched a cry, gagged. She leaned towards him, her mandibles protruding through the silk, her liquid mouth, her teeth grazing his neck. Her voice a breath:

'Sleep well, Thibaud.'

Sushirexia

Yellow

Kathrine Sowerby

I'm on the fries, shuffling and scooping salty chips into carton after carton, lining them up and passing them on. The same music has been playing since the start of my shift and I sing along under my breath but the heat is too much. Sweat marks are growing on my standard issue T-shirt and I turn my face to the cool of the restaurant. That's when I see her. Her hair is pulled back off her face into a tight ponytail. Her skin holds an orange glow under layers of foundation. Circling the table, she takes off her kids' coats and hangs them on the back of their chairs. She shakes their chips into a single pile, bites the corner off a sachet of ketchup and squeezes it over the heap; slapping at the children's hands when they reach out too soon.

Growing up, Alyssa's family had ruled the street by sheer quantity. There were four of them, Alyssa and three older brothers. Graeme, the youngest of the boys, had an ink spill birthmark over his right eye and tight black curls.

'Shit.' I blow on my wrist where a line of skin has already wrinkled and turned beige. 'Cover for me, Pete.'

I lock the door of the staff toilets and run the tap until the water is ice cold. My knuckles turn white as I clench my fist in the sink letting the water stream down my arm. I look at myself in the mirror. The light is unkind. My hair is stuck to my forehead and a film of grease coats my cheeks and chin.

Alyssa and Maggie had led me away from the caravans our class was staying in for the week. The same caravans the primary sevens took over every Easter. As we passed the farmhouse Alyssa stopped. 'Keep watch,' she said, and darted into the chicken coop nudging birds out of her path with her feet. She came out with an egg in each hand. 'For later,' she said, 'don't break them.' They were still warm and I held them deep in my pockets; their shells smooth like sea beaten stones in my cupped hands.

We followed a rough track through the trees. I tried to step on the smooth crusts of earth the tractor tyres had left but every few steps the surface broke and mud coated the sides of my white trainers. We passed the pond where the rowboat lay half in the water, half on the shore. There were deep scores in its fibreglass hull as if it had been dragged along the ground. A single oar lay propped on its bench.

We turned uphill where a digger sat stranded in a chewed up mangle of branches until the track came to a clearing with smaller paths running off it. The gentle slope was covered in unruly clumps of gorse sprinkled with yellow flowers. Tufts of fleece caught on stray branches fluttered in the breeze. After going down several dead ends, treading the bracken flat underfoot, we edged between the bushes into a clearing with a tree in the middle. Moss-covered rocks formed a broken circle round its trunk.

'Sit down.' Alyssa said and she plucked a dandelion from the ground. She rubbed its head on one of her plump cheeks then the other as if putting on blusher. With a fresh flower she leaned over and did the same to Maggie then turned to me. 'Maggie's already made a promise,' she said, rubbing the cool pollen onto my face. 'You'll need to prove yourself, Saffron.' Jets from the RAF base roared overhead. 'You want to be part of the gang, don't you?'

I remembered my brother, Boyd, picking a buttercup from our garden, holding it under my chin then passing it to me. The sheen of its petals reflected onto his delicate skin and a golden sphere vanished and reappeared as I waved the flower about. 'You have to hold it still,' he said.

I remembered that day, from the beginning, while Alyssa and Maggie talked out of earshot, Boyd sitting next to me on the low wall in front of our house, the boys from down the road coming out and waving at us to follow them. There can't have been school that day. 'I'll watch out for you,' Boyd told me.

The boys crossed the field, took the path through the woods. It was the furthest I'd ever ventured and we stood on the embankment knee high in daffodils looking out over the dual carriageway. It was mid morning and quiet. I hung back from the group as they went down the slope to the road. Graeme, Alyssa's brother, bent over Boyd and whispered something in his ear. I saw Boyd shake his head. The sun caught a hint of red in his blonde hair. Graeme put his hand on Boyd's back, disturbing the horizontal stripes on his T-shirt, and together they looked up and down the curve of the road. Then Boyd was running. Across one lane then another. He touched the barrier on the central reservation and turned. A van came from nowhere. There was a sound like someone kicking a football and I saw Boyd flip into the air, his body arched. The boys ran past me and up the hill, flattening the flowers, as the van spun in circles across the road. I felt something hot running down the insides of my legs.

'Take your top off.' I didn't move. 'Come on.' I looked at Maggie and she looked away. I unzipped my hoodie and laid it on the ground being careful not to break the eggs. I pulled my T-shirt over my head and dropped it, clutching my hands to my chin to cover my chest. Alyssa stood up and pulled at my elbow. 'Let's see how grown up you are.' She and Maggie laughed. 'Okay, you're going to follow me. Saffron in the middle.'

Alyssa ducked under an overhanging branch. She crouched down on all fours at the mouth of a tunnel that ran at sheep height through the thicket of gorse.

'Come on,' she shouted and sped off. Maggie gave me a shove from behind. I heard the thorns spike and catch on Alyssa's cagoule and tried to push the branches away from me but they sprung back, puncturing my bare skin. I kept going. My arms and shoulders got the worst of it. Thin trails of blood rose to the surface of the white scrapes as we wove through the tunnels until Alyssa started swearing.

'My jacket's getting ripped to shreds,' she yelled and, after a few wrong turns, led us back to the rocks. The three of us stood in the clearing looking at each other. I didn't bother to cover myself.

'Give me the eggs,' Alyssa said. They were cold as I passed them to her. 'Stand against the tree,' she ordered and I stood with my back to the trunk. She turned her finger in the air. 'Other way.' I leant my forehead against the bark and waited while Alyssa and Maggie giggled behind my back then something thumped against my shoulder blade. I cried out, saw the shell fall to the ground, and felt the egg run down my side. I put my hand on my waist where it pooled in the gape of my jeans.

'Last thing,' Alyssa said as she took me by the arm. She led me out of the clearing and down to the burn. She pushed me to the ground, clenched a handful of my hair and dunked my head into the shallow water. I gasped as cold drips fell onto my shoulders. Alyssa cracked the remaining egg on a rock and handed me the bigger half.

'Swallow this and you're done.'

The yolk shone through its transparent white and I knocked it back, gagging as it slid down my throat. I threw the shell into the bushes. Maggie and Alyssa clapped.

'We'll leave you here. You can get cleaned up,' Alyssa said.

'Don't take too long,' Maggie called back as they disappeared over the curve of hill and into the trees. Sprouts of milky primroses lined the side of the burn. My jeans were damp at the knees.

I went back to the clearing and gathered up my clothes. Spots of watery blood seeped through my T-shirt as I pulled it on. Raw egg lined the insides of my mouth so I picked a handful of gorse flowers and ate them a few at a time. They tasted sweet, like coconut, as I chewed on them but a bitter aftertaste lingered after each mouthful. I pulled up my hood, lay down on a bed of moss and listened to the muffled bleating of newborn lambs from the other side of the glen.

Bending over the sink I gulp down mouthfuls of cold water, dry myself with a paper towel and go back out to the kitchen. 'Thanks, Pete.'

'You okay?' he asks, handing back the chip scoop.

'I will be.'

I wasn't the youngest in the street. Chloe, an only child, was the one who got left behind on the bikes, laughed at when she couldn't keep up. I went unnoticed, Boyd's little sister. I tagged along. We lived on the edge of the town. There were fields, woods, the chimney of an old gasworks. I still live there. Every day I drive down the same stretch of road, take the same exit from the roundabout to get to work and every Spring I cut a bunch of daffodils, cross the lanes, and tie them to the barrier where Boyd's hand rested for that brief moment.

Alyssa's family moved to an estate on the other side of town before we started secondary school. If we passed each other in town she looked away or kept on chatting to her friends and pretended not to notice me. I hadn't seen her in a long time.

I glance across. She is sitting with her back to me. The purple strap of her thong has risen above the waistband of her jeans. As the kids eat she stares straight ahead. I check the time and keep the chips coming.

Sushirexia

The Famine

Ulrich Hansen

—

I can't have been more than four or five, but standing on the window sill I could see it all. The fire made the sky darker than I had ever seen it before, and although it was the bakery that was burning, you could see the flames reflected in the windows of the shoe shop and the newly built supermarket. From where I stood the whole world was ablaze.

There are things you experience and things you are told. Over the years the drape between them is eaten away. That it was the third week of advent no one disputed. After that most agreement stopped. One story was that the fire had started in the bakery, most likely the chimney, and from there spread to the living quarters. Another version, mainly circulated in the butcher's shop, saw the fire move in the opposite direction. Fact was, as the butcher put it, that he had heard that the baker's wife had gone upstairs, leaving behind her a wreath with three lit candles, held mid-air by red ribbons.

As people came rushing out of the neighbouring houses it quickly became clear that while the baker had made it out, his wife was nowhere to be seen. It took five men to hold down the baker who would otherwise have gone straight back into the flames. While one group took it upon themselves to prevent him from going in, another group was trying to figure out how to get the wife out. By now the heat was so strong that one after the other, the windows started exploding. All the time the wife was upstairs. From her elevated position she must have been able to see the blue lights from the fire engines coming all the way from Odense, but really, they were nowhere near fast enough.

Whether it was because the flames were the only thing welcoming her at the bottom of the stairs or if it was the smoke, nobody knew. However, next thing the wife appeared in a window and before anyone could start looking for ladders she was out on the roof. Clutching in her hands an early oil painting by Oluf Høst, she took one precise jump into the naked arms of a rhododendron. For the second time that day the emergency services received a call from Sønder Nærå, this time requesting an ambulance.

By the time the fire engines pulled up, one of them driving right into the garden, there was little of the building left to be saved. The next many hours they kept spraying water at a fire that didn't want to die. My last memory of that evening is lying in bed with the lights from the engines flashing across my ceiling.

The following morning the fire fighters were gone leaving only the soot covered walls and a smell of burned toast.

It took the entire spring and summer to rebuild the bakery, and when it finally re-opened the baker's wife was walking again. Up until then we all had to make the six kilometre journey to the bakery in Nørre Lyndelse. While the butcher thought the bread from Nørre Lyndelse was at least as good, to everyone else, that spring was remembered as the famine.

Cocoon

JL Williams

—I was sitting on a porch step. The sun was, as it is now, white, hazy – it came down through the air like a substance. My hands had dirt on them so I rubbed them against the cut-off trousers I was wearing. The dirt came from my hands onto the trousers. There wasn't anything much more to it. Nothing happened. No dog died under the porch. I just looked up into the sun and there wasn't anything there, in me. I mean, I realised there wasn't anything there at all.

He thinks he could leave her tomorrow and it wouldn't bother him.
He's not sure that's the truth.
He looks inside. There is a wall held up with scaffolding and sheets of plywood. He wonders if it's what's left of "history". No blood stains. Quiet of a closed construction site. Muddied windows. Floating motes of dust.

—No, it's wings.

She looks again at the trembling wall of light and colour. Hundreds and hundreds of butterflies. She laughs, stares up at him.

—Name, sir?

He coughs. He looks at his hands. Dirty. He rubs his hands on his trousers.

—Name?

His right foot is itchy, where the arch curves up from the ball. He stamps his foot on the floor. The officer with the gun by the door takes a step closer. The man at the desk lifts his eyes to the officer and the officer steps back.

—It's just for the record, sir. You're not in any trouble.

He rubs his hands on his trousers. He feels too aware of his skin. It is itchy and warm all over. He can't remember his name.

—I was onstage, like in the movies. And I was really happy. I was singing and I had my eyes closed. The voice coming back to me through the monitor sounded like, sounded pure. I was so happy. But then I was floating up, out of myself. I could hear the music getting farther and farther away until it was, sort of an echo.

He is confused. Balance. Clarity. He pictures a marble arcade with a pane of glass hung from a keystone every ten feet along. He imagines the panes rotating.
There isn't much left; the clothes on his back, her smell on the mattress in the corner of the room.
It's a sound like a gut string snapping, then a crash so loud it drowns him out. Explosions of glass every ten feet along.

—I stopped eating the same time I started walking You can go for a long time. Yeah, it hurts at first. Well no, I mean, you'll know what it's like at first. Nothing, then the regular old, "Oh, I'd like a burger right now," then after a while you get grumpy and tired, a little faint. The walking helped. Blisters really helped.

—Yeah, I think he walked too. He was trying to find something, wasn't he?

—I don't know, like, getting lighter and lighter. Like feeling as if you're see-through, like things could pass right through you.

—In the hospital? Well I didn't want them too but I couldn't stop them. You know what that's like?

—I don't know what perfect'd be.

She turns to him. The sky is glass blue, blown by a light the source of which cannot yet be seen. He is sleeping. She smiles. Her heart is full as a bucket pulled up from a well in the rain.

—My cup runneth over, she whispers. It runneth over.

He tries to get his clothes off but they grapple him to the ground. Millions of invisible needles impale every nerve. It takes four men to hold him. He can be heard on the street.

Hush little baby don't say a word, momma's gonna buy you a mockingbird and if that mockingbird don't sing momma's gonna buy you a diamond ring and if that diamond ring don't shine…

It stops there. She doesn't remember what comes next. Searches her mind. A moth jitters along a steamed-up pane of glass.

—But do they eat? What do they live on? Don't they get hungry?

—They don't need food or water in there. Ah, I just realised – the "skin of glass", it's the pupa. Looks just like glass. And when they come out, it takes a while for the wings to dry. Before that they're crumpled-up towels. But watch, see – they have to pump them full and climb up someplace high so the wings dry out. Then they can fly.

—Cell was empty in the morning. His clothes in a pile; dirty, wet. Gave the officer on guard hell but there was no explanation. Nothing tampered with. All the locks and alarms working fine. He'd never touched his dinner. Managed to keep it out of the papers, that's all.

—I guess I wanted to be… to get rid of all the bad things I'd done. I wanted to go away somewhere, to get cleaned up of all that stuff and come out like something else.

—What so many people don't realise is it's feeding we need. To store up for the change. All the hurt people in the world doing bad things, they're just hungry.

—True, you couldn't have told me that. Have you seen how a butterfly wing is, so powdery, you can see right through? That's how I wanted to be. Thin enough.

—I got pretty damn near. He didn't rescue me, no. No, sir. I rescued me. It was later. It was when I was finally ready to eat.

He lifts a sheet thrown over a pile of boards. Hundreds of wings explode into the air. He stumbles and falls back onto the rubbish-strewn ground, a storm of moths wheeling and glinting.

She touches his hand. He turns to look at her, and then at what she has found; hanging from a branch, a row of empty cocoons.
He realises that he couldn't do without her, but doesn't say anything. Just touches her, so gently, on her face.

—I'm not sure what's right. I go, and then I come back. Ever since that time when I was a boy. It's like, sometimes I'm here, sometimes I'm not. I don't know if I'm best off trying to be here, or trying to be away. I feel like I'm in between, like something in me is changing.

An Act of Desperation

Arthur Ker

I don't expect pity. I know that anyone hearing the story over coffee break or in the pub is going to smile. They'll file it away so they can entertain their friends and dinner guests for years to come. And who can blame them. I would do the same myself. It's one of those 'You'll never believe this' stories.

I've asked myself a hundred times: Why did I do it? It was an act of desperation, but what was I so desperate for? The money? No. Another six grand would have been nice but I didn't need it. With my salary, plus what I got from her father, Melanie and I were doing fine. I made sure she wanted for nothing. We had a comfortable home, a car, and a foreign holiday, most years, through the last minute deals. There wasn't enough to indulge my old passion for designer clothes and handbags, but there was always the sales.

No, it was something to do with the constant rejection, watching people I considered less experienced leapfrogging over me just because they have the gift of the gab. My problem is that I ramble – so I was told at the feedback session after my last interview. They didn't use the word *ramble* of course, they said I missed key points, lost my focus, got diverted, side-tracked, flew off at tangents. I talked complete crap in other words. The thing is, outside that pressured situation I can be perfectly coherent, it's just in the heat of the moment I go to pieces. Any presentations I do are great, because I spend hours planning them, and hours more getting every last word off by heart.

Of course that was my downfall on this occasion. Getting it off by heart.

At the time I wasn't sure what happened. They asked me the same question twice, or so I thought. I was so hyped up that I went into automatic answer mode before I realised what I was doing. I remember thinking, this is weird why don't they stop me? Why doesn't one of them say I'm sorry we've repeated that last question? But nobody said a word. The five of them just sat staring at me with blank expressions.

The one thing I was aware of was that none of them made notes or ticked their response sheets. There's a procedure to these interviews and they strictly adhere to the five or six set questions and never offer any prompts or follow-on questions. It's so they can't be accused of directing the interviewees, or favouring one candidate over another. But surely they should've admitted to a simple mistake like this and moved on to the next question.

Just as I was coming to the end of my answer, for the second time, the sun appeared from behind the clouds and the panel members were silhouetted against the glare. It was difficult to read the expressions on their faces as I waited for the next question. There was a long silence in which Derek from personnel, who was chairing the interview, glanced at Walter, the Depute Principal, before asking me the final question.

I immediately launched into my response, but I could sense that the atmosphere had changed. There were no encouraging smiles or nods of the head. As soon as I looked at them they looked at their notes – even Walter, who up until then had been grinning into my face when he wasn't surreptitiously ogling my legs. They all avoided eye contact with me, especially Sarah, the Head of Faculty

At the end of the interview they asked if I had any questions. I'd prepared a couple on topics that I knew were close to Sarah's heart. I thought they were brilliant. They were designed to show that I was clued up on the latest educational developments, and that I recognised Sarah was a forward-looking faculty head, determined to get these programmes up and running. So I couldn't believe how curt, and cold, she was in her reply. She was always friendly enough in the past. We live two streets from each other and quite often shared taxis back to the west end after college functions. On a couple of occasions we even dropped into the bar in the converted church at the end of her street for a nightcap and a gossip.

Sarah's on the big side, and has absolutely no sense of style. So maybe I should have dressed down on this occasion rather than making the best of myself. What worked for me where Walter was concerned obviously worked against me in her case. You sometimes find that with successful women, especially plain ones, they surround themselves with young syco- phantic men and keep more attractive female rivals at arms length. But if I'm honest, Sarah wasn't really like that, she'd appointed younger women to promoted posts in the past. If it were down to Walter the job would be mine, of that I was certain. He'd been pestering me for years and I'd always been careful to keep the flirtation at simmering point. He'd made some indecent proposals when he'd been the worse for drink but never followed through when he was sober. He was like a lot of men in that way. At the start of the interview he was definitely rooting for me, but now even he looked frosty.

Derek thanked me for attending and said the successful candidate would be informed the next day. Not one of them looked at me as I thanked them and got up to leave.

As soon as I got outside the room I started shaking and had to reach for the wall to steady myself. The next candidate was sitting waiting to go in. She'd looked up and smiled as soon as she heard the door shut, but when she saw the state I was in she stood up and grabbed me by the arms.

'Are you alright? You're as white as a sheet.'

I think she was frightened that I was going to faint so she tried to steer me to a seat.

'I'll be fine,' I said. 'There's a water cooler at the end of the corridor. Once I've had a glass of water I'll be okay.'

'Do you want me to come with you?'

'No. No. They could come out at any minute and call you in. You better stay here.'

She was attractive, probably in her late thirties or early forties. I almost asked her who her colourist was. The glasses, the suit and the shoes were all quite conservative but with a clever modish twist only a former label freak like me would notice. The material of her grey suit looked like a silk and linen blend and had a delicate striped effect. If the job was awarded on personal presentation she'd get my vote. She escorted me to the glass doors leading into the corridor.

'Were they really that bad?' she asked.

'No. It's just the after effect of the adrenaline rush. You know what it's like.'

'Yeah,' she said, frowning and holding the door open for me.

After I got myself a glass of water I went out to the back door for a breath of fresh air. Nikki from Learning Support was leaning against the railing having a cigarette. Suddenly it wasn't fresh air I wanted.

'Can I cadge one of those?' I said.

'Sure, Jacqui,' she said, handing over the pack and her lighter. 'I can't think the last time I saw you out here with a coffin nail in your hand.'

'It's been years,' I said, sucking the nicotine deep into my lungs. 'But God it tastes fabulous.'

'Really? Anytime I've restarted the first one's always tasted like shit. It's never stopped me reaching for the next one, mind you. Had a hard day?'

'I've just had an interview for the HOD post in Business and Accounting.'

'Brilliant. How did it go?'

'Really badly I think.'

'Och never mind, there's always next time.'

'I don't know. That was my fifth interview for one of these posts. I wanted it so much too. I don't understand how it went so wrong, I couldn't have been better prepared.'

Just after three o' clock my phone rang.

It was Sarah, asking me to come down to her office, straight away.

I went into my desk drawer and got out my little stand mirror. My face was still fresh from the touch-up after lunch but I reached over to my make-up bag for my lipstick and gave my lips a second coat, for good luck. I blotted off the excess with a tissue and shook my hair, running my fingers through it to give it some volume.

As I walked along the corridor to Sarah's office I had an unexpected rush of optimism. They usually only contact the successful candidate on the day of the interview, the rest are always forced to wait till the next day to be informed of their failure. I'd been over the interview again and again in my head during the afternoon and there were a couple of moments I thought it wasn't a complete disaster. There was that sticky point when they repeated the question, but that was their fault not mine. The strained atmosphere afterwards was probably due to their embarrassment.

I straightened my top and entered the outer office where Jane and Eileen have their desks. Eileen looked up and smiled. Sarah's door was closed, which was strange because she operates a literal open-door policy.

'Sarah's expecting me,' I said to Jane.

'She's having a quick word with the Depute Principle and Derek from personnel. Take a seat, Jacqui, I'm sure they won't be a minute.'

I sat on the seat outside Sarah's door. I was feeling a lot more positive now. Apart from that unfortunate hiccup I was certain all my other answers were near faultless. It doesn't all hinge on the set questions anyway, there's experience, academic and professional qualifications, and personal qualities to consider. I'd made sure in my CV and during the interview to highlight my personal qualities. I was committed, competent, flexible, friendly. I got on well with other people but was also an independent worker. I was methodical, positive, practical, receptive, relaxed, and above all reliable.

'Sit down, Jacqui, we want to discuss your performance at the interview this morning.'

It didn't sound as though they were about to offer me the job. As soon as I'd entered the room and seen the expressions on their faces I knew something was up. Walter didn't even look at me, he kept his eyes fixed on Sarah. I crossed my fingers under the table.

'You must have had time to consider how the interview went,' said Sarah. 'Did you find it unusual in any way?'

'Well, yes.'

'How exactly?'

'Well, you asked me the same question twice, and you let me go through the entire response again.'

Sarah looked at Derek and Walter, then lifted a sheet of paper from a pile in front of her and pushed it across the table to me.

'We didn't ask any question twice, Jacqui. Those are the questions we asked you. Have a look at them.'

I scanned down the list of questions. My heart thumped and started racing when I read question four, where the hell had that come from? I felt the colour draining from my face.

'Can you explain, Jacqui, why when we asked you question four you responded with the answer to question five?'

'Well, I must have misheard you. I'd anticipated most of these questions coming up and practiced my responses.'

'Read the two questions. Do you see any similarity?'

'No.'

'Neither do we. Which is why we've asked you in here to explain yourself. Take your time.'

'I've told you.'

When Walter turned and looked at me for the first time his eyes tightened and his crows feet sprung into sharp relief.

'The technicians are looking at Sarah's computer. She had her suspicions that someone had accessed her interview files which is why we inserted that extra question. This could become a matter for the police. We would rather it didn't come to that. Do you understand?'

'Yes.'

Walter folded his arms and leaned back in his seat.

'So can you explain these extraordinary anticipatory powers that you have?'

Derek accompanied me back to my office and stood over me while I cleared the personal things from my desk. Thankfully the other two senior lecturers I shared the office with were in class. Both of them had been up against me for the post so I wouldn't have been able to look either of them in the face.

When I was ready to go Derek helped me on with my coat.

'You were the last person we suspected,' he said.

We'd always got on well together. I remember, before the interview, he stopped me in the corridor one day and wished me all the best. 'It's your turn this time, Jacqui, I'm certain. Just relax and let your sparkling personality do the work. You know the format, you know the answers.' Of course he had no idea how prophetic he was.

I'm not sacked. Not yet. I've been suspended on full pay until the Senior Management Team and the Board of Governors have discussed the matter and come to some decision. It's all a formality. My life is completely fucked, and I have nobody to blame but myself.

I don't know how I'll ever be able to face my friends or colleagues again, but the one thing I absolutely dread is telling Melanie.

Sushirexia

Speaking in Tongues

Jose Velazquez

At the outer edge of the Milky Way galaxy there is a great blue planet called Rizon. It is one hundred times the size of Earth and contains cities with populations that approach and exceed one billion inhabitants. One such city, Fleghn-X1, is home to hundreds of skyscrapers and they are all, by law, green glass. Except one. The natives call it the Orange Blight. It stands 15,000 meters tall and sits atop the highest hill in the city. On the 4,256th floor, a resident is stirring. Ciacco Cosmopolitan stands in front of a large saucepot. If you were to try and describe Ciacco's carriage in human terms, you could consider an upright zebra, with three fingered hands and three toed feet in place of hoofs. The head could be a zebra's except for the third nostril, third eye and three mouths. Wash this mishmash of animal parts with bright red stripes and a pink base and you would have a Cerulean male[1]. Ciacco is holding his tongue with a pair of tongs while he waves a glowing red baton in his other hand. With a conductor's flick, Ciacco's tongue, severed from its stem by the 1693 degree Celsius implement, falls towards the preparation table. Impact seems inevitable but a Poinsettia leaf stretches out across the gunmetal surface. The leaf flexes, sending the mass into the air where a yellow gloved hand snatches it. Another glove cups it as the cut slithers in its own saliva. Ciacco raises the chunk to his eye level, turns it over and around a few times, and looses three big, happy grins.

He looks around his apartment windows to make sure the windows are set to the correct opaqueness even though he knows it is far too late.

---

1 Besides the necessary differences, the females are the same except the base colouring is gold and the stripes are green.

He already checked before he removed his clamp and blade from the safe behind the paint-by-numbers portrait he made of Pancho Villa. And again before he poured the goose fat into the pot. If anyone were scoping at either juncture, the caregivers would have sent their orderlies by now.

They would reattach his tongue. They would not use anaesthetic.

He didn't understand why he couldn't eat himself. Limbs grew back. In his opinion, the Doctrine of Unknown Potential (DUP) was absolute bullshit. But the politicians and most Ceruleans cherished it. DUPes, as the apologists were called, screamed that your hand might grow back but it could possess the slightest difference from its previous incarnation. This infinitesimal could mean symphonies. Ciacco was certain there were no grand movements coming from his hands. He had been on this planet alone for over three hundred years and had accomplished little more than a few hundred offspring (much to his mothers' chagrin) and a mountain of angry hive keepers. He could not even manage his families. Frustrated, he had taken them all[2], including his mother, on holiday and eaten them all . If found out, he would have countless forms to fill out and hours of community offering. He would rather face the orderlies than milk the worms again.

He plops the meat into the boiling pot of goose fat. The tongue convulses as it soaks in the scalding liquid, turning it a slight shade of blue. 'Perfect,' he thinks. As his tongue boils in the pot, Ciacco hands the clamp and blade to the Poinsettia standing next to him. The flora takes the instruments away.

The odour from the pot made him smile. No matter how many body parts he had consumed, he always enjoyed the smell of his boiling flesh. The scent fills his nostrils and he shivers. Ciacco, now erect, leans his entire head into the large pot when a bead of drool from his secondary mouth drops. Too engorged to notice the drop until the broth turns green and begins to hiss, Ciacco snaps out of his coma and screams with all three of his mouths. The Poinsettia, now watching his financial guild program, increases the volume on the viewer.

---

2 According to the Planetary Bureau of Statistics, this misdemeanour occurs roughly six times a day and has no significant effect on population growth. It is, however, considered impolite.

Next door, Klaus Ni, his new neighbour, an arthropod alchemist with metal claws (a typical accident for young metallurgists and not at all indicative of competency), is not as accustomed to Ciacco's screams because he has just moved in to the place with his brand new hive keeper and over 40,000 larvae. He hears the scream just as he is about to put his Worm Milk to his mouth. His fists tense up, and being coated in metal, crush his glass and spray the acidic drink all over his greater mandibles and onto his remodelled food island. He spews clicks and roars and stamps his lowest pair of feet. He scurries across his living room and punches the walls, screaming at his neighbour.

Ciacco, meanwhile, pours the contents of the pot onto the preparation stone, sending the tongue skidding off the edge and landing on the floor. He punches himself in his secondary mouth, punishing it for yet another mishap. He scoops up the tongue; gaining some new second degree burns and throws it into the mini reactor. He punches in the security code. A flash of red symbols appears on the display and they speed up until they are a purple blur. A shrill ding sounds from the reactor and Ciacco kisses the keypad. He slices open his palm with a free blade to produce a small amount of plasma. He opens the reactor door. Ciacco counts to X, as his psychic had advised him to do, and settles the tongue meat into his palm. He starts to massage the tongue into the blood, making sure to coat the meat when a furious rapping comes at his entryway. Ciacco motions to his Poinsettia, who is busy with currency exchange charts. Ciacco grunts and jumps up and down on the floor, forcing the plant to look his way.

'What do you want?' asks the flora, knowing full well its domestic responsibilities and full well its employer could not speak due to the delicacies of this particular ritual.

Ciacco pulls his peacekeeper from behind his back and blasts a warning shot that misses the view screen by millimetres. The Poinsettia bristles and leans over to pause the broadcast. He jumps out of his pot and hops to the door. Ciacco waves his fist at him and returns to the preparation. His secondary mouth is now drooling and a large and ever growing saliva stain is creating an umber spot in the middle of his apricot robe. But, at this point, Ciacco is near the end so he does not care for his couture.

A tugging at his robe makes him look down and the Poinsettia stands, drenched. Ciacco leans over and inhales for a full ten seconds. It smells like berries. It is wonderful.

'It is the arthropod and his hive keeper,' says the Poinsettia. 'They both protest and want to know the cause of your scream. As you instructed, I said you were preparing illegal self-body foods and made another careless error. As this is fact, they refused to believe it. They then proceeded to make a disparaging comment about my heritage and requested your presence for a personal explanation. I asked if I could be of further assistance. At this point, the one covered in worm's milk urinated on me. Let me correct myself. I believe it is urine but I am not familiar with this particular ethnicity's biology. I attempted to close the entryway, fearing this was not a prelude to more productive intercourse but the arthropod reached for me. I shut the hatch and five of his limbs are now pinched tight. As security[3] is outside the purview of my contract, may I return to my investments?'

Ciacco bellows. He does not have a security detail because he spends all of his extra money on goose fat. The Poinsettia shrugs and takes the absence of explicit prohibition as assent. Ciacco lumbers to the entryway and the five hands are scraping and causing a clanging racket as their owner tries to free himself. Ciacco reduces the opaqueness on the glass and he is now visible to and he can now see the frenzied Arthropod and his hive keeper as they screech at each other. He taps on the glass to get their attention and the couple stop their discussion and turn to him. Instead of being angry at each other, they now have a singular focus. Klaus' hive keeper stands behind him, offering a polite smile and then ducks out of sight. Klaus, despite full knowledge that Ciacco knows none of his native tongue, screeches a monologue at Ciacco. A rough translation follows: 'You too few legged beast. You have ruined my dinner for the last time. I am forced to buy new cups every week because of your bellows fun. You have an odour of vomit. What do you have to say?'

'I stubbed my toe. It was very painful. Don't you multi-legged freaks know anything about pain?' Ciacco asks knowing full well that they do not speak his dialect. Despite the vocabulary deficit, Arthropods from the

---

3 Euphorbia pulchirrima, when tasked with protection, have an excellent work record.

south sea of Delilah are quite adept at reading moods, lies and sarcasm. The Arthropod's eyes glow yellow and begin to ooze green puss. His hive keeper starts to slink away, knowing full well what is coming.

A torrent of profanity spews forth from the Arthropod's mouth. The hive keeper is now retreating in full gallop. Ciacco presses the door release and the Arthropod, who had been thrashing against his immobilization, falls backwards against the hallway wall. He sits there for a moment before unfurling himself to his full nine-foot height and stares down at Ciacco, who at five feet tall, is quite sizeable for a member of his people. Klaus' twenty metal hands ball into fists and his twenty biceps stiffen. Fourteen lives ago, he might have reasoned with the Arthropod but he knows he has just three minutes and forty two seconds left before his piece of tongue is useless.

Ciacco just sighs, rears back his beefy arm as Klaus' eyes widen in disbelief. There is no way he is about to be assaulted by this disgusting subspecies when he is in the right. Alas, he is wrong. Ciacco's arm meets Klaus' upper mandible claws with a loud crack. His hive keeper screams and, expels a red gas. Ciacco is trying to shake Klaus' mandible fluid off his hand but it is so viscous that it just bounces up and down. Klaus is hollering in pain, expelling spit and an untranslatable slew while trying to maintain his balance. Ciacco looks at his messy hand and Klaus' long, uncovered torso and proceeds to wipe the fluid off onto Klaus' exoskeleton. He has now so infuriated the Arthropod that it has turned from its usual shade of lemon to sapphire.

Ciacco recognizes the not-so-subtle change but all he can think about is his tongue soaking on the plate and the fact that he would not be able to get high again for at least another month. He steps back from the frantic Arthropod and presses the button on his door panel. A green mist sprays onto Klaus and he lets out a guttural scream, not from pain but, rather, indignation. Within seconds, Klaus is a statue, covered in a thin layer of green sauce that tastes like thyme[4]. Ciacco drags the statue into his foyer and moans at the Poinsettia, who is trying to ignore the entire situation

---

4 Ciacco knew it tasted like thyme was because he had once been parched after self-digesting and security
  system spray was the only liquid he could find.

and listen to a commentator discuss the milk trade market.

Despite Ciacco's recreational drug use, he was not such a bad employer so the Poinsettia turns and smiles. Generally, his employer's civil violations were not so grand. He had kidnapped and later consumed plenty of other citizens before but never the next door neighbour. This level of stupidity was unprecedented. The Poinsettia un-pots itself again and walks over to the frozen Arthropod and begins to size him up.

Ciacco storms out the door and the sound of an entryway opening and the Arthropod's hive keeper shrieking fills the hallway. Ciacco's bellows soon follow. The Poinsettia is retrieving ten jars from the cabinet when Ciacco, dragging the Arthropod's hive keeper by her legs and sporting six new deep gashes on his chest and face, seals the entryway behind him. The Poinsettia sharpens the saw while Ciacco forces the hive keeper into his laundry chambers and slams the door, sealing her in.

Ciacco exhales and looks at the clock. Only fifty eight seconds till the tongue is completely worthless. He moans. The sound of the saw going through the Arthropod's exoskeleton is grating and Ciacco shoots the Poinsettia an impatient look that the Poinsettia ignores. The Poinsettia knows full well that if he waits too long, the Arthropod's meat would go bad and there is nothing that smells worse. There are documented cases of death due to inhalation of the odour.

Ciacco looks down at his plate of tongue and sees that it is starting to steam. He knows he has less than twenty eight seconds before the tongue would eat through the plate and become inedible. Ciacco eschews the normal etiquette[5], grabs the tongue and jams it into his secondary mouth. The mouth chews once and swallows, causing Ciacco to nearly choke. But he could now feel the warmth in his belly as the goose fat batter, tongue meat and initial acids mix into a combination both illegal and intoxicating.

He begins to lose balance and half-waddles, half-falls over to his cleaning room. His bath is already drawn in preparation for this event and he shucks off his robe. His skin is already turning a deep shade

---

5 A complex ritual that is said to release the flavours in the body mass and heighten the hallucinatory effects.

of vermillion and his eyes are crusting over. He just wants to stop and enjoy the sensation but he knows that would be a waste of good tongue. He winces at the initial sensation of the water but the millennia old mix begins to work its chemical reaction. Ciacco's skin is now a deep burgundy and his eyes are covered by mustard coloured crust. His secondary mouth is pursed and chapped while his primary mouth hums like an oversized honeybee.

In the living room, the Poinsettia dims the lights, as he has done so many times before. He looks into the cleaning room and lifts a sample of burgundy cloth to make sure his employer is the correct hue, smiles and shuts the cleaning room door. He now has to deal with the usual preparation room cleaning and the additional inconvenience of putting down a hive keeper and putting both Arthropods into preserves. He begins to pull another ten jars from the storage shelves.

The water around Ciacco starts to boil and the entire cleaning room begins to fill with a steam that smells like oil. Ciacco is twisted at this point and even his ears fill up with an abnormal amount of wax. His swollen capillaries clog his nasal passages so he is forced to breathe out of his primary mouth. His secondary mouth is useless. He is in a sensory cloister. He can only taste the steam from the boiling water as it lurches around him. He strokes his belly and falls asleep.

Sushirexia

As Hard as it Gets

Alison Ryan

—◄—

Not many people are awake within the hostel, despite the lateness of the day. The park, which the hostel edges onto, is tinged in yellows and browns. Leaves lie in armful bundles. Mainly chestnut, each perfectly formed with five crinkly long fingers; each dying alone as they separate from the whole. The bandstand in the centre has fallen into disrepair. Concrete steps around it have worn away, anaemic looking grass attempts to thrive amongst the stones, and random pieces of litter are trapped in its circularity. People used to gather here to listen to brass bands on Sunday afternoons.

Man-made paths circle the park. They steepen in the middle, climbing until they reach the tall monument in the centre. Behind the monument are allotments and large Victorian greenhouses. Trails have been formed by centuries of footsteps. The top of the park has large bushes with soft, damp undergrowth. The wardens cut these back as they harbour many forms of life leaving sinister tracks. Rolls of long grass cascade down from the bush area until they reach the large pond with a boat shed at one end. It's painted local authority green and covered in graffiti. A pair of swans nests on the island within the pond, along with ducks and moorhens, amidst the discarded chip bags and sodden bread. In spring they all have young.

The pond can't be seen from the hostel. The residents would have to come out and walk away from the town and enter the park through the side entrance. Sometimes they do this. If they want to get away from the others. But mainly they walk out in a straight line, direct to the swings, where they gather to open up their space.

Someone is waking in one of the bedrooms: Michael. One long, thin arm hangs over the side of the bed. The Maori tattoo on his bicep looks like it is attacking him. His black hair lies flat against the side of his face. Small knots of muscle twitch under the white skin of his back. The room is large and dark, cocooned against the dimming autumn sunshine. The walls are the colour of good claret that has soured over many years. The dullness of the room hides the peeling paint. A large wardrobe stands alone at one end of the room, its doors bulge open with layers of fallen clothes.

Michael opens his eyes and then rolls onto his back. Instinctively he stretches his arm and feels under his pillow, fingering his three mobile phones and wallet. There are mud marks on the carpet and his trainers have grass wedged into the grooves of the soles. He closes his eyes again and thinks of the night before.

It hadn't been busy in the park. After a time of wandering and sitting, ignoring the other boys wandering and sitting, he had skinned up a fat joint of dark tobacco sprinkled with ketamine powder. He had lain on an old piece of fencing, torn from one of the allotments, discarded into the long area of grass. His hands dug into the soft earth, nourished by decaying leaves. With the cooling air spiking the line of hair on his bare stomach, he had left his body behind and glided over the venomous city.

Many hours later, when the wind began its howling and the branches above him shook like a murderous man with hands around a lover's neck, he had got up and walked down the hill towards the quiet of the pond. Another day was forcing its way in. Not bright enough to kick away the heavy darkness, but rather a reluctant grey dawn. Birds still woke with songs in their throats, and foxes stopped whining their baby cries. Michael turned off his phones and headed back to the hostel.

He forces himself to get up and takes the time to slip on his Diesel jeans that lie on the floor beside his bed, and puts his mobiles and wallet into the back pockets before he goes out to the small bathroom off the hallway. The ice cold linoleum shoots a pain up his legs as he washes himself at the sink with a disintegrating piece of soap. Looking in the mirror he pulls his long fringe to the side to check his face for stubble. His skin is almost smooth, even when he strokes his fingers across his chin. Only a few stray hairs can be seen around the high arch of his eyebrows. He takes each one between his almond shaped nails and pulls it out.

Back in his room he lifts his trainers, holding them away from his clothes until he's outside, where he scrapes them against the high pavement at the front of the hostel. He puts them on and walks over to the park.

The late afternoon sun is dropping and a cold chill hangs in the air. A couple of young kids from the hostel have settled around the swings.

The late afternoon dossers sit on the memorial benches, brown bags at their sides. As he wanders past, scanning them, he nods his head now and then.

—Okay son. They smile at him with a chuckle in their eyes.

He strolls down by the endless charity shops on Victoria Road. The women who volunteer pucker their faces as they shoo away the skinny, glazed eyed junkies who hang around outside. He recognises some of them from their occasional stays at the hostel. They look at him with their empty eyes. He pulls down his face and walks by.

Jumping on the number 66, he walks to a seat at the back, his head still low. The bus is busy and it seems like everyone has shuffled closer to him. Without looking up, he shortens his breathing to stop his body being invaded by theirs.

By the time he gets off, every part of him is trembling and a film of sweat has crept over his skin. He rests his hands on his mobiles. Each of his phones represents a different persona; young, hot and active; Latino lover looking for lust; sweet, gentle and submissive. Each contact detail attracts a different type of punter, and Michael catalogues them by storing their numbers in different mobiles; a kind of reference library.

He turns towards Merchant City. The wide streets and bright shops start to restore him. He crosses under a large archway, the feel of cobbles on his feet. Something catches his eye. Shoes, wicked shoes, long and slim with upturned points. There is no price label. A movement in the window makes him raise his head. A boy around his age is stretching over the display to pick up a shirt. He looks up and, for a moment, their eyes eyes hook onto one another. The boy smiles now. Not in a shy way, but open, confident, a grin maybe. Michael raises his eyebrows, and the boy smiles wider, his teeth showing. They stay like this until one of them has to move.

It's the boy. He sticks a little of his tongue out and cocks his head to the side. Then he leaves the window.

Michael walks on passing Armani, Gucci, Diesel. He slows at each window, his eyes hungry with desire. He remembers when a famous Scottish author came to visit the children's home. He was dressed in a way that Michael never imagined real people dressed. The care workers only smartened up when they attended panel meetings. This guy had a silk yellow hankie, bold as you like, hanging out of the pocket of a deep blue waistcoat. His trousers were light brown and fitted around his bum like they had been cut especially for it, and his shoes; his shoes, they were like a new world altogether, a parallel universe. Actually that is what the author talked about, he wrote fantasy novels and talked about other lives as Michael looked up and down from his shoes to his eyes. The author talked to a group of them, but his eyes held Michael's for a second or two longer than anyone else's. Michael had become aware of nerve endings he never knew existed. His stomach felt like it was flipping inside him like a gymnast on ropes and, for weeks, he couldn't wait to go to bed so that he could dream of him.

It's not long before he arrives at a large converted warehouse. Each brick is the same shade of deep red and slotted in perfectly, like pieces of Lego. Small windows sit depressed into the brickwork. He wonders why people pay a fortune for a small flat in something that looks like a prison.

He walks up some steps and presses the buzzer. There is no answer. He holds it in for a long time, aware that his wallet is thin and the rain is starting.

The light fades around him as he moves back down the steps and the noise of the build up of traffic on wet roads get louder. The city's pulse is quickening. It's a man in an expensive suit. He walks up. Michael stops, drops his hands into his pockets and leans against the steel railing at the steps.

—What you hanging about here for son? The man asks.

Michael smiles at him without parting his lips.

— I've seen you before, you visiting someone?

Michael doesn't move. His eyes stay level with the man.

—Someone isn't in. It's getting a bit cold waiting for him, fancy inviting me in?

Michel knows he's tempted, these types always are.

With one hand on the door, and the other guiding Michael ahead, they walk along the large hallway with a large mesh stairwell.

A prison, Michael thinks to himself.

The lift stops at the top floor, and the man taps in a code then walks through to a large grey panelled door.

There is only one wall in the living area; the rest is windowed from ceiling to floor. Michael stands and looks out. Blue and pink and white fairy lights, from the city's bridges, fizzle and splodge behind the streams of rain now battering against the glass. Sounds go on behind him. Fire sparking into life; ice clinking in a glass; cork being screwed in slowly then released. This is the life he will have one day.

Not too much later he is walking against the beating rain, crossing the bridge to the south-side of the city. Buses carrying grim faced workers file past him. The blue lanterns are now within a hand clasp away. He thinks of the man he has left behind, standing there naked and majestic at his long window, looking down.

Sushirexia

Moment of Silence

Elisabeth Ingram

Mhairi, 1979

From the beginning, our baby ruled us. I fell for her, fattening into a padded cell: I slept and woke and pumped milk according to her screams, hoping to make contact with her above the surface one day.

From that year, Owen and I ricocheted around the greedy sound of our crying child, wounding each other without target. Mhairi's body was quickly dissatisfied, she astounded us, becoming hungry again within minutes; out of control, she controlled everything, as madmen and dictators do. But we had elected her to join our house, so Mhairi became head of state, and she hung the halls with screams.

She grew, painfully, slowly.

She became a small howl, punctuating the hours with silences that made me think she was dead.

Aberfan, 1979

Aberfan is a ghost story. The place only exists because of the mine.

Thirty years ago, the week I turned sixteen in 1979, I married Owen. He was twenty-three, already a miner for nearly five years. His Da was a miner, my Da was a miner – that's the way it went. I always knew Owen – he lived next door – and I always liked him. He was too bright to live his life in the dark though. He knew everything there was to know about the world, but he kept it inside. Except for once. After he proposed, lying in the grass, he told me about the blackness. It made him cough, it was caked so thick upon his tongue, he had to spit it out. The light cut from his eyes into a slurry of words, broken down from deep inside, they grabbed the breath right out of him. He told me about days inhaled in a pit that didn't care if he ever breathed out again. Cased by black pressures of gas, thick indifference in shifting concentrations that strained the fault lines until the rock groaned, deeply, for miles.

Everything about my life before Owen noticed me sunk back from that day. Compared to what was black, what could burn, and earn enough to keep a town alive, what did I matter? Nothing was as important as his days gone under the hill. When he came home at night, his eyes shone brighter than the rest of him, and they were what I began to see through.

All mining men are men of few words. Owen was a man of action, especially that first hot spring he noticed me, the pit manager's daughter, growing up in spurts and curves. Each Sunday we would walk for hours, quietly out of it, away from the deep valley town and the black slagheap Mountains, into the green cradling rounds of the river paths. I looked over his silence at the flowers, blushing the ground into colour. I would bow my head with the river bank bluebells, their slight petals unsettled by the water throwing speckles of coal dust in their faces. After a time walking further, far away from the town, the bells would start to chime clear and blue, their stamens straight, green tones in the gentle wind; peals of clean petals unfurled down the hours, and he'd began to talk, as everything opened up around us, and began. After a few weeks, he whistled with the birds, falling into their swooped calls and upward flights into mating song. His lips would push the air into music. We lay on the ground, blanketed in white and yellow, and Owen stroked the earth, brushing his hand over the flowers, he smiled, 'Someone's pushing up daisies for you'. He picked them, threaded them, and hung the chain around my neck. I got pregnant out in the woods, the daisies wilting and snapping in my sweat.

We kept it secret for a while, we always shared our silences. That spring, the stream rushed full to bursting, white around town, fizzing down towards the green, dumping bubbles of wet black coal dust from the slag heap onto the river banks. There has always been something black running underground in Aberfan. Walking along I felt the undercurrent of men, sweating under my feet, drilling and digging, leaving something hollow beneath me. We walked on, all day, until Owen stopped for a cigarette. Rolling up tightly, he turned us back for home, back to the black fringed path, which closed up around us into the silence of Merthyr Vale.

Aberfan, 1966

I was only three years old in 1966.

Owen remembers everything about the year Aberfan became an event, not a place. He was ten and it was the last day before half term. He had been at school less than half an hour.

It had rained heavily, for two days. The children in the rear of the school had a view up the mountain, at the wave of skyline formed from seven giant piles of coal waste. Everyone took lessons in the shadow of this unwanted rock from the local mine. Someone must have known when they put a thousand tonnes of rubble on top of a stream, on top of a mountain, that it would end.

It was like thunder, but a thousand, thousand times louder.

Owen remembers every second of that sound. It seemed like ages, but it must have taken only minutes for the waste tip to fall down the mountain, onto the school: and then there was silence. The black wave of slurry had engulfed the room, and carried him along.

It went straight through the school, from back to front, half burying it.

Immediately after, Owen could hear all the other children. They weren't screaming, they were breathing out, trapped beneath, amongst, their desks. From a tall old classroom with echoes and sounds, there was nothing, and all the school went dead.

Slurry had cracked over walls, knocked the town unconscious.

Mothers were still at the gates after dropping off their children. In that silence, you couldn't hear a bird or a child.

Then the women dug, clawing the earth with their bare hands, breaking windows, shovelling sharp black sludge. In fifteen minutes, they had no skin left on their hands, they were down to the blood. They shovelled on, they were women like stone.

Hard men, miners, were afraid of that silence. Arriving at the school in a hurtle of lamplight and orders, they found the grit; the women, dug in, hard faces black, blank as the ground.

My parents dug for my brothers. Owen's parents dug for him, for his sister. Teams of fifty worked in long rows, digging, emptying the classrooms that had just been filled, hauling slurry back up the mountainside. At intervals, everything would come to a halt – the scrapes, the shovels, the shouts. Not a breath would be heard among the parents. They stood still, tense for the slightest sound from the wreckage. A shout, a creak, anything. They didn't find Owen's little sister for a week, but Owen was pulled out in minutes and taken to hospital. His parents dug all day not knowing if he or his sister were alive. They never talked about it. He just knew.

I was luckier. Both my brothers died, but I remember nothing at all about the day, only the facts I learned later. One-hundred-and-sixteen children dead and twenty-eight adults killed.

I grew up in a buried alive town, a near childless town. That is what I remember.

We were part of the missing generation of Aberfan. Me and Owen have always known that. We both knew what it was like to not go out to play because those who'd lost their own children couldn't bear to see us. We knew what they were feeling, and we felt guilty for being alive. Staying in was bad too, our parents had lost too much to let us out of their sight. We were the elite with new bikes and new clothes, a disaster fund. We lost out on our schooling. None of us travelled far, our generation, we all stayed here.

Every street has a house or a person that sticks like a lump in my throat. There were fatalities from every street in that school. All those years unlearned. 'Buried alive by the coal board' is what my Da said.

Mhairi, 1983

When Mhairi was downstairs napping, I'd run upstairs and do the housework. I'd see her hollow shape left behind in the bed.

That's what was left when the school fell down, Owen remembers.
For months there was rubble spiked with small wooden chairs, desks, carved wood still holding the shape of little bodies. For a year some of it sat around, heavy fragments of the school, chunks of green-painted classroom walls. For years our terrace looked right out on the abandoned rubble, a whole other terrace that liquefied slag had squeezed through like toothpaste. It must have been many years, because even I have half-lit infant memories of sagging, gaping frames, noises breaking down and leaving. Owen remembers looking through broken windows at scattered letters, coat hangers, and an open jar of pickles on a kitchen table. Coats left hang-

ing on a door that had no walls about it, just a frame. I remember a small brown pullover hanging there, and the rain hitting it, dirty sleeves cuffing damp beats on the door, slapping out a rhythm, the slow knitted presence of a narrative. A knot fingered Nan, a tied down Ma, hunched unspooling wool, measuring their child into the winter ahead.

Then it was all gone. The authorities came and knocked the houses down, and then the school. There's a remembrance garden there now. I don't remember any of it, solidly. There are the shapes though, patterns – a hanging, knotted dampness.

I'd try to ignore all this when Mhairi was a little girl. I'd get on with the housework. I'd smooth Mhairi's bed for her, make it new.

I grew up caring for my parents, stooping down to the graves of my brothers, of all the children. Cleaning the stones, bringing them flowers, tending to them.

I'd rush through Mhairi's room to finish the housework. I'd clean the windows, polishing my reflection into the town. I'd empty the bins, and when she screamed, I'd go downstairs to wash Mhairi's clothes, to make her some lunch, to wait for Owen to come home and the day to move on.

Mhairi played on the floor. Slicing up chicken, I noticed the kitchen door was always open, and the concrete steps leading down into the garden, inevitably positioned for Mhairi to trip over and fall down broken. I pared the bone from the chicken thigh, seeing how quickly it could be done, how cold the flesh felt, how efficient a mother can be.

There was a dead silence after the fall, while I questioned whether I had been willing this event to happen. Mhairi answered with a scream; it had a new tempo, like blood circulating in a brain that wasn't watertight, it heaved, raw with newborn fears.

The wound on her leg was deep. She wept big, lucid tears as the cut bled. Tears overwhelmed screams, and Mhairi fell into a word that tremored and came from her whole body, quietly and covered in snot:

'Daddy.'

Her eyes so full with emptiness I could see her heart beating out syllables through her eyelids. The throbs lengthened, widened, and fell:

'Daaady. Daaaaaaaddeeeey!'

Owen was working, and I would have to do. I took her to the Hospital.

The Doctor said the bone would heal, she was young and strong. He did not waste time on the surface, the ripped pink grazing her leg; he thought it cosmetic and irrelevant to address the hardening bruises, the blood diverted from her heart, bursting her veins.

When Owen came home that evening, Mhairi's crying began again as he stroked her hair and looked at her plaster cast. I left them alone in the kitchen. I sat down next door by the broken gas fire, eating a bowl of ice cream defrosted and re-frozen countless times into churned watery ice-crystals. I had shut the door, put the radio on loud. A comedy was playing. I let the day melt on my tongue, and through the window grey collided with grey in clouded silence. The garden was rain, concluded with Holly bushes, spikes hedging around us stubbornly evergreen.

Aberfan, 2009

I eat to keep going.

I see colours, and I hear too well, but as I age, my other senses are failing me. I can't taste, only sense texture or temperature. I can't smell. Food is either hot, or cold. It's slimy, or dry. I can't tell the difference between good or bad. It's hard to know what matters, or even what matter is.

The poster in our kitchen reads 'KEEP CALM AND CARRY ON'. I make the kettle boil, and cook a month old egg. It was best-before a week ago.

The rest of the day has the dry clogging texture of yolk embalmed by the slime of white.

I sit and watch the shadows on the dinner table swallowing up one cup, one plate, one egg.

'I'm sorry, he's gone.'

That's what the doctor said, with the snapped electric tone of a light switched off in a hospital room.

A flicker in a circuit, followed by a long black hum in a frequency only I can hear.

At dusk there is the heavy presence in the bin bag of one cracked empty shell.

The mine closed twenty years ago, what was a man to do, unemployed since 1989? Owen started drinking a bit heavier, to try and forget. But it doesn't work that way, if anything, it comes back twice as bad. He knew how sick he was – he worked underground for years, he knew when he was buried. It was the booze and fags that finally finished it. But it was the coal that undermined him from the day he started work. The dust seemed light, but airborn, it was something terrible. It inhaled through him, thickening his lungs, blowing him away.

Me, 1963

Long before I had a child, I was a child, and there was lightning.

I hid afraid in the half light of the night kitchen, underneath the dinner table. The wireless was on next door in the living room, talking loudly over my parents, who swelled together in occasional laughter, caught in the rise and fall of the evening's narrative. They loved listening to far away stories.

The night that there was lightning, I was torn between my fear of this new darkness, sharpened to black by shocks of white light, and my greatest fear: that of interrupting my parents' escape into story time. I was scared to be silent, and I was scared to cry, to remind them of everyday fears, to remind them of how a child feels alone in the dark. So I hid in the cave under the kitchen table, and listened. Without understanding any words clearly, I could hear the story was moving on. Somewhere through a wall, outside the kitchen and above the black, came laughter that could cut through lightning.

That laughter played through the evening, into the corners of the night, and I did not need them to hold me, anymore. When their story ended they went softly up to bed. I waited, hidden under the table, awake for a last touch to stir from their bodies. I heard them pass overhead, floorboards creaking them towards bed, pulled along by their shared stories.

Tomorrow, you'll come home for your Da's funeral, Mhairi. You'll sweep in wearing black, a long skirt touching the floor, brushing over steps, reminding the ground of your pain.

You're wordless, full of sentence. I'm afraid of the conclusion in your silence. You bury me in it, in your volume, the way you fill the room with your isolation. But your father said the only way to experience complete silence is upon death. Complete silence is when not the smallest sound is heard. Until then, there is always the sound of yourself breathing, and the wind blowing.

And there is a thrill that comes with fresh snow.

You'll make everything clear, appraising the house, its contents, evaluating your father's worth.

I will sit alone in the living room; with the radio turned high, life will go on as scheduled, through the news, on the hour, to a story, a comedy; the day playing out through the radio.

You will hear me, laughing, when I can. You will harden, strengthen, dig. You are a mining town woman, a woman like stone.

Acknowledgment:
Inspired by news and witness reports collected in Iain McLean & Martin Johnes, *Aberfan: Government and Disasters* (Cardiff: Welsh Academic Press, 2000). This is entirely a work of fiction, and all characters and events are products of the author's imagination.

Thwarted Little Redskins

Martin Shannon

◆

The hypnotherapist pulled an old, scuffed, wooden stool up close and perched beside me. The stool creaked loudly in protest whenever he shifted position and I fretted for his unsupported back.

'Relax!' he said, 'breathe deeply.'

I tried a few half-hearted, half-lungfuls then stopped abruptly – self-hypnosis I can do at home for free.

'What is it about your confidence you're concerned about?' he said, hugging his knee.

'I blush very easily,' I said.

Mr Cairney BSc, DHyp, blinked.

'Far too easily,' I added for emphasis, 'slightest thing sets me off.' He looked unconvinced. 'No, really,' I said, 'I can barely talk to anyone these days without having an episode. It's really holding me back at…'

'An episode?' he butted in.

'Yeah, an episode, that's what I call it when it goes beyond the point of no return. Completely out of control, y'know? Scarlet like no scarlet you've ever seen.' I flicked my fingers open above my cheeks in a face-exploding-into-flames gesture. 'That's an episode.'

'O-kay,' he said neutrally, which really pissed me off. Can't £40-an-hour buy a little empathy these days?

'You don't seem to understand,' I went on, 'my name's been a life sentence since school.'

Mr Cairney looked puzzled.

'Burns,' I said, 'Rory Burns.'

He nodded, eyes blank.

'This afternoon,' I went on, 'I was in a meeting. The Chief Executive,

Heads of Department, my boss and me. They were talking round and round the best way to present the half yearly results at the AGM and I didn't say anything for about three quarters of an hour then the Chief Executive, seeing that everyone else in the room had contributed 'cept me, said: what do you think, Rory?

'Well, let me tell you, I've got a head full of ideas that'd really make a difference but my mind went totally blank. I mumbled some incoherent nonsense – and I'm not just saying that, it really was incoherent nonsense – and there was this terrible stunned silence when I stopped. The Chief Exec shook his head a couple of times like he was waking from a bad dream, then he ignored me – completely blanked me – as an act of *kindness*, acted as if I hadn't spoken at all, and asked someone else for their input.'

'Go on…'

'As soon as the Chief Exec focussed the meeting on me I felt this 'click' inside me – a physiological click – followed by a whirring inside my chest like a little motor had just cranked up. Unmistakable. Unstoppable.'

'An episode!'

'A *full blown* episode.'

'So what happened?'

'Well, the discussion moved on and all the normal people started chipping in with their oh-so-clever suggestions of what to do, some of which, I swear, were ones I'd thought of too and they all seemed to speak with a spring in their step. Like they were rejoicing in the fact they weren't me.'

Mr Cairney said nothing.

'I corpsed,' I said.

It was true. Disfiguring blotches surfaced on my forehead, neck and cheeks. Not soft, muted pinks but violent, raw meat reds. Fight or flight prickly heat itched my skin all over and I ran, trying to shake off an army of colonising ants, racing to the zenith of my discomfort without even leaving my seat.

Men loosened their ties and unfastened the top button of their shirts in the insufferable heat. Women fanned themselves with papers. Someone opened a window, wedged the door ajar. Iced water turned lukewarm in the cooler then bubbled to a boil. Heat shimmers distorted the air creating mirages of puddles on the boardroom table. The wood creaked and warped. Seats drooped haphazardly as metal legs buckled. Watches melted on wrists, hands and faces wilted, numbers dripped to the floor. At the epicentre of my own microclimate, I sizzled silently, the very picture of awkwardness. Better I could achieve the natural conclusion of these episodes and spontaneously combust. Burst into glorious, purifying, sanctifying flames.

Instead, episodes peak quickly before the whirring slowly, slowly, slowly tails off. Taking hours to return to the pale palette of nondescript inscrutability I yearn for.

'Very common problem,' Mr Cairney said. 'These are elementary social skills I can help you with. Everyone gets these feelings – it's just that they've developed coping strategies to disguise their inadequacies. But we can work on that.'

Mr Cairney, I guessed, thought my condition was small beer. Didn't rate it compared with some of the more exotic cases he'd dealt with. 'Everything from agoraphobia to zelophobia,' it said in the airmail paper thin endorsement of his Yellow Pages listing. Red skin must pale in comparison. It didn't help my case that for some unfathomable reason my face right now was an alabaster mask. I was able to speak to him fluently and confidently without so much as the merest hint of a wine stain blotting my cheeks.

'I had one woman who came to see me, Rory,' said Mr Cairney, using the repetition of my name as a form of pre-hypnosis, unaware he'd already lost me, 'who had a self-destructive and self-defeating relationship with food.

'She didn't derive any pleasure from food whatsoever. She ate so fast she hardly tasted it. She suffered heartburn and dyspepsia. Even when she was so stuffed she felt ill, she never felt satiated or satisfied. During the day, when people could see her, she'd eat like a tiny bird but when she got home she'd race to reach the elusive well-being of a full stomach as fast as she possibly could. Only she couldn't stop, Rory, and she'd gallop right past the point of fullness into physical discomfort, bloated pain, heartburn, constipation but, above all, mental guilt and anguish. Only when she slept could she escape food until she woke again in the wee small hours and her first thought – before husband or family – was for what, Rory?'

'More food?'

'Exactly. More food. Can you believe it?'

'So what did you do?' I asked politely, prodding him towards the point of the story and its £40-an-hour relevance to me.

'I said, why do you feel the need to overeat? I'm unhappy, she said. Why are you unhappy? I said. Because I'm fat, she said. No! I said. That's not the real reason you're unhappy. Have you always been overweight? I asked her. No, she said. Have you always been unhappy? No, she said. Well, why do you eat so much? I asked her.

'She said – now listen to this, Rory – she said: I eat…because I'm hungry.' He threw his head back and laughed. 'Because I'm hungry!'

I nodded and smiled too, more at him laughing than for what he was saying. Frankly, I was perplexed. Couldn't for the life of me see what he was driving at.

'Because I'm hungry,' he repeated. 'It was the right answer. She wasn't hungry for food, mind you. She was hungry for something just as fundamental for her wellbeing. The hunger for something she couldn't readily obtain was finding its warped manifestation in an over-indulgence in food. Do you see?'

I nodded. Shook my head. Shrugged.

'Then I put her under hypnosis…imagine you've eaten a sumptuous six course banquet and no sooner have you eaten your last mint chocolate and drunk your coffee than the waiter returns with the first course all over again. He's not being judgemental. He doesn't even acknowledge he's served you before. You have unlimited funds and unlimited time. So you eat again and manage to eat the whole meal for a second time when, lo and behold, the waiter returns once more with the first course. And that is how it actually is. For there is no end to the food that's waiting to be eaten. You know this will go on for as long as you let it. No-one can stop this perpetual meal except yourself.

'Before, you were unable to say: enough! But now you feel so full, so brimming over, that you really couldn't eat another thing. The slightest taste of any food, even the merest morsel of mint chocolate would make you violently ill. You recognise that feeling of fullness now. It feels good. You couldn't eat another thing. When you wake, Karen – no, Caroline we'll call her – you will remember that feeling of well-being. A feeling you will always achieve now long before you've eaten too much. You will drink a large glass of water before every meal. You will eat slowly. You will savour tastes and textures. You will always leave some food on your plate. You will never ask for seconds. Your hunger will always be satisfied in this way.'

'We had a few more sessions then she came to the door six months later and I hardly recognised her. It wasn't just that she'd lost weight physically, she'd lost weight here too,' he tapped his temple meaningfully.

'Why do you blush, Rory?' he asked.

'I don't know. I'm embarrassed. Self-conscious.'

'Why are you self-conscious, Rory?'

'I don't know.'

'Ah, but you do know, Rory,' he pressed.

'No,' I said slowly, as if speaking to a child, 'I do not know.'

'You do. Think, Rory, think. Why are you so self-conscious?'

I cannot tell a lie but I was getting a mite tetchy with his line of enquiry. There was a clock on the desk behind him and I could quite clearly see that we'd run over the hour mark and he hadn't even begun to try and hypnotise me.

'Because I'm hungry?' I said flippantly. The words hung ugly as fly paper as Mr Cairney let the silence grow wings and flap manically around. My skin crawled. I expected short shrift. Instead, his neutral expression broke into a smile.

'That's right,' he said, 'because you're hungry. Not hungry for food, mind. No, no. Hungry for something else just as fundamental as food for your wellbeing, huh? A hunger that's finding its warped manifestation in an overblown self consciousness. Can you see?'

I just blinked.

'What are you hungry for, Rory?'

Cheesecake, I wanted to say. Money, women, success, I didn't know. My head was spinning with possible answers but which one to choose here? Which one did he want? Mr Cairney checked his wristwatch with a subtle flick of the eye but I clocked him. It put me off. Why bother? I was simply a time slot.

'Self esteem, Rory,' he said, reeling me back. 'Self worth. R-E-S-P-E-C-T as Aretha Franklin eloquently put it. Now,' he began in a brisk business-like manner as if everything that had gone before had all been mere preliminaries: 'sit back and relax.'

Hypnosis! At last! I sat back all eager. Closed my eyes then opened them straight away in case he was going to start swinging a watch on a chain. He wasn't. I closed my eyes again and peeked through my lashes to see what he was up to.

'Don't close your eyes,' he said.

'Oh.'

'I want you to place your hands on the armrests of the chair and keep them still. Very still. All the time relaxing. Letting the muscles in your arms relax. Your hands are feeling very heavy. You cannot lift your hands from the armrests they're so heavy. Very heavy.'

He lifted my wrist and shook it slightly as if to check for life then dropped it limply onto the armrest. He walked round to my other side and did the same. I was trying to let my hand flop without resistance but he clumsily dropped my hand to the edge of the armrest and I was forced to re-awaken my wasted muscles at jarringly short notice to place it back on the armrest. If he noticed he didn't let on.

He repeated the process and I grew a little less tense and a little more relaxed each time until: 'Lift your right hand two inches,' he said, and for a few moments I couldn't do it. For a few choice seconds, my hand responded with inert mutiny. Just long enough for me to get a glimpse of how hypnosis must actually work. But it didn't last. A single breath later I could clearly feel my hand begin to lift up, no bother, so I fought the impulse and kept it still. Pretended I couldn't move it. He'd prised open the window of my suggestibility for a moment but now it was firmly locked shut again. No way back in. I didn't want to spoil things though, so I played along.

'Now relax, Rory,' said Mr Cairney. 'Breathe deeply. Do you have gas or electricity at home?'

'Em, both.'

'Gas cooker?'

'Em, yeah, gas cooker.'

'Okay, I want you to think of your gas cooker at home. Imagine you can see inside the oven when it's on.'

'I can. It's got a glass door. You can see right in.'

'Good, good, well, picture the oven. In terms of gas mark 1, 2 and 3 etcetera, how embarrassed do you feel now?'

'I'm fine. Cool. Not embarrassed at all.'

'In terms of gas marks?'

'Not even ignited.'

'Good,' he paused, 'now imagine you're in a supermarket, Tescos, ASDA, whatever, it really doesn't matter, just so long as you can visualise it clearly. You've finished shopping. It's very busy. There are long queues at every checkout and you join one of them with your basket. All sorts of people join the queue behind you. An elderly couple, a family with small children, a business suited woman, three pretty teenage girls... what gas mark would you imagine being in this situation, Rory?'

'One,' I think, 'maybe two.'

'Good. Finally, it's your turn at the checkout. You begin placing your shopping onto the conveyor belt: bread, milk, baked beans, the usual groceries… How are you doing?'

'Same, I think, gas mark one.'

'Head and Shoulders dandruff shampoo?'

'One,' I laugh, 'maybe two.'

'Athlete foot spray.'

'Two.'

'Haemorrhoid cream.'

I just laugh.

'Condoms?'

'One.'

'What about a copy of The Sun with a banner headline of some lurid sex scandal.'

'Three, maybe four.'

'Do you have a girlfriend, Rory?'

'Married.'

'Good, well imagine you've bought a few items for your wife. What gas mark would you be placing tampons onto the conveyor belt?'

'This is a bit like the Generation Game.'

'It has a serious purpose. Answer me, Rory.'

'Tampons?'

'Em, one.'

'Good. Oranges?'

'Zero.'

'A packet of tan coloured tights.'

'Three.'

'A packet of women's panties.'

'Four, maybe five.'

'But wait, there's a problem with the bar code. The checkout operator holds up the packet of panties and shouts to the floor manager three tills down. "Can I get a price for a packet of assorted women's briefs?" Maybe fifty people are looking at you, Rory, from your own queue and others. In terms of gas marks, what number would you put on your discomfort in that situation?'

'Ooh, six and rising fast, I should imagine. How far do they go up to, I forget.'

'Well, I'm not sure either… ten? Let's say ten.'

'In that case, I think it'd probably be hitting ten then.'

'Ten, really?' he seemed impressed. I was flattered.

'Oh, yes, if it was a proper episode. Then ten. No bother. Definitely.'

'What is it about that particular scenario that would cause such a violent reaction in you?'

Mr Cairney had shifted position on his stool and seemed to be taking an interest in me for the first time. I sensed he was actually listening which made me want to unload a little more but I couldn't articulate it and sat there mute.

'No matter, Rory,' he said, 'here's where we start fighting back. Relax, close your eyes, take deep breaths. Imagine the heat you're wasting at gas mark ten!' he scolded. 'Take back control, Rory, take back control. Imagine you're turning the gas burner down slowly. Slowly through the numbers, 10, 9, 8, 7, 6… and so on until it clicks off and everything rapidly cools down. This is what I want you to do. Whenever you feel an episode coming on. Take charge. Fight back. Visualise the gas burner being turned slowly down the numbers 10, 9, 8, 7, 6, 5, 4, 3, 2, 1 until it switches off and everything cools down. Will you do that for me, Rory?'

'Yes.'

'Will you come back next week for another session?'

'Oh, yes, definitely.'

'We need to build on this session, Rory. You weren't properly hypnotised this time but you can come back, tell me how you've got on and we
can work more on your hunger for respect, okay? Will you do that Rory?'

'Oh, yes, uh-huh,' I nodded but no, I knew I would never go back
even though Mr Cairney was perfectly nice, kind and well-meaning. If I
went back we'd have to develop a proper hypnotherapist-patient relationship and I don't do relationships. Oh, no. We'd have to establish a kind of
intimacy. We'd recognise each other in the street. I wouldn't know whether
to pretend I hadn't seen him or say hello. It would be awkward and embarrassing. In fact, it would be highly likely to provoke an episode. And I
make every possible effort to avoid all episodes.

As Mr Cairney showed me out, a middle-aged woman arrived at the
door. His next client. It was obvious at a glance she had a self-destructive
and self-defeating relationship with food and, without word or gesture from
either of them, I knew for certain she was the client Mr Cairney had told
me earlier he'd cured. Yeah, once maybe, but look at her now!

Her fat defined her.

I blushed at the thought.

Sushirexia

The Lady's not for Beetroot

Rob A. Smith

Our glasses are nearly empty. I've decided upon the goat's cheese soufflé, followed by the sea bream. She has played safe with soup of the day, carrot and coriander, and the homemade steak pie as her main.

I peer around the solitary bloom, lolling in the long-necked vase, to where Joan is fighting off the leather sofa's attempt to swallow her plump form.

'If they don't bring it soon, there'll be no time to eat it.'

'Relax. There's plenty of time for two courses and the odd glass.'

Joan's words gush forth as she sinks a little deeper into the brown hide.

'As for the interview, it'll be fine. As far as I'm concerned you've always been the "Brains behind the Beetroot", Celia Baldwin.'

"Brains behind the Beetroot": I like the title Joan's given me. It sounds almost as good as when they crowned you the mighty "Iron Lady".

'And so it should be. It's your turn by rights. About time this bloomin' society had a woman at the top. You tell me why we should choose anyone else?'

I muster a smile at my friend's reassurance. Our waitress approaches and spares me from replying.

'Your table's ready, ladies; if you'd like to follow me.'

We take hold of our glasses, and move through to a table in the bay. The view across the groomed lawns to the lily pond soothes me as only a garden can. The formal rose beds beyond are a blaze of colour: the head gardener's homage to Capability Brown's original design. I am at one with their beauty: all will be well.

Joan prattles on between scoops from the pool of orange set before her. All that's required from me is the odd grunt in the right places. I pick at my soufflé; I let my thoughts wander.

The appointment of the first woman President is indeed long overdue. And yes, I do deserve it. I want it more than even dear Joan can imagine. I've given years of dedication to this Society. They owe me. I was an active member long before Willie joined. I was the one who knew what needed doing as the seasons raced by: when to cut back hard, what to plant in the herbaceous borders. It was Celia, not Willie, Baldwin whose know-how made our flowerbeds the talk of the Open Gardens programme across the county.

I was devastated the day Derek and Frank came round and asked for Willie. The committee wanted him for President. It was a man's job. I was only fit to play first lady. No better really than all the other dutiful spouses suffering in supporting roles: only destined to smile at society events and conventions.

You would not have let them trample over you: you would have known what to do.

Worse was to follow: how I hated the sniggering brigade as they gossiped about Willie's indiscretion. All talk of the best way to propagate fuchsias was buried for many weeks. I ventured into vegetables as an escape. I specialised in soft fruits, determined that the accolades bestowed on my plums would, if I bided my time, earn me the number one spot one day.

Reputations are built on achievements. I for one admired you for your Falklands Conquest; for the way you crushed the Miners; even for your tank driving in the Gulf. And all these kept you safely at the helm.

Until six months ago, all was going to plan. My Victorias brought national recognition. Appearances on Gardener's Question Time made me the talk of enthusiasts throughout the country. And at last the committee of our Organic Gardening Society was ready to adopt its first woman leader. Even the staunchest chauvinists agreed I would do the job better than anyone else.

Other saplings had sprung up fleetingly, but their candidacies were destined to wither on stony ground. I, on the other hand, made sure not to fall by the wayside.

You showed us how to win: how to keep men in their place.

Recently however, it's been hard to say how it will go. A challenger for the presidency threatens. His rapid rise in popularity, especially with the younger members, can't be ignored. What right did he have to put his name forward? He only moved to the area a couple of years ago, and is still a novice in the practicalities of gardening: even with his Honours degree in horticulture. But his oratory has proved more effective in nurturing hope than any organic compost could. The desire for change has grown as the months passed by. I knew radical action was needed if I was to stop his intentions.

I wipe away the last remnant of soufflé from the corner of my mouth before speaking.

'It's not a good sign. When it comes to having a new President, the committee has always just approached someone; voting unnecessary. We never interview. Who pushed for it this time?'

Joan shuffles in her seat.

'Er… Derek, I think. Although once he'd mentioned it, most folks liked the idea.'

She is no longer looking at me. And I don't like the way she is fidgeting with her napkin, twisting the corner of it round and round her left index finger.

'You too, Joan?'

Her silence is answer enough.

'So, you're having second thoughts, are you? Great.'

I feel the heat rise up my neck; certain that it's turning the same shade as the roses outside.

'That's really going to boost my confidence when I'm sitting in front of the bloody lot of you. My oldest friend; and you're no longer sure I'd be the best. All these years, and now I might as well throw down my gardening gloves if I can't rely even on you. You stupid, stupid cow.'

I choke to a halt as the waitress clears the plates.

'Don't take it like that, Celia. Once they're reminded of all you've done for the Society I'm sure you'll get you what you deserve.'

She is saying something else, but I no longer hear. I'm forfeiting the bream and dashing out in need of air. God, if only I could just get in the car and drive.

My strength returns. I'm determined to do whatever is necessary to win.

The interviews are to take place in the Conference Room, here at the Country Club. Derek thought it best to have a neutral venue. The lemmings followed without questioning.

I kill time in the gardens, and even bump into my rival as I'm walking amongst the delphiniums. His boyish smile is as sweet as the scented stocks.

We pause and chorus in unison.

'May the best man win.'

An unfortunate choice of words I fear.

Going into that first ballot I marvelled at your bravado; convinced you'd defeat your opponent.

They have decided on ladies first; or perhaps it's alphabetical, or maybe an age thing, rather than beauty. Whatever, I enter the arena as the clock strikes. As expected, Derek is chairing.

'Sit down Celia. As you know, we're introducing an informal chat with both candidates before reaching a decision this time.'

I smile.

I hear him say something about how they appreciate the years of service I've given the Society.

His drawl continues, 'We all admired the way you stood by Willie after he was forced to resign. You showed guts by staying with us after that.'

The rest of them are nodding like those infuriating toy dogs you see in the back of car windows. Did he really have to bring that up? I hear the distinct note of envy as he splutters on about the glory I've brought to the Society since becoming a well-known Radio 4 personality.

But I don't catch everything he is saying: I am looking at Joan. She is wrapping the corner of her tissue around her finger in her attempts not to look at me.

The interrogator changes to Frank. He mutters; but then Frank always mutters. He sounds serious however; so I ask him to repeat his last sentence.

And he does.

'Some of us are worried, Celia.'

The tip of Joan's poor finger is turning a deep purple.

'You're aware of the Society's Byelaw Thirteen, aren't you?' Frank leans forwards, gripping the edge of the table.

Suddenly I am uneasy.

'Of course: why do you ask?'

'Well, it's your plums; and your roses.'

Frank pauses, seeking the agreement of the rest of the committee before spitting out the last of my three accusers:

'But worst of all, it seems your beetroot are not all they should be.'

He rocks back in triumph, and continues, 'I am afraid it has come to our attention that you may have contravened Byelaw Thirteen with each of these. Perhaps you could tell us whether our information is correct or not.'

Joan. It can only be Joan. Over the years, she has caught me spraying my plum tree and rose bushes with the deadliest of insecticides and fungicides. She always laughed it off though, acknowledging that, "We all do it." But my secret weapon to ensure I grew the largest beetroot this season; when did she discover this heinous crime? Tears trickle down my cheeks. I taste their saltiness as I stutter to withdraw my application.

You saw your support crumble; a second ballot was out of the question. Jump: it's the only way out.

I proffer my resignation from the Society. Promises are made not to give interviews that might embarrass them; assurances too of my decision to retire from public life with immediate effect.

A couple of days later, I read in the local paper that the young man has been confirmed as the next President. There is a photograph of him, displaying a fine set of teeth, with Derek and Frank by his side. She is there too. The article expresses shock at the choice as it had been widely tipped that Mrs Celia Baldwin would make history by becoming the first woman head. There is speculation also as to why I'm stepping down from my radio commitments. At least they are kind enough to note that my wit and integrity will be missed by many.

Weeks pass before Joan rings the bell. I'm undecided on whether to answer or not. In the end I do.

'If it isn't Mata Hari; finally come to gloat have we?'

Sarcasm does not become me.

She says nothing. Instead, she's looking in horror at the wood chippings strewn where Victoria once stood. Her gaze scans next the patch formerly inhabited by my beetroot.

'I wasn't going to mention the non-organic fertiliser, honest I wasn't.'

She's focussing straight at me now, and with a resolve I've not seen before.

'I had a good idea what you were doing to your beetroots.'

I'm about to ask how, but her confidence throws me into confusion.

'I'd decided to keep quiet; I knew what the President thing meant to you. But at lunch on the day of the interviews you scared me.'

No nervous wringing of hands; today her index finger gets a lucky break.

'Your reaction when you found out I'd agreed with Derek. For the first time I saw just how all the scheming to be President had changed you. I couldn't let you be eaten up by it any longer. Cheating, Celia; it was cheating.'

She is done. I shun the hand that's offered. She turns and leaves.

I go back inside the house and turn on the television:

You wave from the back of the limousine. You manage a brave smile. The car draws away from outside the black door guarded by a policeman. The reporter comments on your tears. He reminds us that it was one of your closest allies who had finally put a stop to your way of doing things. Vanquished, and yet still able to impress your public. I share your audacity to hunger for the power you have lost. Next door a man peeps out from behind a curtain. He watches. He bides his time.

Sushirexia

The Hum of Gargantua

Juana Adcock

For a long time I had been waking up at night with a painful, high-pitched hum in my left ear. I was convinced it came to me when I slept in an awkward position, so on waking I would straighten myself up, lie very still, breathe deeply and try to visualize the hum-pain as a warm, orange cloud I could nestle in. And fade back into sleep.

But one night the pain was so loud I couldn't hear my own cries. My neighbour José was so worried that he climbed in through the kitchen window and took me to the hospital to have my ear cut open.

Inside they found the pinto bean I hid when I was three, rescuing it from the cruel meal Mum was preparing. I had been made the executioner; I had to take the beans one by one from the sticky flowery tablecloth to the pot of water where they would be soaked and cooked to death. And be careful to leave out all the stones. But why should I care about them? Us unworthy humans should be eating the dead stones, and not the poor baby beans. I wanted to save the life of just one and so I hid it in my ear where it was never to be found.

For almost my entire existence I had been hatching it near the entrance to the tube of my Eustachian. Which, as the doctor explained, is the conduit that carries music to the pharynx. And now, at last, it had begun to sprout.

'We'll have to kill it,' said the white-coated man, dangerously balancing his surgical knife towards my little one.

'No, don't! Do what ever you like to me but don't hurt it! I'd like to plant it, see if it wants to keep on growing.'

'You should call it "Gargantua",' said José the next day. My little one lay snugly wrapped in a wad of damp cotton in a jar on the kitchen window-sill.

'Why Gargantua?'

'Gargantua is a famous character written by Rabelais. He was also born through his mother's left ear.'

'It seems very odd to me. It isn't a gargling sound people make before they are born through an ear. It's a humming sound, a high-pitched one. Don't you think Mr. Rabelais was confused, and should have called him "Hummingtua"?'

But after José left, I whispered to my little one, 'Is your name Gargantua?'

And he said, 'Yes.' I had already asked him a few questions, and he replied by quivering slightly, or bending forward almost imperceptibly in that way plants like to do. I don't quite know how I came to understand what it all meant – call it a motherly thing if you like. You can't have a bean sprout its first little arm through your ear in search for the sky, and not make a magical connection with it.

During his pre-plantation childhood, Gargantua and I had the best of times. His incubator was so practical he didn't have to stay alone on the windowsill when I went out. He liked to ride in the basket of my bike, or in the car, especially on the motorway. To avoid accidents, I would tie the jar to the headrest of the passenger's seat with cellotape. And so my little one received the perfect amount of sun and air. But plants are not nomads by nature, and in time we both came to understand it was best if we didn't jiggle around so much. I grew aware of how pointless people's movements are. They sit down only to get up again a few minutes later, absurdly going from one room to another and from one building to the next carrying objects and paperwork and other people to their so-called proper place. They think they're going somewhere, but they're just restless.

I started out by lingering at the table after breakfast, Gargantua on my lap, sitting perfectly still, not quite sure what to do. José showed me a book once – sitting still with your back straight and your eyes closed listening to yourself breathe is good for curing all sorts of things – anxiety reduction, weight loss, business success, even cancer. I'm not sure if that's what

I was doing, though. I just sat there, listening to Gargantua. I managed to slow right down the act of breakfast by careful contemplation of the toast after every millimetre buttered, by shelling the egg in the tiniest pieces my fingers could break, by flavouring each particle of each infinitesimal bite. For tea, I brewed one teaspoon at a time, re-boiling the kettle every time, and I didn't sip but let the tea melt into my tongue. I found I could make it all the way till lunchtime like this, without leaving the table once, not even for the toilet. Eventually I found it was better to just put the table in the bathroom and so, breakfast blended into lunch blended into dinner. An endless feast filled my days.

'You can't go on like this for ever.' José told me one day, peering in nervously through the open bathroom door. 'And besides, you do know one day you'll have to plant it, don't you?' Gargantua was getting taller and taller.

'Shhh, don't *say* that, he might hear you!' I whispered between clenched teeth. 'And of course I know, what sort of person do you think I am?' It came out a little defensive as I hadn't really stopped to think about this since the day I rescued Gargantua from the killer hands of the white-coated man.

'Son,' I told my little one that very night, 'the time will come in which you shall have to abandon your incubator and grow roots into the earth. This saddens me, as you will never again sit on my lap. I shall live indoors, moving about absurdly, and you shall live outside, in the garden.'

'Out in the open?' Gargantua bent slightly forwards. 'And what shall become of me when it freezes? I could die out there! Do you not care at all for your only son?'

'You must understand, my sweet, gorgeous Gargantua, that if you don't grow roots into the earth you will not be able to survive long. The earth and the sun have nutrients I cannot give you. It will take a while to get used to it, but in the end you'll see it's far better than being indoors with me.' My voice was shaky as I spoke.

'I don't ever want to part with you! If you put me in the garden and watch me from the kitchen window I shall die just to spite you!'

'Please don't be upset, fruit of my ear. Tomorrow we'll have a long breakfast together and find a way to solve this.'

My whole life will never get past the breakfast we had next day.

I stayed up all night preparing all the food I could find in the house. After we were done, Gargantua would live outside, in the ground, and me indoors, moving about pointlessly. I baked a cake with all the flour and eggs, and laid out six plastic trays with eighteen sausages, two strips of bacon, one black pudding, three chicken wings, six pre-packed skewers with green peppers, onions and mushrooms, two frozen pepperoni pizzas, one broccoli quiche, five-hundred grams of peas, two loaves of garlic bread and four microwave dinners: enchilada, lasagne, korma, Sunday roast. I made one heap of instant yellow rice, one heap of instant mash, and laid out all six boxes of cereal, half a packet of digestive biscuits, one tin of sardines and one of spam, one jar each of raspberry jam, pickled onions, mustard, mayonnaise, pasta sauce. Plus everything else left in the cupboard: two pounds of potatoes, fruitcake, six oranges, an apple and a banana, a bar of cooking chocolate, three Belgian waffles, two and a half packets of custard powder, sugar, salt, pepper, butter, chocolate sprinkles, an unopened loaf of bread, sultanas, fudge, icing sugar, black treacle and marzipan. Everything except the poor, baby beans.

'Today I become a plant with you, Gargantua. Tomorrow we shall part.' I lay all the food on a long strip of fabric to pull towards me as I finished eating each dish, the plates I threw into a pile behind me.

I felt my hips grow wide and my shoulders hunch, my chin double and triple. I was a continuous pile of stuff from head to table to toilet to floor. José came in sometimes, and nibbled a chicken wing, shaking his head in bitter disappointment.

'You can't go on like this,' he'd say. 'You can't go on like this.'

'It's just this one meal,' I'd say and besides, 'it's between my son and I. You have no right.'

How much time went past? Weeks, months? I don't know but, slowly as I was eating, the food started to run out. I ate the crumbs on the ground,

I ate the rotting fruit peel, I licked the broken plates, I scratched the fat off the bottom of pans and sucked it from under my nails, just to make this meal last longer, Gargantua, just to make this meal last longer. When the banquet was finished and the time had come for him to go outdoors, I camped in the garden to keep him company. Two weeks of squishy grass and rain bashing on the sagging walls of the tent. But José showed me a psychology book that said that giving children unconditional love can bring nothing but disasters. I soon abandoned the project.

I could hear him crying in the garden, and I thought of the child that cannot ask his mother for a second kiss because his father does not approve of this petty sentimentalism. Exiled in his room, tucked in bed, he must listen to the world of grown-ups: *even pudding seemed to hide evil pleasures because mother enjoyed them far from me*. Whenever I was about to run to the garden and hug Gargantua, or when I was about to burst into tears over our separation, I had to tell myself: 'Get a hold of yourself. Gargantua will be better off without you.'

I sold the house, and with it the garden where Gargantua lived. He had stopped speaking to me. I decided to travel to the sea, but didn't get further than a tiny, stuffy hotel room in London. I didn't want to move. I spent the whole time crying and fighting the withdrawals from my meal with Gargantua. Everything made me ill. The wallpaper, the sink, the plug in the sink, the narrow bed, the television screwed to the wall, the carpet stinky of feet. If I looked out the window the sky made me ill, the street, the people, the traffic. But, most of all, I couldn't bear those civilized trees in their little squares of earth, framed by the pavement. Those trees that, ignored by everyone, hum sweetly to themselves, and rattle their leaves against the wind.

Sushirexia

Won with the Egg, Lost with the Shell

John Jennett

➤

If the isolated house didn't look as if it had been built in the last few hundred years it might be taken for ice-age debris, like the moraine of huge boulders that were scattered across the acres of island bog. Why the twee-looking cottage came to be there nobody could remember, although when the man moved in it caused people to try. In the town pub, twenty miles away, they could not agree if it was built by the GPO (something to do with telegraphs), by the Army (rockets) or by a southern Lord (grouse). The cottage had fallen grey, and braced itself against the south-westerlies which so scoured its corners that even the swallows, searching the endless moor for nest sites, shunned its shallow worn-out eaves. In summer, the deep window sills dammed black with midges and in winter filled with rain. The men in the pub did agree that this was the only semi-detached house they knew of, and that nothing good could come to a man with a wall between himself and a woman.

On the night when Stephen Fair first arrived in his half of the cottage, the rain stung so hard he thought it might rip the slates. On the ferry, any locals who noticed him assumed he was a tourist. Probably here for the wildlife, if his careless hair, glasses and expensive looking waterproofs were anything to go by. To the yellow-clad marshals on the vehicle deck, the laden Volvo estate, crouched down on its back wheels, was just a typical early holiday-maker's car, not someone planning to be in the Hebrides for good.

The cottage was no more, or less, than Stephen expected. "The property has been unoccupied for some years," the Letting Agent's flyer had said. "Although fully furnished it provides a unique opportunity to personalise the surroundings and this is reflected in the long contract period and competitive rent." Stephen pushed open all the doors and dipped his head into each room, inspecting the plain cornice and the splitting matchboard corners. It was tidy but smelled of old fires and mice; it was fine.

Stephen Fair did not want to encounter anyone by daylight so he trudged his belongings from the car the same night, the rain needling his hood. It was past one in the morning by the time he had found places for all his things, shaken off his jacket and slumped into a chair. Mark's name almost sneaked out on a sigh then, a stowaway on his breath. Stephen patted the damp patches on his shirt, counting them to distract himself. He'd stowed the cardboard box, still freckled with rain, out of reach on top of an old dresser. He twisted his top lip as if it was a bottle-top that wouldn't close: the box seemed to be everywhere he looked, the rest of the room a foggy sunburn red. There was the familiar tide of hunger for it, the hook like he was holding back a pee, butterfly-tingles twining through his legs, his arms. Stephen was not aware of his hands closing like crocuses under a dark cloud, his toes arching, lips parting, dampened by a flick of his adder's tongue.

He carried the carton to the back room as if it might have been a bowlful of liquid he was trying not to spill, a hair-trigger bomb. Underneath a lampshade that brimmed with bluebottle husks, Stephen laid out some of the dozen eggs he had yet to part with, three each from golden eagles and ospreys and two from a black throated diver. Out of habit he glanced over his shoulder to check the door, delaying to draw the mildewed curtains before setting the first egg in a stand. He moved his head around the exhibit, admiring the unique ivory lustre of the shell, its rusty splashes of autumn bracken: brown flakes a memory, the tight mosaic of feathers on the eagle that had swooped tirelessly on him the day he'd taken the eggs. As he leaned over the table, he did not notice his hands unfurl, like a pianist stretching for octaves. There was no need to scrape a fingernail over the shell to know the sandpaper texture, as rough as the granite handholds that had grazed him raw when he'd edged towards the eyrie. Stephen had cursed the stain of his bloody fingerprints on the warm clutch that day, the bird mewing overhead, her ragged wings twitching on the thermals.

Peigi MacDonald tells her boy about his father on the day of his eighteenth birthday. She can no longer reach her tall son's shoulder so settles her arm around his waist as she recalls the months when Stephen Fair lived next door. As they speak, mother and son watch the empty windows of the other half of the cottage, the glass standing like blank pages for Peigi to fill.

She says she'd woken on the morning after Stephen Fair arrived and known someone was there because the tilt to the house was gone. Peigi tells her son how she'd wondered, as she did every morning then, whether cancer had taken root in the night. That she realised she'd lived so long with no-one in the other half of the cottage, waiting for the disease to strike, that she was used to the building leaning her way in the soft peat like a sailing boat in a gust. She recalls how she held her breath that morning, heard the rain was off and listened to the sound of an everyday island breeze coiling round the house. How the wind hadn't pressed hard enough that day to shut out the welcome chatter of peewits and skylarks.

Peigi never could sleep without the rush of the wind and the noise of the birds, learned in the draughty rafters of her parents' croft. As an infant, she had been hoisted there, whenever she wasn't screaming for food, to make more room for the big family on the cramped floor. Hoisted by a horsehair rope her father had wefted, in the cot used in turn by her six sisters before her, the last one dead nine years and forty two days before Stephen Fair moved in next door. The cot had swung near the place in the thatch where the pied wagtails nested, the family's ill fortune to disturb them.

When Peigi rose on the morning the cottage lost its tilt, it was into the usual cold morning smell of her fire, still smoored from the night before. She was unsteady at first on the unusually level deck of the room. From the window she could see a long silver car lying at an angle to the house like a tender moored to a ship. It was surrounded by fifty two blackface hogs. Although they were scarcely more than a year old, the faces of the sheep were already greying; their horns smooth as the glass she collected from the beach, their backs tatty where winter had tried to wrench off their fleeces. The animals stared at Peigi's half of the house, waiting for a cud to ripple their throats.

A month passed before Peigi set eyes on Stephen Fair, the April days stretching so it became harder for him to come and go in the dark. On the eve of *bealtainn*, Peigi lit the usual two fires although she couldn't remember exactly why she was supposed to. Nor, if she was asked, could she explain the tradition of taking a peat brand from one of them and walking sunwise around the outside of the house when the next day, the First of May, was wearing in.

"Every peat has its own smoke; and every person her own sorrow," her mother would have said.

Peigi usually circled the house six times with the smouldering turf, once for each sister, always listening out for the mournful call of the golden plover, wishing she could whistle the bird's sad cadence herself. She tried to picture her sisters but saw the impostors instead: gaunt sacks in quiet hospital side rooms that according to their plastic bracelets were supposed to be the girls she grew up with.

As the two fires roared she heard her neighbour's car on the track, a lazy wasp buzzing in her stomach, like hunger. She hunted a mirror, pushed vaguely at her black hair and pulled on her boots.

'Peigi,' she said. 'Next door?' as if even she wasn't convinced. From the distant machair she heard a corn bunting, its song of jangling keys.

'Thought it was time I said hello?'

The tall man looked furtive, as if she had caught him with his finger in the butter. She saw him glance over her shoulder down the track, maybe looking to see if she had come in a car.

'I mean next door. Right here,' she raised her arm towards her own half of the house and he looked relieved.

'Of course,' he said. 'Is there anything wrong?'

'No, just saying hello. No there's nothing wrong.'

The wind blew something around their feet and she looked down to see what might be passing through the open door, speaking without lifting her eyes,

'There's a tradition. It's Beltane tomorrow. It means you might see me walking past your door a few times tonight. I'll be no bother. That'll be it until next year'

'OK.'

'Didn't want you phoning the police if you saw me.'

'OK.'

Peigi looked up.

'Are you sure?'

'Of course.'

'How are you finding it?'

'Finding it? The house? Yes, it's fine. It's great. Just right.'

Beyond his ear, she noticed binoculars hanging in the porch.

'Are you getting out and about and seeing the wildlife?'

'That's what I'm here for.'

'Really?'

After he closed the door on the short woman, Stephen hurried to the table. There were four eggs left now, none of them raptors'. Since he arrived, he'd smashed the other eight on the island skerries, or hurled them into the Atlantic surf, laughing at the gull that gulped a hollow osprey egg. The four conical eggs left in the box belonged to common guillemots. Stephen set them spinning on the table, their peculiar length meant to keep them from rolling off the precarious ledges where the birds laid. Mark had fallen from the cliffs the day they took these eggs.

Stephen did not watch or listen for his neighbour, who smelled of sheep, or stop rubbing his fingers when his shower turned cold. Later the sheep-woman appeared in his dreams. Her black hair still hung to her waist, but she had grown his mother's clean hands and held his eye as she stretched on a bed. She used those familiar palms to disguise her breasts before her arms fell to her side as she arched her back with the effort of pushing; a grey egg as big as a whooper swan's inching out of her dark crotch.

Most mornings, Peigi released the white collie from the shed onto the un-fenced moor. She felt the dog's keen eyes on her before she gave breath to a long, liquid whistle. It ran like a starling's tune, shaping the dog wide to gather the scattered sheep. She counted them each day, pencilling fifty two in her grass-stained notebook before telling the dog, 'come by,' to split the flock again like billiard balls.

One wet July Wednesday when the hogs were counted, she did not go back inside to listen to the kettle creak on the range and smell her boots drying, but hissed at the dog to keep the animals in a huddle and steer them to the fank. The sheep shifted uneasily in the pens, the dog canny on the other side of the fence, the spoon of its tongue dripping. Peigi opened a narrow gate and shoved the first animal into the crush. It splashed through the dip and she followed it to the dead-end, banging at her pockets for the castration pliers.

She used the tool to stretch open a strong rubber ring, no bigger than a Polo-mint, and slip it over the catkin of the animal's tail. After reloading the device, she reached between its legs, her strong milking fingers feeling for the place to set the second strangling band. Each beast in turn swallowed its bleat when she released the pliers and let the ring bite. In a few weeks time she'd expect to catch the dog chewing at the withered pouches that would litter the field. As she yelled warnings of bad luck at him, she'd know that the tight castration rings had neatly done their job: made the hogs into wethers.

By *Oidhche Shamhna*, the evenings were dark and Peigi shut the oven door on the final cut of last year's lamb. Earlier that day she'd picked two beasts for next year, which now dangled by their hind legs in the darkening Halloween byre, slit necks puddling into black-pudding buckets. In the kitchen she wiped her hands, ran the tap cold, and filled three jars with water.

She had three eggs put by from her favourite hen, and cracked one above each jar. Nursing the whites into the water she shucked the yokes for the dog. As she knelt to watch the slow-motion syrup of the three whites settling in the water, Peigi fumbled for the prayer she'd been taught by her mother for this divination. She shook her head as the pale columns of the egg-whites clotted into shapes. This, the first year they had ever split in two: there was to be a child after all. The wasp in her belly became a busy hive, her neck turned cold. Herself and a child.

Peigi brushed out the spiders before filling the brackish bath, the steam making her cheeks shine like sea-pinks. The cottage sweetened with cooking mutton as she made two places at the table with the mismatched cutlery and the good plates; took mugs to the byre and filled them to the brim straight from the cow, the cream forming slicks as she set them down. She pressed her hand to her prickling stomach as if she might iron out the craving, but pulled on the funeral coat anyway, all the while listening out for the car in the gloaming. When its long silver roof passed her window she was out the front door to follow in the last few yards of its wake, her arms feeling strong as she hugged the coat to herself, hems luffing in the mustering gale.

Stephen could not make himself fight the woman, who turned out to be naked under her long sheepskin, only struggling to see if the hands that manhandled him were his mother's. When she straddled him he pulled off his glasses. A dog was barking somewhere and he sheltered in the memory of Mark's hard grip, the urgency in his lovemaking before they had set out together for the guillemot cliffs. His teeth sinking into Mark's shoulder, their desire for each other muddled with the anticipation of taking the eggs. The smell of Mark lingering on his fingers, finding his stiff hairs for days after the thick black bag had been zipped up at the foot of the cliff.

The steel wool of the woman's groin rasped against Stephen and he felt her long hair brushing his knees when she threw back her head. Mark learned to be an egger from his dad. The only secret Stephen shared with his own father was the pills he'd seen him powder daily into mum's tea. He wouldn't want a brother, heaven forbid, a sister would he? When he nodded understanding, his father leathered him anyway, said he had no idea how much worse the pain would be if he let on about the pills. Mam would be killed, his father said, twisting the last inch of a cigarette into Stephen's thigh, the hand that smelled of tyres over his mouth until he learned to gulp down his screams.

Peigi and her son stop talking and tilt their heads back when they hear the rush of wings, the story of Stephen Fair - lover, father - still newborn in the midsummer air.

'Peregrine,' whispers Peigi, shielding her eyes from the sun.

She is remembering the place by the shieling where she found the falcon's nest when she was pregnant, Stephen Fair gone. It was a day when the moor was thick with clouds of clegs and midges but she'd stayed anyway to watch the young peregrines thrashing their wings. Six of them tumbling and hopping as they discovered power, lifting themselves a hesitant foot or two in the air. She wanted to clap when they were suddenly aloft, beating off, the adults cackling harshly as the fledglings spread out from the nest. She watched their awkward landings, the shuffling of feathers as they recovered, beaks open in a pant.

Peigi wonders if she will blur the end of this, if she will tell the boy what happened two weeks after she took Stephen Fair. It was the day he showed her the eggs as if they were trophies, his eyes misty, the beef sandwiches and wine abandoned in the kitchen, her period already late. Did she need to explain the rage she'd felt to her son, recount the man's pleas, say she'd told Stephen Fair that she'd already milked any good out of him? Tell him how she'd stretched the rubber ring with the pliers, wider than they went for the sheep and that Stephen Fair had not made a sound when she let the band snap shut.

Smile Nice Now for the Yearbook

Genevieve Schrier

—◆—

School picture day was my most hated day of the whole year. That was the day that my mother always made me wear a collared shirt and a sweater to school, and told me that I couldn't play football at recess because I might get my good clothes dirty. Last year I wore a white t-shirt under my collared shirt and sweater, and when I got to school, I ducked into the bathroom, pulled them off, and stuffed them into my backpack. But I didn't know was that there was a leak in my thermos. By lunch, both were stained with grape juice. My dad had thought my school picture in my undershirt was funny; my mother didn't.

Last week she sent a note to my teacher, asking her to be sure that on picture day this year, I was indeed wearing my sweater and collared shirt all day long. This was especially important because now that I was in third grade, my mother didn't take me to school every day. As long as she didn't get any reports from my teacher about tardiness, I was sometimes allowed to walk alone, with the responsibility of being home by 4:00pm every afternoon, the punishment being that I'd go to bed without supper if I wasn't. One time I got caught up playing football, and Uncle Bill came to the school yard looking for me. He'd driven his Buick over, and when I got into the car after he hollered my name, he sat there with his hand over the key in the ignition, not turning it.

'Henry,' he said, sounding serious. 'You can't just disappear on your mother like that.'

'I wasn't disappeared,' I argued. 'I just forgot what time it was.'

'Henry,' he said, though lower this time. 'Men of the house don't disappear on the women of it. You be home when you promise to be home, whether you're done playing or not. That's responsibility.'

I just nodded, and Uncle Bill started the car. After that day, I wasn't late again. It had nothing to do with not wanting to go to bed hungry.

I loved that my mother was beautiful, especially considering how all the other mothers of the kids in my class at Benjamin Robbins Curtis Elementary were lumpy and old, waiting in the schoolyard wearing flannel housecoats and snowboots. On the days my mother walked me to school, I stood up straighter and didn't fuss when she leaned down to kiss me goodbye, even if her lipstick rubbed off on my cheek. Uncle Bill once said my father had been the luckiest man in the world for convincing her to marry him. My mother snapped back at him that she had nothing to do with it – it was me who did all the convincing – which made Uncle Bill turn bright red and say, 'Evelyn! Not in front of Henry.'

My mother snapped a lot when my father was mentioned, but there were still afternoons when I would come home from school and she'd be sitting on the sofa wearing her pink bathrobe, with a balled-up tissue in her hand, staring at the gold star in our front window. She had refused to take it down, even though my gammy and poppop said it might make things easier.

'Easier on Henry, at least, Evie,' Gammy said to her a few weeks ago. They didn't know that I was standing at the backdoor and could hear them in the kitchen. 'It's been seven months.'

Gammy wasn't the only one. Last Tuesday, my mother received a telegram from the War Department reminding her that stars were only to be displayed in wartime and that the war was over. When the doorbell rang and the Western Union boy stood there holding out a telegram for her, she snapped at him that what did he want, her husband was already dead, and then she slammed the door. Uncle Bill got up from the table and tried to hug her, but she walked right by him and went upstairs without cooking supper, even though I'd gotten home from school on time. That night, Uncle Bill took me to the diner and bought me a club sandwich and a root beer float because he said he didn't want me to go to bed without eating.

Then he dropped me off at Gammy and Poppop's, telling me it might be better if I spent the night there instead.

'Henry Fontain! What are you wearing?' my teacher called out when I walked into the classroom on school picture day. My dad had told me our last name was a French one, from some old ancestors who'd mixed with Indians up in Quebec, and my teacher could say it perfectly.

I stood up and raised my chin so that she could see the collar sticking out of my sweater. Gammy had taken clippers to my head last night, so I knew that my hair was tidy too. My teacher smiled and I sat down. Across the aisle from me, Jackie Pederson was whispering. Of all the boys in my class, I liked Jackie the least. Not because he was poor and lived in county housing down past the Kroger. And not because the star in his window never changed from blue. I didn't like Jackie because he was big, dumb, smelled bad, always had a finger up his nose, and made comments about my mother. The last time he did, I promised I'd sock him if he didn't shut up and said his mother looked like a walrus, mustache and all.

'Hey Fowntan,' Jackie hissed, saying my last name like the thing you drink out of. 'I saw your mom this morning.'

'You shut it, Pederson.' I could feel the tips of my ears get hot.

'Boys,' my teacher said, turning around from putting up the five times table on the board. Jackie and I sat still and faced the front of the room. When she turned around again, Jackie turned back to me.

'She looked all pretty, Fowntan. Maybe I can be your new daddy?'

'You're darn sure old enough,' Joey Harman whispered right back at Jackie from two seats in front of me before I could. 'How many times you been in third grade now?'

'You still got baby teeth?' Jackie said at Joey. My face was burning.

'Hows about I help you lose…'

My teacher slammed down the chalk in her right hand and the arithmetic book in her left. She wasn't as pretty as my mother.

'Sorry, ma'am,' Joey said and slumped down in his chair. Joey's dad belted him when he got in trouble. And I didn't want him belted on account of me, especially when there was no chance of it happening on my end. In August, I'd asked Uncle Bill if he was going to belt me when Joey and I broke Mrs. Lawrence's window playing baseball, because I knew for certain that Joey was getting belted at that very moment, but Uncle Bill just laughed and said, 'No, Henry, that's a daddy's job, and lucky for you, yours didn't believe in it.' And then he laughed again, but in a strange way, the way my mother laughed whenever someone would tell a funny story about my father, before excusing herself and going to the powder room and not coming back until they were talking about someone else.

My teacher glared at us for a few seconds longer before picking up the arithmetic book again. Jackie Pederson made a face at me, and I responded by pointing at him and drawing a line across my throat with my finger. My mistake was making the choking sound that I imagined someone made when their throat was slit, and my teacher looked up, slammed down the arithmetic book again, and yelled, "Henry Joseph Fontain, that's enough!" before sending me straight to the principal's office.

It wasn't the first time.

The principal's secretary Mrs. Horsham smiled and raised an eyebrow and nudged the candy dish that sat on her desk towards me when I walked in. I shook my head.

'That's some scowl you got there.'

I shrugged.

'Jackie Pederson?'

I nodded. My hands were clenched and my arms were folded across my chest, pressing into my school picture day sweater.

'Sure you don't want a caramel?'

I shook my head again, though my mother said Mrs. Horsham wasn't the type of lady to take no for an answer. My mother complained that she knew everyone's business because her husband was the butcher at the Kroger and overheard all the gossip. The door to the principal's office opened and he waved me inside, pointing to the brown leather chair where I was to sit.

'Henry,' he said. 'The fighting has to stop.'

'I wasn't fighting.' I balled my fists up even tighter, then remembered something Uncle Bill told me, and said again, 'I wasn't fighting, sir.'

'Yes, well, you were disrupting the classroom with your 'not fighting'.'

I didn't say anything.

'This is your fifth trip to my office this month, Henry,' he said. His voice got a bit softer and he was leaning towards me. 'I know things are hard for you without your father around, but you can't go picking fights, not in...'

'Uncle Bill told me that if Jackie Pederson said one more thing about my mother, I better sock him good!' I jutted my chin out and unfolded my arms, pulling at my sweater, trying to get rid of the wrinkles that had formed when my arms were crossed.

The principal tugged on the skin of his throat.

'Henry,' he said the way that Uncle Bill said my name when he's about to say something important. 'Henry, listen to me. Bill Walters is a good man for sticking by your mother since your father died, and Lord knows she needs all the help with a little boy that she can get, but it's just not his place.'

'But, I'm not picking fights.' My ears were getting warm again. 'And Uncle Bill didn't tell me...'

'Henry.'

'...to start fights, he told me...'

'Henry.'

'...that if stupid Jackie Pederson talked about my mother...'

'Henry Fontain, that's enough!'

'...to make sure I knocked out all his teeth.'

I was breathing hard and my whole face was hot. That last part – about all of Jackie Pederson's teeth – was a lie, and I felt bad because I hoped it wasn't going to get Uncle Bill in trouble.

'Henry, I'm calling your mother in. We're going to have to have a talk – you, your mother, and myself – about this. '

'But I'm just being responsible,' I said. 'Uncle Bill says I'm the man of the house now,' and then I added for good measure, 'Sir.'

'Henry, go back to class till your mother gets here.'

The principal stood up. I got up too and left before he could tell me again.

On my way back down the hallway, I realized that in all my arm-crossing, my collared shirt had come untucked from my slacks, and there were pencil smudges on the front of my sweater. I rubbed at them and hoped that my mother wouldn't be able to see them in the picture. As I walked past the auditorium, I could see the fourth graders getting their pictures taken, which meant that third grade would be next, right after lunch, which was now. My stomach rumbled, and I realized that my lunchbox was locked in the empty classroom. I had been in the principal's office when the third grade lined up and walked to the cafeteria, and I didn't have the quarter for a baloney sandwich and a chocolate milk.

When I got out to blacktop for recess, Jackie Pederson and Ron Belladucci were sitting on top of the slide, not letting anyone else go down. Joey Harman was kicking a rock against the red brick wall. He ran over when he saw me.

'Henry, you're back!'

I nodded.

'Are you in trouble?' Joey looked worried. 'Because if you did and it's all 'cause stupid Jackie Pe...'

'Takes one to know one, Harman,' Jackie said from behind me. He had come off the slide, but Ron was still blocking it.

'Why don't you just scram,' I said. Because he was as old as most fifth graders, Jackie was a lot bigger than me. I only came up to his chin.

'Why don't you make me.'

'Maybe I will.'

'Maybe I'll scram right to your house.' Jackie leaned in close. His breath smelled rotten and there were lines of dirt around the collar of his white t-shirt. 'Maybe your mom will rub my back. That's all my mom says she's good for.'

I didn't know anything about back-rubbing, but when my knuckles made contact with Jackie's mouth, I knew that it hurt.

My first punch knocked him backwards, the second one knocked him down, and with the third one, the one that sent teeth flying across the blacktop, my entire third grade class came running over, screaming. But I only knew this because I saw their mouths moving. My ears had gone fuzzy again, like they were plugged with the wax my mother put in them when I went swimming. Jackie was down on the blacktop and I kept wailing away, throwing punches at his head, when suddenly his fist came up and went straight into my face, and then someone reached down and pulled me up, pinning my arms against the side of my body, and holding me two feet off the ground.

'Henry, enough!' Uncle Bill yelled, and I kicked my feet back and forth.

'PUT ME DOWN PUT ME DOWN PUT ME DOWN. '

The principal, Mrs. Horsham, and the school nurse had run out to the schoolyard. My teacher started to round up the rest of the third graders, shooing them into the building. The nurse hovered over Jackie, and the principal picked up small, white rectangles from the blacktop. Uncle Bill kept his arms wrapped around me from behind and started walking back into school, still holding me two feet above the ground. I could feel hot tears in the back of my eyes. The principal followed us.

'Bill. Bill,' he said in the same angry tone he'd used for me earlier.

'Not now, Richard,' Uncle Bill said in an angry voice too. The principal chased us into the main hallway and was out of breath. There was blood on the cuffs of his white shirt.

'Bill, this has got to stop,' the principal kept going. 'Henry can't keep getting in...'

'Henry's learning to defend himself.'

'...fights with a bully just because he calls his mother...'

'He's standing up for his family, Richard.'

'...names, that's just not how the world works. And the sooner you realize...'

'Realize what?'

'...you're not his father, the better off...'

'Don't you dare, you arrogant sonofabitch. What goes on between me and Evie is...'

'...Bill.'

The principal suddenly stopped walking, and motioned at me with his chin. I'd never heard Uncle Bill curse. And I realized that my left hand was throbbing, and when I looked down, I saw it was bleeding too. There was blood all over my sweater. I couldn't hold it in any longer, and tears came down my cheeks and into my mouth. Somewhere in the scuffle, my lip had split open, and the tears were stinging it. I shook my head and turned my face away, blinking quickly, hoping that no one would see me.

'Bill,' the principal said again. I was still two feet up in the air. Uncle Bill looked over at me and his eyes widened. He set me down.

'Henry,' Uncle Bill dropped down to one knee. 'Henry, let me take a look at that.'

I shook my head. Another hot tear plopped down onto my sweater, which now had bloody polka dots all over the front of it from my lip.

'Richard,' Uncle Bill said quietly. 'I'm going to go ahead and take him home for the day, okay?'

The principal pressed his lips together and nodded.

'Come on, champ,' Uncle Bill stood up and put his hand on my shoulder. 'Let's go get you cleaned up before your mother sees.'

I didn't want to speak; I was afraid I'd just cry harder. Uncle Bill ruffled my newly-buzzed hair, handing me his handkerchief to press against my lip, and as we turned to walk out of the school to his Buick, he took my hand and squeezed it, then dropped it as we walked by the auditorium where the rest of the third grade was having their pictures taken.

When we got home that afternoon, after Uncle Bill stopped to buy me an ice cream cone ('Evie, it's to help his lip, for chrissakes') and the new Superman comic ('Ev, the kid got socked in the mouth, cut him some slack'), my mother washed my face off and sent me straight to bed without supper, even though it was only 2pm, and I'd gotten home before 4.

I changed out of my bloody day clothes, put on my flannel pajama pants, pulled back the sheets, and climbed into bed with my new comic book. A scab was starting to form on my lower lip and it felt hard when I touched it. I was so hungry from no lunch, no supper, and only ice cream that my stomach was growling, but I didn't care. All I could think about was how bad Jackie Pederson smelled and how his teeth went flying from his mouth when I punched him and what I was going to do for two days because I'd been suspended and how last year, everyone laughed because in my school picture, I was wearing a white undershirt with grape juice stains, and how this year my school picture didn't even get taken at all.

A Place

Jill Creighton

—

She wasn't wearing the right shoes to get up the wet grass. He tensed as he saw her slip, but she stayed upright. At the brow of the hill she placed her handbag at the foot of a leafless hawthorn, then wrapped her arms round the most solid looking branch, leaned her forehead in, and made contact with the bark. He turned his attention back to the rose bush.

She had found it on her second visit. The first time she hadn't looked, just wept. The weather had kept the bereaved at home that day and she'd sat in the rose garden alone, head bent. The hood of her jacket had lain down her back, redundant; the rain found the gap at the nape of her neck.

Later, she felt cheated when she learned that unclaimed ashes are disposed of two weeks after a funeral. How was she to have known that instead of sitting her O'Grades she should have been picking up his ashes? It didn't matter now anyway. What would she have done with them? Pride of place on the mantlepiece? Yuk. Take a pleasure boat out on Loch Lomond and hope the wind would scatter them when she tipped the urn? Were there bits of teeth and bone in ashes? It would be awful if the moment turned slapstick; the ashes blowing back into her face, or if she became creeped out, like when she vacuumed up spiders.

The next time she came she returned to the rose garden. Were all these flowers and…things here last time? Her shoulders tensed as she side-stepped the arm of a rag doll which had spilled onto the path. She frowned as she looked down at a Scotland football top which had, *See You Again Pal*, scrawled on it. Ahead, sitting cross legged on the ground, a woman cried silently as she placed a still-priced bunch of flowers beside the photograph of a teenage girl. A man stood over them, staring ahead.

She walked towards a spindly tree on the open ground. The card read *Daniel Thompson 1942 – 2008. Rest in Peace my Darling*. The laminate coating blurred the photograph of Daniel. She looked around and realised that identical trees were dotted throughout grounds; cards flapped in the wind.

The light started to fade. She returned to her car. She pulled down the driver's visor and looked in the mirror. Why was she here, after all these years? She wondered if she would cry. Instead, she watched her mouth as it said, 'I need a place.'

As she drove round the curve of the road towards the gates she looked up at the row of trees, which created a natural boundary. Then she saw it: silhouetted against the greying sky, a gnarled tree. Three branches formed a crooked W.

The car door lay open as she climbed the hill. She scratched her hand as she reached out to it. A bramble bush climbed up the trunk, protecting it. She smiled as she looked into the field beyond where a crowd of boys were playing football, squeezing the last bit of fun out of the daylight. A dog walker hurried towards the houses at the bottom of the field and in the distance The Campsies formed a protective arc.

'No. I'm afraid it's not possible to use a boundary tree as a memorial. You can however lease a blossom tree for a minimum period of five years, at a cost of £349, which includes a laminated memorial card with one photograph and up to 50 words. Another option would be to take out a page in the Book of Remembrance, which can be viewed in person or online. That would cost…' She hung up.

She was glad of the rain as she released the tree from her hug. He looked down at his spade as she scanned the grounds. When he returned his gaze she was on tiptoes, her arms were at a strange angle and her body was leaning heavily in to the tree. After a while he saw her reach into her handbag. Her hands emerged clad in yellow gloves. She cut away some of the bramble bush with, what looked like, kitchen scissors.

When she grabbed on to a solid bough he thought she was going to attempt to climb the tree. Instead she manoeuvred her body into the neuk created at the base of the three branches. His cheeks puffed out as he exhaled his relief. She sat in the nest. She was safe. She remembered.

When he returned from his lunch break she was gone. His heavy boots took him effortlessly up the slippy hill. The rain had stopped and the sun glinted off the small bronze plaque. It was squint. He pulled the sleeve of his sweatshirt over his thumb and wiped away her fingerprints. The plaque wobbled.

WILLIAM'S TREE
This is a place to remember my dad, William Bruce
A very good man
1930 – 1984

He looked around the grounds, pulled a screwdriver from his jacket pocket and tightened the four screws.

Sushirexia

In the Park

Julie McDowall

—

The man and woman stopped at the duck pond. The man stepped over the fence and waded in. He dropped on all-fours and thrashed the water, swiping his hands across the bed of the pond. Nothing. Anger rose in his chest like a snake.

'Nothing,' he said. 'Nothing!'

The woman gripped the scarf around her throat. 'What are you looking for?'

He came out of the pond. Grey froth stuck to his trousers like soup.

'Anything. Christ, we must eat.'

The man and woman did not know where to go. They looked up at the blackened shard of the university spire. They went out to Argyle Street, where broken glass had settled like alien snow. They crunched through it, and looked down Radnor Street. Empty. They turned the corner. A green council lorry was abandoned in the road. A bin bag fluttered like a black flag. Beside the lorry lay a pile of bodies: a clumsy pyramid of elbows and knees. A head lolled, its eyes pressed too deep in the plasticine of the face. The wind lifted. Something moved in the front seat of the lorry. They retreated to the park.

They sat on an iron bench. It had warped in the blast and was shaped like a wacky fairground seat. They sat askew.

'Why'd you still wear that?' the woman said. She gestured at the ID badge round his neck.

He lifted the badge and stared at it. 'I was at work when it happened. In the basement. I felt the floor move. Thought it was an earthquake.'

'I saw the flash. It made me go blind for a while. White light, like heaven.'

'Heaven.' He looked up. 'Only thing in the sky is fallout.'

'There has to be something.'

'There's nothing. We're just dying animals.'

'I'm hungry.'

'Better say a prayer.'

They gathered sticks. He lit a fire with his green plastic lighter. They frowned into the flames. Around them rose the smooth concrete hills of the skate park.

'I don't like it here,' she said.

He didn't look up. 'There's no-one coming.'

There had been people four days ago. The man and woman had squatted between the trees and watched the silent group journey through the scarred park, halting once when one of them stopped by the swings, gripped the gnarled chains and vomited. The man and the woman had debated furiously whether to follow them. She had won. Stay hidden. Trust nobody. So they remained amidst the mute sticks of the trees. That had been the last sighting of people. Since then, one crow. The bird had simply stopped beating its wings and dropped to the ground like a parcel. It fed them for two days. He kept the beak in his pocket. Might be useful one day.

It started to snow. It covered the wrecked landscape, like an embarrassed child covering his mother's nakedness. But the fallout came down with it, bringing ash from the cancered sky. The man looked out across the whiteness and saw a squirrel dart across the park. He chased it. The meat on a squirrel! As he ran across the snow, he felt the white light gleam on his cheekbones and remembered: the joy of stamping in a snowy field. School's off! *Dashing through the snow*. Then he stopped. His hands fell to his sides. There is no squirrel. And there is no joy. There is nothing to lift your eyes to. Only this endless grey bolt of fabric which keeps on unwinding.

They found an apple. Now they sat huddled together, observing it. The man held the apple: a leathery brown tennis ball.

He looked at the woman. 'We need to ration this.'

'We're starving.'

'It'll get worse.' He weighed the apple in his palm. 'We can't eat it yet.'

The woman knocked it out of his hand. It thumped over the grass and rolled down the slope of the skate park. She ran after it. The man saw her squat and cram it whole into her mouth. Starving. He felt something in his head flex and then snap like a wafer. He scrambled down beside her. He seized the woman's hair and rammed her face into the concrete. He felt her nose crumple. *Spit it out spit it out.* He grabbed her neck and rattled it. Blood and apple sprayed onto the snow.

He sat quietly and bumped his fingernail over the grooves of her teeth, prising out the last shreds of apple. Scrape your plate, mum would say. A tooth came loose and adhered to his pulpy fingertip. He pinged it away.

Nothing to eat now.

As he moved her body, he felt her springy flesh, still warm.

Sushirexia

Heat

Harry McDonald

There was me and there was Ange and Candie and her husband Cal at the table. It was the same bar we went to every Thursday after the bowling. Thursday was bowling night.

There was a whole gang of us who would go along on the night. Sometimes it was because it was a match night in the bowling league and sometimes it was just informal, friends playing together, shooting the routine.

During the evening different people would stop at the table, sit for a while and talk, maybe buy a drink. Who had their eye in and who had blown everything with a lousy shot. That kind of talk. Or exchange courtesies; ask about the family, the job. We had two kids. Two girls. Cal and Candie didn't have any kids. They went out a lot. We were all about the same age, in our thirties, but I used to say to Cal,

'Cal, you make us feel like a couple of old stay-at-home farts.'

Me and Ange had known Cal and Candie for years. Sometimes, maybe once a month, we went for a meal together or took in a movie. Come the holidays, especially Christmas, we would go over to their house or they would come over to us for a seasonal dinner. That kind of thing. Cal and Candie always bought expensive presents for the girls at Christmas.

They were a good couple. Candie was a good looking woman for her age; for any age. She was tall; maybe a little taller than Cal. She was thin and had a narrow face that drew to a soft point at her chin. Her hair was coloured blonde, straightened and tapered at the front where it framed her face. Cal was proud of her. It was in his talk when we were at the bar getting the drinks in and talking about the women. Candie still went to the beauty salon once a week. I can remember at least two occasions across the years when Cal nearly got into a fight with guys who were coming on to Candie.

So this night I'm talking about was the same as any other Thursday night. Except it had been raining and that turned out to be significant. But what happened all started with Al Pacino. I came back from the toilet and sat down at the table. Cal leaned at me.

'Bernie: Pacino or De Niro?' Cal said.

'What about them?' I said. I swallowed a mouthful of beer.

Ange touched the back of my hand. 'Cal and Candie are deciding their best actor,' Ange said.

'Best actor of their generation,' Cal said. 'Let's not complicate things, Ange.'

'Well, they're the best,' Candie said. She cradled her wine glass. Candie always drank white wine.

'We know they're the best, Candie. Bernie, they're the best; you agree that?' Cal said.

'Yeah, they're the best. No doubt about it,' I said. Ange nodded. Cal went back to Candie.

'Nobody's disagreeing on that,' Cal said. 'I mean, what dummy's going to disagree with that. What I'm saying is De Niro – he's the man. El numero uno. He's the godfather.' Cal leaned back and took a long, lazy victory drink from his beer.

'Pacino is the godfather, too,' Candie said.

Cal said, 'I just said De Niro is the godfather, the number one. You can't have two number ones, Candie.'

'Al Pacino was the godfather in three films. Robert De Niro was only in one. And I could see on the screen who was the best actor,' Candie said.

'They weren't on the screen together in that film. They were in the same film but they never appeared together,' Cal said. 'And Bobby D got an Oscar for that one.'

'Some people might say Brando was the godfather,' I said.

Cal said, ' I know what you're saying, Bernie. And I respect that. But it's a different generation; a different style, and I don't want to go there. It's hard enough trying to persuade Candie.'

'You can't persuade me. It's not something you persuade people on anyway. People just know. I know who the best is and it's Al Pacino,' Candie said.

'I go to the movies; I have eyes. I can see who's the better actor,' Cal said.

'And who do you go see these movies with, Cal? I'm there too, you know,' Candie said.

Ange said, 'What about *Heat*? That was a good film. I remember they had some scenes in that together.'

'That's right,' I said. 'Maybe that's where you should go for a comparison.'

Cal said, 'I can talk about *Heat*. Two great actors on the screen together. Who was the best in Heat? Bobby De Niro. Come on, I'm right. Ange, I'm right?'

'I don't know, Cal,' Ange said. 'I think I remember liking Pacino more. I think he maybe had a better part to play.'

'Sure, the part matters,' Cal said. 'Might be a lot of people saw it like you did, Ange. But you need to think on what the actor's got to work with. Pacino gets to be this rebel cop, bad mouthing and bleedin' emotions all over the place.'

'He was good,' I said.

Candie said, 'Who else could have played that part the way he did? Nobody: that's who!'

'Chrissake, Candie. I'm not saying he wasn't good,' Cal said.

'I don't get what you're saying, Cal,' Ange said.

'Ange. It's just the Pacino part had more juice, you know. Just Bobby De Niro had to play this cold, calculating genius of a master criminal. He's cool, he doesn't lose it. That's his thing. How many people like that do you know? Right. And how many guys like the Pacino character, guys watching their lives go down the toilet do you know?' Cal said.

'I get it, Cal,' I said. 'There must be guys out there like the guy De Niro played. But because we don't know them so well…'

'That's it, Bernie. That's it exactly,' Cal said.

Later, we went for a smoke in the covered terrace out back. Me and Cal. It was no more than a wooden canopy skirting the back wall of the bar and slanting into the yard. There were a few tables and chairs sprawled beneath it. It was dark and there were puddles lying in the uneven dips where the concrete hadn't been laid properly. They caught the reflected light from the bar and scrambled it. Earlier the rain had been coming at us fast and full of pace. Now it was petering out like a runner at the end of a race.

Cal passed me a *Cubano*. We'd given up smoking years ago but we still liked the routine of a good cigar.

'Candie wants to try and have a kid,' Cal said.

'That's great. Kids are great. A lot of work…' I said.

'Like I don't have eyes. We tried to have a kid before,' Cal said.

'I didn't know. I just thought you'd made a decision,' I said. I blew smoke into the night.

'She miscarried,' Cal said. 'Something wrong with her womb, something technical. Anyways, the doctors told us years back if we tried again that ninety-nine to one for sure the same thing would happen. And that's not something you want to go through twice in one lifetime. You know what I'm saying? You have kids yourself.'

'It must have been hard,' I said. 'I mean, I love my kids. You don't even let yourself think about anything bad happening to them. Suppose that's why people fuss about kids so much.'

Cal said, 'So what's happened now, she's seen something on TV, one of these medical programs they're always showing – she loves them – saying they can fix this type of problem. The type of problem we had. Now she wants to try again for a kid. Says she's never stopped thinking about it. All these years. But what if it doesn't work? I mean this thing's new. What if it doesn't work?'

I tried to think of something clever or snappy to say to Cal but then I thought about my own kids and I knew the best thing was to say nothing. The best thing was just to be there and share a smoke.

Back at the table Ange was looking tired, dimmed. Or maybe it was because I could tell that Candie had freshened up with her makeup and stuff and was all glowing again, sucking up the light. I thought we should leave soon.

Cal sat down. I stayed standing. I said, 'One for the road?' I saw Ange give me a look. Then she looked at her watch.

She said. 'Okay. I'll help you get the drinks in.'

At the bar, Ange said to me: 'I've never seen them like this.'

'I know. They have problems,' I said. I waited for Ange to say something. She didn't.

I said, 'Candie wants to try for a kid. But there's some kind of medical problem from the past. Cal seems pretty cut up about it. Might be he's right, maybe they should leave things the way they are.'

Ange pinned me down with her eyes. She said, 'Christ, Bernie. Is that what you told him?'

'No. I didn't say anything. I'm not stupid. I don't think he really wanted advice anyway. Just somebody to talk to,' I said.

'Candie says if they don't try for this kid then she's leaving him,' Ange said.

We took the drinks back to the table. Cal and Candie were cuddling, kissing.

I said, 'Hey, this is a family bar, you know.'

We sat down. Cal said, 'We want to apologise for earlier.' Candie was nodding; they were holding hands. Cal had his juice back. 'We got a bit carried away. What can I say?'

'It's okay. We do the same thing sometimes. Don't we, Bernie?' Ange said.

I nodded. My beer tasted better than it had all night. I said, 'Let's make a toast. Good Friends!' Everybody touched glasses: four separate little chinks of glass with different tones.

After a while we finished our drinks and gathered up coats and hats and bags and umbrellas and headed out into the night to get a cab. Ange and me were outside first with Cal and then Candie following. The rain had stopped. A shallow puddle lapped at our feet. Our friends were behind us. I heard Candie speak first; something like hold on or wait up, Cal. Then I heard Cal do his Robert De Niro impersonation, the one from *Taxi Driver*.

He said. 'Are you talkin' to me? Are you talkin' to me? Cause there aint nobody else here.' That's what I heard Cal say. The thing De Niro says in *Taxi Driver*. I didn't hear Candie say anything. Not a word. No shrieks or anything.

I heard Cal scream. When I turned around he was teetering against the outside wall of the bar. Candie was stood in the doorway, completely still like everything inside had shut down. Cal was screaming. Jesusfuckingchrist. Over and over. The metal point of Candie's umbrella was spiked in his left eye. There was blood all over one side of his face. Cal was pawing at the umbrella, trying to get it loose I suppose. Nothing is easy when you're in pain and you can only see out of one eye. But he must have touched the little trigger mechanism because the umbrella suddenly flew open and just for that awful moment it looked like he had a satellite dish coming out of his head.

Cal lost his eye. The doctors said he was lucky. The three inch point of the umbrella went real close to his brain. A half inch the other way and there would have been a different story to tell. Cal and Candie are still our friends. We still go bowling. Even with one eye Cal can still bowl a six pack. Candie got her technical problem sorted out and now they have a little boy. A cute kid called Robert. We never really talk about that night. It's just that sometimes, like a weird kind of tourettes, out of nowhere in the middle of something else, Cal will suddenly splutter – *Al Pacino*

Waiting at the Big Red Rabbit

Mark Russell

—◆—

At 11.15 am on Monday 18th September 2006 I waited in the lobby of the White Spa Hotel to interview Daniella Escoffier. She didn't show.

For a while, I stood by a pillar in the lobby watching people come and go. I was fifteen minutes early and chose the pillar on the left as you enter the hotel. Facing the entrance of a hotel from this side makes you more conspicuous to the arriving guests. Don't ask me why but our brains tell us to look left before we look right.

Before long I started to get twitchy about Jonty's absence. I needed a photograph and the desk always insisted on Jonty shooting the pictures of pretty girls. I dialled Features on my mobile.

'Jenny? It's Grant. Where the fuck is Jonty?'

'Think I'm his fucking secretary? Prick.'

'Put me on to Des.'

'Put yourself on to Des.' Jenny hung up on me.

I shrugged and rang Des. 'Des? It's Grant. Where the fuck is Jonty?'

'How the fuck do I know? Shouldn't you be speaking to that model? I'm running out of space, Grant. You want the inches, give me the copy.'

'She's due here any minute.'

'You said that last week. Listen, I'm busy. Copy, photo, or fuck off.' Des hung up on me.

Smooth, firm and cold to the touch, the pillar reminded me of Diane Morris, particularly her fourteen-year-old bottom. Diane and I spent Wednesday afternoons in her bedroom rather than French with Miss Demeurre and English with Mr Rankin. It did my studies no harm. I was good at both subjects. I suppose it didn't really do Diane any harm. She could have done double French and English and never been able to conjugate a verb in either language. But when it came to PE and sex, Diane Morris excelled. The girl had talents. She represented the county on the pommel horse.

After thirty minutes I nipped outside to have a fag and a flick through the cuttings I'd brought. Sitting between two flowerpots, a bum cheek on each, I reminded myself of Escoffier's short life. Twenty-years-old next month. Endorsements for perfume, jeans, a crappy sports car, some line of jewellery, an American soft drink not sold in the U.K. and a range of 'power' bars made of sugar, food colouring, two peanuts and a heavy dollop of irony when you considered her battles with anorexia and bulimia. It seemed a trifle greedy to be bothered by two eating disorders at the same time. Escoffier was hoping to move into the film industry.

My mobile burred. I looked at the caller's number and name.

'Jonty, where the fuck are you?'

'Hampstead.'

'Hampstead? What the fuck are you doing in Hampstead?'

'I'm on my way to you.'

'For fuck's sake, Jonty.'

'Won't be long. She won't turn up anyway.'

'Oh, is that right?'

'Waste of my time.'

'Just get your arse down here. I need this fucking copy and I need you to get a shot of her.'

'I'll do my best.'

'You'll do better than that, you tart.'

'Oh, wait, here's a taxi now…' Jonty hung up on me.

I thumbed the photographs in my folder. Hackneyed portraits that could have been dashed off in an agency's lunch break. Escoffier was the colour of burnt sienna. She rolled around on carpets, was topless in showers, wrapped around trees or emerging from the ocean's surf peering straight into the lens, lips parted, as if my looking at her had given her an orgasm. Black bikinis were intended to make her mature and domineering; white bikinis were designed to make her innocent and seductive. She looked like a little girl in underwear. The memory of Diane Morris returned. Diane was tactile. She had a smell. She had faults.

I moved back inside to the reception desk itself and rested my elbow on its polished surface. The receptionist, intent on her computer monitor, didn't even glance at me. 'Journalist?' she said.

'Either that or a detective, eh?'

'Oh no. Detectives are older and fatter.'

'Thanks.'

She clicked her mouse. 'You were fondling that pillar.'

'"Fondling" is a touch strong.'

A wisp of hair fell from her forehead across her left eye. 'You into ersatz marble?'

'It reminded me of something.'

'Everything's fake in this place. This isn't even wood,' she said tapping the desk. She looked up and tucked the stray hair into a black kirby grip set with a single mock ruby stone. 'People love it.'

'You think?'

'Oh yea. We get a lot of that type here.'

'What type?'

'Stinking rich and no fucking taste.'

'Right.'

'Who you waiting for?'

'Daniella Escoffier.'

'Wow. The model?'

'Yes.'

'She's Argentinean, isn't she? Or Brazilian or something?'

'French Guiana.'

'Yea? Where the fuck's that, eh?' she laughed.

Her phone rang. She picked it up and a bleached-tooth smile erupted from her mouth. Her voice switched from estuary English to Transatlantic formality. She sounded like a British reporter who had been working on the Fox Network for far too long.

I checked my watch. 'Shit.' I said.

She put the phone down and her fingers raced across her keyboard.

'I'm on my break in a second. Want a coffee?'

At that precise moment, another receptionist appeared from behind a wall hung with a hundred sets of keys.

'This place runs like clockwork,' I said.

The two women said a cursory hello and goodbye and she led me to the coffee shop to the right of the desk.

'You can see the entrance from here,' she said, stopping at a table from which you could indeed see all the comings and goings in the lobby. 'Black, no sugar?' She'd obviously met a few journalists in her time.

'I'll get them,' I said.

'Don't worry. I don't pay.' She went to the counter and I parked myself with my back to the rest of the room, the windows to the street on my left. Taxis cruised past, smartly dressed executives paused to speak on mobile phones, middle aged women returned to hotels laden with shopping, detachments of foreign language students with identical rucksacks and peaked caps marched past clutching street maps of central London.

'Here,' she said, putting my coffee in front of me and sitting opposite. She had a bottle of still mineral water.

'You not having one?' I said.

'Coffee's bad for you.'

'So they say.'

'It's a drug. I don't do drugs.'

'OK.'

'It causes fatigue and exhaustion. First you get confused and then you get headaches. Your body thinks it's been told to produce adrenalin.'

'Nothing wrong with a little buzz from time to time, surely?'

'Course there is. You become hyper-alert, like you were on constant standby for war.'

'Well, it's not that bad…'

'I'm telling you. You can only take it for so long. Then you crash and burn.'

'Bloody hell.' I blew into my coffee to cool it down.

'You're nothing but a junkie getting his next fix.' She sipped her water. A rim of crimson remained on the neck of her plastic bottle. 'What's in your folder?'

I reached for the folder in my briefcase and passed it over to her.

'I'm going to be famous,' she said as she opened it. 'Fuck me, she looks like a stick of cinnamon.'

'What are you going to be famous for?' I asked, looking into the lobby. No photographer. No model.

'Not sure yet.' She turned over a page. 'Something on the telly. A reality show.'

I laughed. 'Which one?'

'Big Brother, maybe.'

'You'll have to be careful. The camera adds twenty pounds.'

'You saying I'm fat?'

'No…'

'There's not an ounce of fat on this body. I work out.'

'I can see that.'

'I'm five foot ten inches tall. I weigh nine stone, ten pounds and my body mass index is 19.2.'

'You look great,' I said. She smiled. I checked my mobile for messages. Nothing.

'Or singing,' she said.

'What?'

'The singing one. You know, where you have to sing in front of those wanky judges.'

'Oh, right. Yea,' I nodded. 'Can you sing?'

'What difference does that make? Jesus, you don't know much do you?' she said, her eyes buried in the folder. 'You got to have the look. I've got the look.' She looked up at me, tilted her head and pouted. 'Haven't I?'

'You've got all the right attributes.'

'Yea. I have. And you know what else I've got?'

'What?'

'I want it. I want it bad.'

'Right.'

'I'll do anything.'

'Course.'

'Anything.' I was about to ask her to qualify that statement but she was way ahead of me. 'Any-fucking-thing.'

'I believe you,' I said.

'If I thought you could help me, I'd suck your dick. Right here, under the table. Nobody would see. I'd drink you dry.' She swigged water from her bottle. 'But you're a journalist. You can't help anybody.'

I glanced through to the lobby. Nothing.

'Jesus. Look at this.' She held up a recent photograph of Escoffier. 'Is this for real?'

'She's having trouble controlling her weight.'

'You can say that again!' she screeched, drawing several faces our way. She noticed and her voice softened. 'What a state. How can somebody do that to themselves?'

'I guess somebody got into her head. Said she was too fat or something.'

'Eeuuhh,' she shuddered and put the photographs back in the folder.

I sipped my coffee. She passed the folder back to me.

'Listen,' I started, looking at the further reddening of her water bottle. 'I realise you don't have a very high opinion of us journos…'

'Right.'

'But, and this is straight up, I happen to know a producer on the X-Factor.'

'Eh?'

'Yea, well, I know a few of them, as it happens, but one of them's a good friend of mine.'

'You're shitting me. Fucker.'

'No. Really. His name's Kirt.'

'Fuck off.'

'Google him.' My phone burred. 'Excuse me a sec.' I pressed 'answer'. 'Fuck's sake, Jonty. Where are you?'

'Where you should be heading.'

'What does that mean?'

'I'm diverting to Heathrow.'

'Heathrow?'

'And you better get your lovely, tight little arse over there as well.'

'Why?'

'Your little honey bunny has gone into a coma on her delayed flight from New York. She'll be landing in half an hour. You really do need to refresh your contacts.'

'Coma?'

'Apparently she weighs about fifty kilos.'

'Fifty kilos, what the fuck does that mean in real money?'

'I'm jiggered if I know, sunshine.'

'It's about seven-and-a-half stone,' the receptionist offered, staring at me.

'Thanks,' I nodded to her and smiled.

Jonty had heard the receptionist. 'Oh my god. You've pulled.'

'Leave it out, Jonty,' I said.

'Are you coming, or am I going to write the story as well, you randy bastard?' Jonty said.

'I'm on my way.' I hung up on Jonty.

'Developments?' she asked.

'Listen, I'm sorry. My name's Grant.' I put out my hand and she shook it.

'Lisa.' She stood up. 'You've got to go.'

'Yes.' I put the folder in my briefcase and began to zip it up.

'What did you say your friend's name was?'

'Kirt. With an 'i'. It's Indian. We can discuss it later if you want.' I handed her my card. 'What are you doing tonight?'

'I'm going to the Big Red Rabbit off Covent Garden to wait for you to join me for a drink.'

'What time will I be there?'

'Nine-fifteen.'

'Great. I've got to fly. No story means no money means I don't eat tonight.'

'Oh, you'll be eating tonight.'

And with that, she turned and walked back to the reception area.

Heathrow was a madhouse. The TV and tabloids were everywhere. I'd spoken to several passengers on the flight and picked up some background from some mates by the time I found Jonty. He had already bagged deals with five hacks lacking a photographer and was on the phone to another desk. He looked up at me for a second, covered the phone and whispered 'It's fucking Christmas'. When he finished his call, I grabbed his arm.

'You're coming with me,' I said, as a police contingent arrived to corral us onto the pavement outside. 'Let's get the jump on these fuckers,' I said, pushing him into a taxi. 'St Paul's Hospital,' I told the driver.

We'd been less than five minutes on the M4 when a Yamaha screamed past us, the pillion rider giving us the middle finger. Jonty smiled and waved. 'Hello, Gavin!' He turned back to me. 'I don't think we're getting the jump on anybody. It's like a scene from the Keystone Kops out there,' he said as a series of cars with other hacks raced into the Middlesex suburbs, chased by police.

'And we're the bad guys,' I said, turning over Lisa's earlier comments. The prospect of listening to her reality TV show aspirations followed, no doubt, by sexual reward later that night, made me shudder.

'What's the matter?' Jonty said.

'I was thinking about somebody.'

'That girl at the hotel?'

'A girl I used to know.'

'There have been so many.'

'She had talents.'

'I bet.'

'Her name was Diane. She had real talents.'

'I hope she did something with them.'

'Dunno. She's probably a size 20 divorcee with five children and working as a dinner lady.'

'Supremely talented, by the sounds of it.'

'I'm tired of this shit, Jonty.'

Jonty was quiet for a moment. 'I hope we're not going to talk about anything of substance.' He wiped one of his lenses. 'We really need to get there a little quicker than this.'

He leaned forward to speak to the driver but before he could open his mouth the driver said, 'I ain't driving no faster.'

An hour later, Jonty and I shared a cigarette outside the Accident and Emergency department having interviewed Daniella Escoffier. I barked questions at the stretcher on which she was being carried, while Jonty got some rather good pictures. She didn't say much because she was busy dying that afternoon and the police escort she had been detailed was busy kicking the arses of the Fourth Estate in retribution for our disrespectful actions. I rubbed a sore spot underneath my left eye where I'd caught a stray elbow.

'That's going to bruise,' Jonty said.

'Not the first time.'

'Police brutality. Want me to take a shot of it, for evidence?'

'Fuck it.'

'You're some miserable sod today,' Jonty said as he changed a roll of film in his camera. I finished the cigarette and stamped it out with my foot. He looked at me. 'Why don't you ring her?'

'Who?' I said. Jonty raised his eyebrows at me. 'I've no idea where she is, what her name might be now, nothing.'

'You're a fucking journalist. You can find anybody.'

I was trying to imagine Diane Morris, now in her thirties, when a text arrived.

'Who is it?' Jonty said.

I opened the message. It was from Lisa. 'Just some girl, waiting for me in Covent Garden.'

'Go.'

'You coming?' I said.

'There are bound to be celebrity ambulance chasers here this evening. I'll snap their sorry arses for them.'

'Don't you get fed up with it, Jonty?'

Jonty's eyes widened in horror. 'It's the best game in the world. And don't you forget it. Now, fuck off and get yourself laid or call your fat, old dinner lady. I'll see you tomorrow.'

At 9.25 pm on Monday 18th September 2006 Lisa the receptionist waited at the bar of the Big Red Rabbit ready to suck my dick. I didn't show.

Sushirexia

Lily

Vicki Husband

He tells the others she's fierce, she hus a gun under hur bed, she grew up oan a country estate wi a gamekeeper fir a faither who taught hur tae shoot. She hus contacts, he says, she kens the Lafferty crew fae Hillside. But they're always mair interested in the Tavern story, where aw eighteen stone o hur comes oot the pub and punches Rab Riley oan the jaw, again and again, until he falls o'er. It's legend. Kyle wisnae born then, and she disnae talk aboot it, so he bluffs it every time. He tells them she's still roond as a barrel, forty a day, lungs like kippers.

The day the champagne's delivered they're aw stood ootside the block. Ryan whistles, look at this, he says, whit fucker hus the money fir this wi a recession. He likes that word, recession; thinks he knows something aboot the world, knows fuck aw. Moet et Chandon, it says oan the van. Kyle recognises it, directs the delivery boy tae the lift and gets in wi him. Once they're oan the way up he lets the boy know the lift only goes as far as the 18th flair; Lily's is oan the 19th. He helps him wi the crate up the final flight fir a small fee. The delivery boy insists oan gettin a signature aff the customer, so he rings the doorbell and they baith wait. A small figure opens the door, eyes the two o them and the crate. Aboot bloody time, she says, the letter came a month ago, making it yirsel were you? Mashing it wi yir muckle feet? Well it does come all the way from France luv, the English boy says. France, ma arse, says Lily, ma bloody arse. Kyle slips in the door before she bangs it shut. She leans against the wall, breathing loud. Hullo stranger, she says, no lookin at him. He feels that. Whit you needing, Lily? Ah cannae stay long, ony messages? Ay, she says, but you'll huvtae sell a bottle o this first, tilts her head towards the crate. Put the word oot, ten quid a pop.

Kyle tells the boys that the Moet is for sale, but only Ryan husa bird and its no the drink she's intae so it wid be wasted oanur. Frankie's dad says he'll get wan for the missus when he's flush, but Frankie's dad's niver flush. He's surprised Tuesday when Graeme says he needs a Moet soon as. He's a dark horse, gies him the tenner there and then. Kyle goes to Rashid's to get the messages: tea, digestives and milk. He takes his cut then feels bad and adds a packet uf Ritz biscuits; heads up tae Lily's. The door's locked so he bangs and waits; leans against the wall feeling knackered then gies himsel a shake, tries to look cheery. He looks doon oanur as she stands at the door gulping air; she seems to shrink every time. Hur clothes hang aff hur, baggy, like hur skin. She frowns at him but it turns intae a smile; she keeps hur mooth closed as she's no got ur teeth in yet. Hur eyes still glitter.

The smell gets him when he steps inside, wi a hangover it makes him gag. He follows her up the unlit corridor, they head for the crack uf light at the end. She lives in the front room noo, wi her bed in the corner. She sits in a cracked leather chair wi magazines stuffed doon the sides, letters and pens spilling o'er the top. The room hus the smell o yesterday's smoke. Ah've run oot, Lily says. He gies hur his last five and says he'll see whit he can dae. He shows hur the messages and hur eyes take it aw in. Pit them in the kitchen, she says, and put the kettle oan while you're in there. Her voice sounds like she husnae used it in a while.

Out uf habit he opens the cupboard and the fridge. Five jars uf Caribbean jerk sauce, dug biscuits and chilli rice crackers. He offers to shift the dug biscuits. She says it's no worth it for whit they'd fetch. Whit's the rice like Lily? It looks fancy that stuff. Spice is no ma thing, she says, it burns oan its way oot. She gies hawf a laugh. He brings the tea through and the biscuits; he eats three, she disnae touch them. She looks him up and doon, takes in the white trainers he got last week and his Bench jacket. You look smart, she says, wi aw that writing on yi, Ah hope they're paying yi fir the advertisin space.

He takes the Moet oot the case, Eleven left Lily. She gets hur business face oan, It's Valentines in a fortnight, surely there some romance left in this city. She thinks a while then tells him, Look oot fir the ones huvin affairs, son, the guilty aye spend more. There wis a time when Lily wid ken the wans to target, she hud a sharp eye; no noo she can barely get o'er the door.

He looks in oan his auld room as he passes, it husnae changed. His band posters are still there; he's embarrassed by them noo. It's been almost a year since he left. Lily says they make the place look lived in, and they keep in the heat. There's some boxes hawf-filled wi the winnings she couldnae shift. Japanese handkerchiefs, doggy perfume, diet pills. Huv you got a bird yet? she shouts after him. Bring ur next time.

He sells a Moet to John who works at the gym and wunders if he's huvin an affair. John remembers the auld Lily, reminisces aboot hur opening beer bottles wi ur teeth. Kyle pictures hur teeth in the plastic cup by the kitchen sink.

Lily's eyes light up when he brings hur the oranges. Squeeze wan intae a glass fir me love, wid yi. She asks after his girlfriend again and when she's gettin tae meet her. He tells hur she's called Lisa, works in Tesco's. Get hur to collect the competition leaflets, she says, and the coupons. You can get done for it Lily, he tells hur, someone got sacked for two pounds fifty worth o pochled coupons. Lily shakes hur head, makes a face. Tam's hurt his back, Tam who works on the trains; nae magazines, nae competitions. Kyle sits doon on the ither chair. He disnae want to ask ur aboot benefits again. Brenda wi the stomach cancer on the groond floor, she got aw this equipment from the social, an electric armchair that rises yi up and a seat that lowers yi intae the bath. Lily purses hur lips, stupid, she says, electricity in the bathroom. Well you could sell it Lily, they gie you trolleys and things if yir bad on yir feet. My feet are great, she says, held me up fir eighty years and ma heid's jist fine too while we're aboot it, it's the bits in between. It's no worth gettin the social involved, ma sister got caught in their trap Kyle, y' ken the story. If yi call the social work son, you neednae bother comin up here again. Her face closes up.

Lisa asks aboot his family and he finds himself telling hur, though he niver did wi the others. There's little to say aboot his father but he talks a bit aboot his mum and how he ended up staying at Lily's when he wis thirteen. He takes Lisa up to see Lily the next week but warns hur it's sink or swim in Lily's company. She's no eatin these days, he says, so dinnae look shocked when you see hur, she'll read yi like a book. Like Ah wid, Lisa says, gie me some credit, Ah've got a Gran too y' know. She's naebody's Gran, he says quickly. She'd hate to hear yi say that. He turns his face away, blowing smoke into the wind. She's no disabled or retarded or onything, but she cannae get aroond so well; sometimes hur place is stinking. Lisa loops hur arm roond his back and coories in. He pulls away to stub oot his fag.

When they get there, he goes intae the kitchen to pit the kettle oan and stands waiting fir it to boil. He busies himsel tidying up though no much hus moved since he wis last here. He listens to them talking. He hears Lisa telling Lily about Tescos and the waste. It's whit she always goes on aboot, that and the freeloaders raiding the bins. It's a mad world, he hears Lily say, throwing away aw that fancy food then folk eating it oot the bin. Then she starts up aboot Lisa's perfume, telling hur it's too strong, probably got awsorts init - cat piss and the like. She complains it's no good fir ur chest, coughs, then lights up a fag. He's thinking of Lisa's face at this point, he imagines hur mooth in a tight line as she looks away. He joins them wi the tea, and sits on the flair, leaning against the bed. Lisa asks aboot the Tavern, just comes oot with it, he'd forgotten to tell hur it wis a no-no. But Lily disnae look bothered. She starts telling Lisa stuff that he's niver heard. He pretends to doze aff. Rab cut a few faces in his time, she says. It was the thing then, knives. Ah've heard they're back in fashion. They used to cut yir face to let you know who the boss wis. But there was rarely a stabbing. Ah only remember the wan, a messy business. You were wan side or the ither. Rab wis aye oan the wrong side. She leans intae Lisa, but he wis a handsome beast, a heartbreaker. A bastard? says Lisa, and the two o them laugh, a private laugh.

Lily gies them a bottle fir Valentines, she's only shifted half a case. They decide to go away fir a weekend, jist the two o them. Lisa's dad lives doon south, they might go there. Kyle takes Lily up a few things afore he goes. You need to make yirsel eat Lily, he says, you'll waste away. Ay, she says, that Ah might. She won't let him ask onywan else to look in oan hur while he's away, besides it's only a few days. He takes hur oot oantae the landing fir some fresh air. They watch the estate below, the tail lights heading up the main road, ootae the city. The tip o Lily's fag glows bright in the wind. She shivers, though she's got two coats oan; he helps hur back inside. She tuts as they pass the boarded up doors; she's the only wan left oan this floor noo.

They huv a guid break in Lowestoft. Its a seaside town, no great but he enjoys being wi Lisa aw that time, mair than he thought he wid. He disnae think aboot Lily much until the bus pulls intae Buchanan Street then he gets that familiar feeling in his gut. He stays at Lisa's when they get back jist for a couple o nights, heads over to Lily's a few days later. He takes up some wee rice puddings, tablet, tins of soup. The front door is unlocked. Lily is usually pretty careful to keep it locked. The light is still no working so he feels his way up the hall, pushes the door at the end. He's relieved when he sees hur shape in the chair and she replies when he calls oot like she's bin asleep. When he gets up close though, pulls the curtains back to see, hur face is a mess: black and blue up ur cheek, yellow o'er ur foreheid. She cannae open wan eye too well. When she sees the look he gies ur, she pulls hursel up in the chair and shapes hur face intae a smile. Its no whit it looks like Kyle, she's starts to say, it's no that bad. How Lily? He takes hur hand in his, feels her bones light as a bird's, slips his fingers to hur wrist, curls them roond it. There's nuthing uv yi.

He makes a pot of tea and pits oan the soup. He finds the oranges felted green in the fridge. She takes a rice pudding, he takes the soup and they eat in silence. Hur teeth clatter, loose in ur mooth. Even hur mooth has lost weight, he thinks. Will you tell someone you're ma next o kin, she asks him. Tell whoever needs to know, make sure it's written on the right piece uf paper when the time comes. What's brought this oan, Lily? Let me call the doctor, she wis guid that wan time, you liked her. Ah wis delirious. Just promise me, you won't put me in onywhere. Ah hud champagne, a glass, that's aw. And y' know Ah'm no wan fir the drink noo. It went tae ma heid. Ah wis goan oot tae the landing tae look at the lights and fell; a simple trip like onybdy can huv; like awbdy hus on a Saturday night. Bubbly oan an empty stomach? Ah bet you were weaving yir way, Lily, whit made you take a drink? Ah remember when a drink used to gie me an appetite. It didnae work though did it? He says. No, she says, no.

He stays over that night, calls Lisa fae oot oan the landing. Lisa gets a bit heavy, says she luvs him. He disnae know whit to say; wishes he was wi hur instead of oan a fucking wind swept balcony uf a hawf empty high rise. She starts telling him aboot the sheltered flats again; hur mum works in a care home, seems to know aw the places. It's fir hur ain guid, he hears

Lisa say. He goes quiet and she asks whit's wrong. He knows he willnae say it right so he hangs up. He stays oot a while longer, listens to some lads singing oan the street below. When he creeps back intae the room, he can hear Lily snoring in the chair. He takes his trainers off and sinks intae the soft mattress. The duvet smells uf smoke and age and something he hopes isnae piss. He pulls his hood up afore pitting his heid oan the pillow, pulls his coat o'er as a blanket.

Lily sleeps maist o the next morning. He pops oot tae buy hur a new blanket. When he gets back, she's awake. She watches him unwrap the blanket but says nuthin. Later she asks if he's planning oan moving in wi Lisa. Not until Ah know yir settled, he says. Where will you go Lily, when they demolish this place? Find me somewhere, she says, Ah'm no bothered where Ah go as long as it's got a view. Ah've spent twenty-five years up here, couldnae stay groond floor noo; people lookin in, breakin in. People roond here don't forget anything fast.

She watches him chewing the nail oan his wee finger. They've sold the Tavern and the land, Kyle tells hur. That rumour's been going roond for ages, Lily replies. Ay, but Ah've heard they're building sheltered flats. Lily gies him a sharp look. He wid usually look away but he stares hur oot on this wan. It's worth thinking aboot, Lily, he says, you're no getting any younger; he hears himself sounding like a tosser. Sheltered, she says, the word curling her tongue. Can you imagine being holed up in some home wi Rab Riley, auld and incontinent, in the next room? They laugh then, both o them, for ages; Lily doing great whooping coughs in between. The view wid be great though Lily, if they build them high enough you wid look right oantae the Campsies. Ay, she says, tilting hur head to the side, considering it, Ah like a view. Then she sets aboot laughing again. Nae chance, she says, nae chance.

Hunger

Joyce Ito

—◆—

'Great party, eh, Clair?'

'Pure awesome, man. Awesome.'

Gary attempted a wink and flopped drunkenly onto the floor. He always winked at her in school. Every Monday at nine o'clock he was there, lazing against the wall as if he was waiting just to give her that weird lop sided smile; every Monday morning she felt sick until she got into history class. She liked Gary, it wasn't that she didn't like him, they used to be friends in primary, but Gary was Isobel Pennie's boyfriend and if anyone saw that smile all hell would break loose. Clair tried to walk away but Gary grabbed her leg.

'Great party, eh, Clair?'

He tried the wink again but both eyes kept closing, so he gave up, shrugged and kissed her ankle instead. She yanked her leg away, grazing the side of his face with her heel as she went.

'Ayah!' he said clutching his cheek, but the noise of the party covered everything, thank God.

The room was hot and dark and sardine-packed with dancing teenagers, the air thick with hairspray, sweet pink wine and perfumed sweat. Clair felt her chest tighten in a spasm of forgotten asthma. She pushed through. For a moment her feet left the floor in the squeeze. Eventually she reached a door but it only led to a set of stairs where some kids were doing more serious snogging. She picked her way through the squirming bodies in her new shoes, terrified she would pierce someone with the pointy heel. How could people wear these things and walk? Mum had smiled and said they would be torture and they were: actual torture. Clair took them off and saw a sticky red mess on the white leather. Blood. Christ! God knows what Isobel Pennie would do now. *Eh, sorry, Izzy, but he was trying to kiss my ankle.* When Clair had calmed down enough to look properly she was pretty sure the blood had come from her own blistered heel and not Gary's face, but it was impossible to be certain it wasn't both.

There was a long queue for the toilet at the top of the stairs. She joined it hoping to escape for a minute but the queue took ages and the kids at the top of the stairs seemed even drunker than the ones at the bottom.

'Pure amazing party, man.'

'Awesome,' said Clair. 'Pure awesome.'

A strange boy passed her a bottle of the pink wine, which she pretended to drink, then shook her head at the pack of cigarettes offered.

'You not smoke, hen? Good for you, don't start.'

The voice was familiar and his face clicked into place: Brian McLeevy's wee brother. My god, she didn't think Brian would have his wee brother at his party. He must be what? Twelve?

Eventually she got to the front of the toilet queue and locked the door. A tall, busty girl leaped out at her. Clair screamed; watched the girl's glossy lipstick mouth stretch wide and her eyes pop; finally recognised her own image in the large mirror; the new clothes; the makeup; the absurd bra.

'Are you all right in there, hen?' said Brian McLeevy's wee brother. He banged on the toilet door.

'That lassie screamed,' he said to no one in particular. 'Are you all right, hen? Does anybody know who she is? It was a pure scream, man. Actual.'

Clair could hear her breath whistling from tight lungs. She tried to breathe slowly. The door banged again.

'Are you okay in there?'

'I'm all right. I saw a spider.'

'Lassies!' he said. 'You gave me a pure fright, man. I thought something had happened. Are you sure you're all right, hen?'

'Aye, I'm fine. It's cool'

'D'you want me to get the spider for you?'

'It's all right. I killed it. Thanks.'

Clair sat down on the toilet seat and stared at her image in the mirror. She pulled the rubbery inserts out of the bra and both boobs dropped into their normal position out of sight. She turned to the sink to wash off the make-up but someone had left it full of pink glutinous vomit that smelled of sherry trifle. She turned on the tap to rinse it away but the water only swirled the lumpy mess around. Her stomach rebelled and she made a loud retching noise.

'Are sure you're all right in there?'

Other kids outside started knocking on the door and asking if she was all right and saying they needed to pee.

'I'm fine, I'll be out in a minute.'

Everyone would think she'd left that mess in the sink. She scooped it into the toilet with a tooth mug so there was only a tiny pink pool left, then used a sponge to soak up the rest. It would fill up again as soon as someone turned on the tap but at least it wouldn't be there when she opened the door. She washed her hands but they smelled of sick so she scrubbed them with toilet cleaner and rinsed them under the bath tap. She breathed carefully, and opened the door. Four boys piled in and lined up at the bath as if it was a public urinal without even waiting for her to leave. She forced her way back down the stairs and through the dancing mass to look for Joanne.

Clair could hear her best friend giggling like crazy before she spotted her perched on Brian McLeevy's knee. Her mouth was all pink wine-stained and her lipstick was all over the place, including Brian's bleached white hair. He was kissing her throat as if he was eating something chewy. Joanne's Dad would go mental when he saw the state of her neck.

'Joanne, I need to go, I'm not feeling well.'

'But you can't. We're not going back till eleven!'

'I'm sorry. I'm not feeling well.'

'But it's only nine o'clock!'

'I'm sorry. I can't help it. I don't feel well.'

'But what about us? Me and Catherine are supposed to stay at your house tonight. I can't go home now.'

'You can stay here,' said Brian coming up for air.

'I'm sorry.'

Her friend drew her a black look.

'Don't bother about us then. Fuck off then, baby, run home to mummy. And don't bother trying to talk to us at school on Monday.'

Clair made it to the door and out into the fresh air before the crying started. Brian McLeevy's wee brother reappeared.

'Are you okay, Clair?'

'Leave me alone.'

'Ma Da says I've to look after the lassies at the party. I'm Kev McLeevy.'

'I'm fine. I don't need a twelve year old following me about.'

'Jesus, you're a hot yin, sure you are. Ma Da says to Brian I've to come to the party and look after the lassies and phone ma Da if anybuddy starts to trash the hoose or looks like they're in bother. So you're screaming and boaking and greeting and I'm thinking you're the kinda lassie ma Da's wanting me to watch so I'm watching you until you get hame. Where d'you stay? I'm thirteen, by the way.'

Kev McLeevy followed her all the way to her front door. It wasn't that far but it took a while because of the shoes. All the while he was staring at her as if he thought she was ill or something.

'It wasn't me was sick in the sink,' she said.

'Course not.'

'I don't even drink.'

'I saw you slugging at the bottle outside the lavvy, hen. Not that I'm caring, I'm just making sure you're all right. My Da says I've to make sure the lassies are okay and nobody goes hame by their selves and I can get a new ipod if the lassies are okay and there's no mess that canny be cleaned up.'

Clair felt her chest loosen in the fresh air.

'You're nothing like your brother,' said Clair.

'Brian's okay. Ma Da says it's his age. He misses wur ma but he says he doesny; says he hates her.'

What was it about drink that made people tell you everything? Clair wasn't in the mood for the McLeevy family history. She took off her shoes and examined her feet.

'Oh man! Look at the state of your feet in they shoes. I couldny be a lassie.'

Kev took off his trainers and insisted she wear them while he went barefoot; he even carried her blood stained white heels. She managed a smile.

When they reached Clair's house she gave him back his shoes.

'Thanks Kev. It really wasn't me was sick in the sink.'

'No worries, Clair, no worries.'

He waited for her to open the front door before speeding back to his duties at the party.

Clair sat on her bed and stared at the clothes still lying about the room. Getting ready for the party had been fun: dressing up, changing, dressing up again. They had spent the whole day trying on each other's clothes and putting on make-up and fake tan and glitter and even shaving their legs. It reminded Clair of the dressing up bags they had when they were little, stuffed full of red riding hood and Cinderella outfits and stickers for their ears and nails. She had photographs of the three of them dressed up as tigers and punks and all sorts, even a video of them as the tellytubbies.

Tinky winky, Dipsy, La La, Po, Clair sang to herself, hugging her knees. She had known Catherine and Joanne would fall out with her, had felt it coming for a while. Mum said that was the way of things when you went to high school but Clair didn't want new friends. Being a teenager looked so great when you were twelve, but now Clair seemed to spend her whole life pretending to have a brilliant time: a pure awesome, cool time. She flicked through her copy of Sugar magazine and wondered if the girls in the magazines with the big smiles and beanpole bodies were pretending too. It was like all the teenagers were acting on a stage with costumes and make up and a script and Clair was left adrift there, begging and borrowing other people's clothes and lines.

Clair had tried to talk to Mum, but she refused to understand how things had changed. When they were getting dressed up for the party Mum had brought them up Irn Bru in Winnie The Pooh cups. Clair had felt her cheeks burning; did Mum think they were still five? Thank god Joanne and Catherine didn't seem to notice.

Don't be so silly, no one will think you're still a Winnie the Pooh fan, Clair.

There was no point in talking to her. It only made things worse. Once Clair told Mum how embarrassing it was when she answered the door in her dressing gown and for the next fortnight she made a point of running off for a dressing gown every time the doorbell rang. Joanne and Catherine thought it was hilarious to see Mum in a business suit and a pink dressing gown, but Clair knew they were laughing at her. And Mum still insisted on picking her up at night.

You can come home yourself for 9.30, or I'll pick you up at 11. Your choice. Of course it was really embarrassing either way, but when Clair tried to explain Mum blew her stack and started ranting and raving.

Do you think I want to stay up till 11 o'clock to drive you around, Lady Muck? I've got my work in the morning! You are a self-obsessed teenage pain in the arse.

Of course Clair could see Mum's point of view, and it was nice to get a lift instead of waiting for buses in the cold, but it was so embarrassing; she felt like a five-year old being collected from a birthday party. Mum was okay, Clair loved her really, but things were different now and Mum just wouldn't see it. She would soon though. No one had noticed yet, but Clair could see the difference. She was careful with the dressing up but Joanne and Catherine didn't give her a second glance; they were too busy looking in the mirror.

Mum was always so busy these days, even when she wasn't working late. Clair would ask her a question and she'd answer without even looking up from the laptop screen. The fridge was full of microwave dinners and a cleaner came during the day when they were out. Clair had always moaned about doing housework but now she even missed washing dishes and vacuuming. There were never proper meals at the table any more. It seemed only a few weeks ago Mum would examine dinner plates for signs of leftover vegetables and start ranting about vitamins and minerals and recommended daily intakes, but now she didn't seem interested.

You're old enough to see to your own meals.

Clair didn't like the microwave meals very much so she started feeding some of them to Joanne and Catherine and eating fruit with a sandwich instead. Mum came home from work in a bad mood one day and went mad because the microwave meals were out of date. She didn't even ask why they hadn't been eaten or anything, just moaned about it being a waste of money. After that Clair put one in the bin every day and ate an apple or a Kiwi instead. She did feel hungry, in fact food was on her mind a lot but it was good not eating it. Then she stopped eating altogether. She felt a bit dizzy, but something good happened as well. It gave her a pure buzz, as Joanne would say: a pure buzz. It was funny how people were always dieting and not getting any thinner, Mum was always at it. The fridge would be full of Weight Watchers meals and she'd be weighing everything and counting calories and reading magazines and exercising and then Clair would come home to find her eating ice cream and chips; Mum never got any thinner.

As Clair turned out the light and tried to sleep her mobile phone bleeped a text message.

"You all right hen? xxx Kev McL"

Sushirexia

The Pig's Head

Frances Corr

—

Way down in the deep south of England, there stood a caravan squeaking and rocking in the wind. And in that caravan lay a young woman in pyjamas worn day in day out, also squeaking and rocking. It was me and my belly was puffed with an unknown future. I would come to resent having to share the caravan with the Pig's Head when it appeared on a plate on the dirty cooker, donated for eating.

This was a foreign land. I was numb at the unplanned happening. Each night he would return from work. The familiar rummel of the clapped out motor. You could hear it from miles away. He'd come in all filthy with his dog and fill the caravan with motion and much awaited noise. The dog was pregnant too. The dog got big pats and rubs and still got to go to work. She was a crazy dog and she ate brambles. Only here they called them brimbles. And tatties teddies. It was a strange land.

He was hungry when he came in from work. One night the dog had scoffed the cheese and he booted her about the caravan and called her a bastard. I felt nervous and stood back. There was only a heel of a loaf left. I'd eaten the rest earlier and wanted the heel, but he'd been out working all day. We fought in the kitchen end of the caravan and rocked it even more.

One time he came back with money and we were heading to the village to get something in the pub. But the motor wouldn't start and he got in a rage and ended up wrecking all the wires. Just like when he couldn't get a picture on the telly so he mashed the ariel. I couldn't tell if this was love.

In a corner on the damp wall there were wee pictures and photos of times before. It was an attempt not to lose my identity. But it was going fast. The social were told at the tribunal that this was still me, the same person as before moving into this caravan so they couldn't stop my money. But the panel in suits and wedding rings only said you can't enjoy the benefits of married life and claim as a single person as well. I looked at the Pig's Head.

Some time later the caravan was still and the light was on. My pyjamas were gone and my belly had filled a dress. The dog had given birth to eight puppies and messed the chair. She'd pushed the puppies over the edge on to the floor and they all squeaked in the night till they were put back next to their mother. One of the puppies got its head stuck in a can. In place of my old capability there was a nervousness about me that was alarming. My hand lay over my big belly with the worry of what was to come.

There was the smooth running of a professional car drawing up, the slam of a door and the awkward squelch of high heels in mud. We sat opposite each other in the caravan. The health visitor with a thick file on her lap. You can't bring a baby up in here, she said. She would see if she could get me a room at the hostel.

The pictures were taken from the damp wall in the corner and quietly packed with my belongings in a bag. Maybe it was good to be going somewhere. The bag was tied at the top and my coat put on, then a pause for a moment to look around at my place of existence. It was strange to think that life would be outside of here now. I slowly stepped out of the caravan and pulled the door shut. The Pig's Head all finished.

The Inferior Cave

William Stevenson

—◆—

I was propping up the bar, finishing off another double vodka when I heard the noise of a man gasping for breath at the door behind me. I turned to find a tall, emaciated young man frantically searching the bar. His face was bright red and the knee length and sleeve-free white robe he was wearing was soaked with sweat. He caught my eye then rushed towards me.

'William?' he asked.

I looked at him blankly.

'Sir, my name is Plax. I have an urgent message for you from the island of Kardia,' he panted urgently.

'Never heard of it,' I replied, quickly turning back to face the bar. I glanced around to see what drama Plax's arrival had caused but no-one else seemed to have noticed. It was a quiet night, except for the bunch of miserable low-lives that called the place their local, and a middle-aged couple making out on the seat next to the fruit machine.

'Regardless, Sir, I must still pass you this message,' he replied, handing me a soggy note.

Realising Plax wasn't about to go away I offered him the seat next to me. I opened the note. The handwriting was familiar.

> *"Kardia is in the gravest danger.*
> *You must help us William, I beg you.*
> *Our island needs you.*
> *We sail tonight at midnight."*

'Is this a joke?'

'No, Sir, our leader, Elder Hamlin, believes that you, and only you, can save our island.'

I scratched my head and forced a nervous laugh, catching the barman's attention as I did so. With a nod towards the empty glass in front of me I ordered another drink.

'What is this grave danger?'

'I am not permitted to say, Sir, I am merely the messenger,' he replied, slowly catching his breath. 'You have read the note, Sir, Kardia is in grave danger. I would not be here otherwise.'

As Plax spoke I realised just how painfully thin he was. I offered to buy him some food but he refused, so instead I downed my drink then re-read the note.

'Where do you sail from?'

'Indigo Quay, our vessel is berthed there. We sail in the dark so that we are not followed.'

'And your clothes,' I said, eyeing his robe, 'does everyone on Kardia dress like that?'

'Yes we do, Sir, it's customary. Men wear a robe and women an orange dress. You will be supplied with a robe when we arrive.'

I rubbed my eyes and tossed the options around in my mind. 'Fine, I'll do it.'

Plax stood up. 'The islanders of *Kardia* cannot thank you enough, Sir.' He bowed then left. I was tempted to follow but didn't have time. I only had two hours to talk myself out of it.

After two more drinks I trudged the short distance home, through the peculiar mist that hung over the city. I packed a bag, downed one last drink then left. I hailed the first taxi that came along. Luckily the driver wasn't overly talkative, allowing me to sip from my hip flask in peace.

'Where do you want dropped?' he asked as we approached.

'No idea.' I looked out the window for a landmark but all I could see were the outlines of disused warehouses. 'Anywhere will do.'

He pulled over instantly. 'Not my kind of place this.'

I ignored him, climbed out then watched as he sped away.

The quay was worryingly dark. I felt my way around for several minutes, but just as I was about to shout for help a tall man wearing a long white robe appeared next to me.

'William, how good of you to come.' The man offered a hand. He looked familiar, his deep set eyes reminded me of my grandfather. 'My name is Hamlin.'

I nodded and shook the man's hand allowing a tentative smile to crack the corners of my lips.

'We are truly privileged to have you join us. Pleasantries later though if you don't mind? There is little time to waste.'

I walked behind him for a short distance until we reached a small galley that I had somehow missed. Plax was there to help me aboard and take me downstairs to the cabin. Hamlin remained on deck until we were away from the city. Sea travel was not my forte and, despite the solidity of the boat, I felt anything but comfortable.

Hamlin appeared in the cabin twenty minutes later. He was leaner than I'd realised onshore. I placed him somewhere in his seventies, but he may have been older.

'I suppose you must be wondering why you are here?'

I shrugged lamely.

The old man paced around the cabin, watching me, trying to read my thoughts. 'I understand you're highly skilled at finding missing people?'

I hadn't worked since the accident, but now wasn't the time to bring that up. 'Depends who I'm looking for.'

'You'll be looking for the young woman who has brought pain, suffering and death to our island. Her name is Demeter.'

'Demeter?'

'Perhaps an unusual name in your world, William, but not in ours.'

'Who is she?'

'No-one in particular, just another islander, although one not used to our ways.'

I poured another tankard of wine. 'And what do I do if I find her?'

'That, I'm afraid, I cannot advise. You must follow your instincts, do what you think is right. We trust you.'

I watched Hamlin intently. 'She doesn't have leprosy does she?'

'Demeter's problems are in the head, or perhaps the heart. It is difficult to say. Rest assured though, what she has is not contagious.'

I thought for a moment. 'But if she's not contagious, why is the island in danger?'

Hamlin sat down opposite me. 'The Kardian people are quite literally connected to the land, William, through their emotions. Therefore any prevalent moods or feelings will be replicated by the land. My job as an Elder is to ensure that equilibrium is maintained. We do that by preventing the islanders from becoming emotional, containing their feelings within certain levels. With Demeter being so emotional, the equilibrium has been thrown into disarray, and it is killing us, literally.'

'Why is she so emotional?'

'We believe she is yearning for something, or angry maybe.'

We docked at first light with the assistance of Hamlin's aide, Felix. Like the city, the light on the island was odd, as though a thin veil had been thrown over us, although even at this early hour the heat was nasty.

Felix was perhaps in his forties and like the others was horribly thin. Yet he too seemed positive, happy almost, despite the drought. I lifted my bag and walked behind as he and Hamlin strode towards three withered, weary-looking horses. Plax remained behind to tend to the galley.

I climbed on my allotted horse. 'I hope I'll be able to rest at your quarters, Hamlin? I didn't sleep on the boat.'

'I offer rest and food, more than can be said for the islanders.'

The journey across the desert-like landscape was painful. Carcasses of pigs, horses, cows and oxen lay sporadically on the roadside. It was a ghastly sight. Fields that would normally have been lush and overflowing with crops and vegetables were completely burnt out, cracks appearing across the soil like the aftermath of a small earthquake. Trees were bare of leaves, without exception.

When we reached Hamlin's home I was ushered into the front room whilst he and Felix conversed with a wretched-looking servant in the hall. Shortly afterwards all three entered, the servant carrying a tray containing cheese, a basket of bread and a jug of water. He dropped it on the dining table with a bump and took his leave immediately.

'Am I not welcome here?'

'Yes of course,' Hamlin replied, 'but these are troubled times. Food is scarce. We try to maintain the equilibrium but tensions are high.' He pulled a chair and ushered me to sit next to him at the table.

I ignored the food that had been crudely dumped in front of me and instead asked if there was any wine.

Hamlin and Felix looked at each other, as if silently debating how to answer. Eventually Hamlin called out a command to the servant. Moments later the man re-appeared with a carafe of red wine and one pristine-looking tankard. I poured some wine and sat back, savouring the heat of the alcohol as it hit the back of my throat. 'So, how long has this drought been going on?'

'Since Demeter vanished,' Felix answered, 'almost six months ago.'

'We're already on the most basic rations and time is running out fast. This is why we had no choice but to find you.' Hamlin continued.

'So Demeter's yearning has caused the drought?'

The men nodded.

'Where might she be hiding, assuming she's not dead?'

'The fact that the drought continues tells us she is alive,' Hamlin replied. 'If she was dead, the yearning would stop, the equilibrium would be restored and growth would return. As to where she might be, only one hiding place remains.'

'Where's that?'

'The Inferior Cave.'

'What's inferior about it?'

'Nothing at all, merely that it is partly disconnected from the land. You will see when you get there. Entering the cave is strictly forbidden for islanders, William. It draws out the emotions, revealing deep-seated feelings that those who enter may not even know exist.'

'But an outsider can enter, allowing you to maintain the equilibrium?'

'Exactly. We hoped that Demeter would return of her own accord, but alas it is not to be.'

'Has she been in the cave all this time?'

'I imagine so. She knows she is safe there after all.' Hamlin stood up as he spoke. 'Anyway, take as much rest as you need, but I implore you not to delay. Time is of the essence.' With that, they left me to enjoy my wine alone.

After I'd changed into my robe Felix and I set out for The Inferior Cave. Hamlin remained behind to maintain the fragile equilibrium. Unlike the skeletal horses that had carried us from the port, the animals for this expedition were strong and healthy, as though they'd been held in reserve especially for this task. On the back of each horse were tied two small blankets, each filled with basic rations.

'If we make good progress,' Felix said, 'we should get there by midday tomorrow. We'll lay camp at the foot of the Unseen Mountain.'

'The Unseen Mountain?'

'Yes, you can only see it when you're at the foot. It suddenly just appears.'

I looked out to the road ahead, straining my eyes against the sun, which was becoming ever more powerful despite the mist that still hung over the island. The land itself was flat as far as the eye could see. It seemed unfeasible that a mountain lay ahead. I began to feel uneasy. My head throbbed and I felt sick. Water streamed from my eyes as they fought off the heat and the sun. I looked over to Felix, but he rode on unfazed.

We arrived at the mountain just before sunset. Its sudden arrival stirred a strangely familiar feeling that sent me into a minor panic. I allowed Felix to set camp and I wandered off to compose myself. Even though we were at the foot of the mountain we were still someway higher than sea level, offering me a view across the island. The once fertile land had turned to dust, the lush greenery replaced with a horrible grey dullness and a distinct sense of wretchedness. I watched two skeletal oxen try to find nourishment amongst the remnants of a dead tree. The rivers and streams that carried water from the mountain down through the island to the town were empty, leaving ugly craters which spread across the land like giant tentacles.

Whilst Felix ate breakfast I readied the horses, feeding them bread and water from the palm of my hand. Lost in my thoughts, I was oblivious to Felix's presence at my side.

'William, I must advise that I can accompany you for only part of the journey. The remainder you must travel alone.'

I grinned mockingly. 'Why?'

'So powerful is the cave that we don't actually have to set foot inside to feel its influence. I have a map for you though.' He passed me a small sketch inked on a square of dirty linen. 'I doubt that you will need it,' he said. 'Your instincts will show you the way.'

The rough terrain made the next stage of the journey painfully slow. I felt weaker by the hour, the heat sapping me of what little energy I had left. Felix too was suffering, yet the horses ploughed on admirably as though they too were aware of the importance of their task. Then, just as the sea came into view, Felix stopped.

'I must leave you here. Good luck, William.'

I pulled the map out and looked around, but Felix was right, I knew where to go. Without looking back I quickly rode off.

An hour later I stood opposite The Inferior Cave. Much smaller than I imagined, it was like a shell-shaped island attached to the mainland by a thin line of rock that looped across the water like a hook. The only way in was to swim into the mouth of the shell. I climbed off my horse, leaving it to find its own shade then made my way down the rocky hillside to the water's edge. I tossed the map aside and dived in.

When I reached the cave I climbed out of the water and sat down on the rock, rubbing salt from my eyes. The cave was deeper and wider than it looked from the outside. Then something changed. The walls began to encroach and the roof seemed to press down on me from above. My heart began to race, I broke out in a cold sweat and my brain throbbed from a pounding noise that bore deep into my soul. My eyesight began to waver, at times throwing me into total blindness, and so my panic worsened. I let out a dreadful, blood curdling roar, a noise I didn't think I was capable of, and then vomited into the water. My whole body was shaking and tears began to escape, slowly at first then en masse through an uncontrollable sob.

After a while I tried to stand up but my legs were shaking and I could only manage it if I held on to the wall. Mindful of my task, I began to look around for Demeter, however the cave seemed empty. Then as my composure returned, I felt a presence behind me. I turned round and there she was about 15 feet away. 'Eleanor, what are you doing here? Where's Demeter?'

'Demeter? Have you finally replaced me then?'

'What?' I staggered towards her in horror, somehow managing to keep my balance on the wet jagged rocks. The closer I got though the thinner she became, her blue eyes seemed lifeless, her clear skin turned an odd yellow colour and her beautiful black hair morphed into a straw-like mess. I stopped just out of reach. 'You're so thin.'

She snorted. 'I'm thin? Take a look in a mirror. You're hardly the picture of health yourself.'

I lifted my hand to my face. My nose and teeth seemed huge, as though they belonged to another man, my skin was rough and dry and my cheeks had all but disappeared. 'What the hell have you done to me?'

'Me? You've done this to yourself, keeping me here like this.'

The thinner she got, the more of a stranger she became, the more her image and her shrill voice began to irritate me. My eyes were pinned to her though. She was wearing a long blue dress, not the orange one Plax had told me about.

'Where's your orange dress?'

'What the hell are you talking about?' she replied as she prowled around in front of me.

A bitter rage began to rise from the centre of my body. 'WHERE IS YOUR ORANGE DRESS?' I roared. 'Like they wear on the island, the one you're destroying with your selfishness.'

She ran at me, pressing her face against mine. 'My selfishness?' she shouted, covering me in saliva in the process. 'This is your fault, not mine. It's you that's causing the drought, not me. Don't you get it?'

I pushed her back. 'Me? What the hell has it got to do with me, I just got here?'

'William, you've always been here, this is your land. It's you that's killing the island by not letting me go. It's you. You have to let me go.'

My heart sank, my knees trembled and I stumbled back as though I'd been punched. She was right, I had to let her go and I had to do it now.

I stretched out, took her hand in mine and caressed her skin softly. We smiled, then I gently placed my other hand around her neck and squeezed. There was no struggle, no scream. She was calm and accepting, it all seemed so necessary. She slumped quickly to the ground. A loose tear tickled down my face as I gently lifted her weightless body into the sea and watched her sink until she disappeared. 'Goodbye, beautiful,' I whispered.

I woke to the cool sensation of rain on my face. The freshness of the water and the air felt wonderful on my skin. The first thing I saw when I opened my eyes was a single yellow flower fluttering in the breeze. I stood up, stretched my arms above me and began to think about home. For the first time in as long as I could remember, I was hungry.

Sushirexia

Tasting the Apple

Anne Hamilton

✦

Barefoot and scrawny, the sombre little girl was balanced aboard a felucca and waving day old English newspapers. Coins changed hands and her eyes, coffee-silk, brightened.

'Lovely jubbily,' she shouted. 'Nice little earner.'

Teresa, leaning over the rail of the cruiser, now moored for the evening, laughed.

'Where do they pick up this language?' Brian wound his arm around Teresa's bare shoulder. 'Don't wave like that, Tess,' he squeezed her. 'You'll only encourage them.'

'Oh, lighten up.' Teresa said. 'You sound like a tourist. It's only a few pence.'

'I am a tourist,' he reminded her, 'following the advice in the guide-book.' He rubbed his hands together. 'Come on, Tess, it's tea time.'

Teresa looked back towards the little girl, who was slipping her earnings underneath her ragged tunic, chattering as her elderly companion rowed the two of them towards the western bank. The desert was so close that the child could pick up handfuls of sand and throw them into the water, yet Teresa was following Brian and the snake of passengers collecting china cups of English tea and balancing dainty pastries on the side. She wanted to scream.

Brian, the guidebook his new bible, was soon reading aloud to the middle-aged and over-friendly Pattersons, *"…Egypt's miracle of the Nile as it cuts defiantly through the burning arid wilderness of the Sahara…"* Teresa heard. She wanted to bash them all over the head with the pages, all of them with their pimply knees exposed, their thighs reddened like under-cooked chicken breasts. Instead, she fed her fury with a tower of cucumber sandwiches. Wiping at a smear of butter already melted into her tee-shirt, she looked up to see Mrs Patterson watching her. Teresa deliberately bit into her last triangle and chewed it slowly, until Mrs Patterson looked away.

'Brian, I'm going to the cabin.' She licked her lips and put her plate down. 'Are you coming?'

'Right you are,' he said, taking her plate and piling it neatly with his own. Teresa pulled him impatiently towards the steps.

In their cabin, they sat side by side, their picture window a cinema from a different age: women scrubbing at tin cooking pots and cotton clothes, men scrubbing themselves and hauling scraggy, dun-coloured cattle to drink. Teresa watched the sun dipping towards the horizon, its alchemy shifting the thick blue sky into irregular reds and golds before sinking into the narrow fields of irrigated crops.

"In this sun the ancient Egyptians saw divinity, the great partner of their river, they named it Ra and raised great temples in its honour." Brian quoted, reverent as a benediction.

Conversely, his sensitivity irritated Teresa, making her remember why she had not, seemingly could not, write him off to experience and move on. She let him lay her down on one of the narrow single beds and make love to her. Methodically. Pleasantly enough.

'I wonder what's for dinner,' she said, pulling her dress down after-wards.

'Hungry again, pudding?' Brian lay propped up on one arm, watching her do her hair. 'You're beautiful,' he said.

'Don't call me that,' Teresa threw her hairbrush at him. He ducked.

'What? Pudding or beautiful?'

'Either. Neither.'

'Don't be daft. Why not? I love you.'

Because she wasn't hungry or beautiful, or anything else, she thought, just, just *empty*.

'Come on, Tess, you need to talk to me,' Brian said. 'I need to know what's wrong.'

Teresa opened her mouth, but the gong sounded before she worked out what she would say.

In the dining room, she engineered it so that she was too far away from the Pattersons to acknowledge their saved seats.

'It might be *Death on the Nile* all over again,' she muttered to Brian's shoulder, 'if I have to listen to any more of her coy references to *trouble down there*.'

'You mean she wasn't talking about the political situation in Cairo?' Brian joked so hopefully that Teresa forced a laugh; he was trying hard on this holiday, trying to give her what she wanted. It wasn't his fault she didn't know what that was.

'Let's sit there,' she pointed, eyeing a couple who stood out amongst sunburned shoulders and tropical eveningwear.

'These free…?' Brian nodded at chairs beside the smart dark-skinned man and a woman swathed, hairline to jewelled stiletto, in a black burkha. The man made as if to stand up.

'Don't, please. Oh–' Teresa, faltered then rallied, as she gazed at the whites of his eyes which rolled without control. 'I'm Teresa and this is Brian,' she said.

'I am Ali. My wife is Rezia Begum,' the man said, holding out his hand in their general direction. The woman just looked at them.

'You will see I am blind,' Ali said, 'and my new bride, she does not yet speak English. We are just married. This is our honeymoon.'

Teresa stiffened, but Brian appeared to take it in his stride. She waited for him to explain that it might have been theirs too, if she hadn't run out on him in the wake of *Gabriel's' Oboe* and a tangle of cream lace.

'Great place for it, Egypt,' he said instead, eyeing the unspecified roast meat being placed before him. 'Where are you two from, then?'

'We are from Pakistan,' Ali explained. 'I, though, have lived many years in London. Rezia now comes there to join with me.'

'It was an arranged marriage then?' Brian said, 'I mean, did you know each other first?'

Teresa frowned at him, but Ali didn't seem to mind.

'We saw photographs. Our families arranged it. Strange to you, my friend.'

'Wow,' said Brian.

Teresa concentrated on her food, guiltily intoxicated by these people, so different to the suffocating ordinariness around her. Rezia ate elegantly but with vigour, helping Ali, Teresa thought, as if he was an employer not a lover. She made no acknowledgment of Teresa's fascinated gaze; like someone behind one-way glass, she appeared to observe everything and gave nothing away.

She's not the child she looks, Teresa thought.

'Tess? Tess, stop dreaming.' Brian squeezed her knee, and she caught the tail end of an unwelcome suggestion. 'Do you fancy seeing the Old Cataract hotel later? Great terrace, apparently.'

'Not really,' she said. 'I'm tired. You go.'

'I think Rezia would prefer to stay here also–' Ali let the words hang.

Teresa accepted the role of chaperone. 'We can keep each other company then,' she said.

Dinner over, they separated and the women made their way silently to the upper deck, where they watched Ali and Brian hail a horse-drawn cab, and haggle over the price. As the contraption rattled away, Teresa flopped into a deckchair by the floodlit plunge pool. She turned to Rezia, who sat precisely, ankles crossed and hands clasped. Teresa smiled.

'Isn't the silence great?' she said. 'I fancy a drink.'

Half a dozen miles away at the Old Cataract Hotel, Brian and Ali were soon dealing with the business of getting down from the carriage. The driver, wanting a bigger tip, refused to help.

'I wonder would you mind…' Ali thrust his elbow towards Brian.

'Oh, right.' Brian took it awkwardly.

Ali smiled. 'You are not comfortable. You find it embarrassing to be with a blind man.'

'Course not. Just don't go in much for touching other chaps, that's all.'

'Ah, the famous repression of the Englishman!'

Teresa was finding the flowery citronella pods more of a torment than the mosquitoes they were there to deter. Sinuses clogged, she sniffed and cleared her throat, prelude to continuing her monologue.

'So, we're trying to work things out,' she said, 'I mean Brian isn't Einstein or Casanova. But he has his good points and not murdering me at the altar was one of them. Would you believe he still wants to marry me? He's going to wait til I ask him, 'til I'm sure. How the hell will I ever be sure?' She gulped at her pink cocktail, distracted. 'If this is cranberry juice it's a bloody boozy cranberry tree that it came from.'

Rezia just looked at her.

'There's something very therapeutic about talking to someone who can't understand a word.' Teresa felt a bit dizzy. She held up her drink. 'Cheers.'

'Yourself and your Teresa are very happily married.' Ali said as the two men sat on the famous terrace, their tea, and a beer on order. 'I hope that Rezia and I will so aspire.'

'Yeah,' said Brian. 'Well, no, not really. Not that happy actually, and definitely not married. I want to be, but Tess is different.' He took a long drink, wondering how to get back onto the neutral ground of football, even cricket would do. 'It must be easier just being told what to do like you lot. No offence,' he added.

Ali laughed. 'We have choice, my friend. I hope I am very lucky.'

'Row, row, row a boat gentle down a steam,
    Melly, melly, melly, melly. Life such a dream.'

Pacing the deck, Teresa was drawn by the high-pitched voices and in the water, saw the little girl of earlier, paddling busily in a narrow wooden canoe, three other tiny bodies jammed in beside her. Illuminated by camera flashes, they were performing for the tourists on the neighbouring boat. 'Goodnight, London, England. Fish and Chips,' they chorused. 'Goodnight, Scotland, Mr McTavish.'

Teresa turned to Rezia, who did not appear to have moved for hours. 'That's what Brian would like. Him, me, and a gang of children, playing the Waltons in a trailer by the sea.' She groaned, 'I love him, I do, but there's just something… *Shit.*' There was a pause and then she brightened. 'Shall we have a snack?'

'It's getting late,' Brian said. 'Should we get back?'

'Surely there is no hurry?' Ali asked. 'Shall we take a stroll around the town's Old Quarter?'

On the boat, the generator roared, hiccupped, failed. Teresa stumbled in the blackout and Rezia took her hand.

'What…?' Cool fingers touched her lips and Teresa stopped, surprised, as they felt their way down steps and into the service area where the smell of foetid drains and rotting vegetables made her retch.

Alongside the boat was a small felucca, a boatman dozing with a cigarette stuck to his moustache. Rezia pointed down the river and, in a low voice, said something, something that caused him to raise his eyebrows and usher them aboard. Minutes away from the moored tourist palaces, there was no sound beyond croaking nocturnal frogs, and the boat splashing through the water. The wind blew, hairdryer warm, yet Teresa drew herself into her shawl, remembering Brian's guidebook; the ancient Egyptian belief that in death they would sail rivers and seas to their final nirvana. Disorientated with pink cocktails and a landscape turned black, Teresa felt an exhilarated and uneasy pull of their faith.

But when the felucca slowed, and they clambered shoreside, she switched to dreaming of Eden. An enclave of trees was cultivated there and behind them, hidden from the river, a flower garden was bleached silver in subdued artificial light. Sunk in the centre a freshwater pool was lit from beneath, the tiles formed from smooth white stone, tribute to the preserved temple, a mirage in the distance.

'Oh,' whispered Teresa. 'It's…magical.'

Rezia tiptoed to the edge of the pool and in one swift and graceful movement removed her heavy cloak and, naked beneath, she dived into the water.

She surfaced and, for the first time, she smiled.

She looked free.

Clumsy and embarrassed Teresa struggled out of her clothes and jumped in too. Without warning, desire flooded the hole inside her.

Brian and Ali were in the backroom of a sidestreet bar somewhere in seediest Kum Ombo. A circle of men in tunics shared a hookah.

'You see mate, me and Tess want different things. She needs all this travelling and stuff. It's like she's always looking for something, never satisfied.' Brian passed the bubbling pipe shakily through the smoke and into Ali's hands. 'All I really want is the telly and a beer with the lads. She cancelled our wedding, you know. I hated her but I love her. What's a man to do?'

Ali took a deep breath and inhaled. 'I worry too, my friend,' he said. 'Why would a beautiful creature like Rezia agree to marry me, a man with a white cane? I worry,' he lowered his voice, 'there is something in her past that is not right.'

'Does it matter? If you love her?'

'I can only love her if she is worthy of love.'

Under the stars, Rezia plaited her long hair whilst Teresa, sobered, swam an uptight breaststroke, hypnotised by that dark hair, the golden skin, tiny breasts, the smoothly rounded stomach. Let loose from her black cocoon Rezia was so small, so perfect. Teresa plunged under water and held her breath.

'She is *nautch* girl'

Ali and Brian stumbled in the sandy, smelly alleyways of the cluttered village. Ali's voice was slurred and Brian held tightly to his arm.

'Steady,' Brian said. 'Mind the dead dog. What's that then?'

'She thinks we do not know. *Nautch* girl – dancing girl. Straight from Heera Mandi, the stigma of Lahore.'

'Not sure I've got you, mate. You've had a bit too much tonight, that's all.'

But Ali's sightless eyes were wild. 'Rezia. *Tawaif* – whore. My wife. Her beauty, her talents – she can dance and sing for royalty – but she is spoiled. Ruined by her nights in a *kotha*, sold by her family.'

'You mean Rezia was a prostitute?' Brian sounded incredulous. 'Like in the red light district?'

'I do not know. I do not know. Perhaps she only entertained. Perhaps more. I feel sick. I love her.' Ali began to cry and sank to the ground.

Brian knelt down beside him. 'Why don't you ask her?'

Teresa flipped over and floated on her back, daring herself not to cover up.

Rezia seemed lifeless, silhouetted on the warm stone, the droplets on her skin crystallised. Teresa, climbing out of the water, and laying down beside her, was tense, willing her own heartbeat to slow. She must have slept because she awoke, suddenly, and Rezia was leaning over her. A silver chain, glittering with three tiny blue sapphires was grazing Teresa's shoulder.

She is going to kiss me, Teresa thought, mind dispassionate, heart thumping. But Rezia didn't. She pursed her lips and blew gently onto Teresa's cheek removing a stray hair. Then she kissed her.

Ali laughed, bitter as lemons. 'My brother, the joke is mine. Ask her you say. That I cannot do. She married me from a picture. My brother and his wife brought her from Lahore. She married me but did not know I was blind. We each have our shame. We are as good as each other. If she is a whore, I am a liar, a cheat. If she is innocent, I am still a liar, a cheat.'

Slowly Rezia raised her head, rose softly, and dressed, looking out towards the Nile. Standing on her toes to reach, she pulled Teresa's clothes gently over her head; like a small child Teresa let her. Hand in hand, they returned to the boatman who, impervious, took them back to the cruiser. Teresa, grappling with elation and a terrible comprehension, vaguely registered the sight of Brian and Ali, slowly making their way up the gang-plank.

'Quite a night,' Brian cleared his throat. 'I'll probably have forgotten most of it in the morning.'

'You have great tact,' Ali grasped his elbow with pressure strong enough to bruise.

Teresa and Rezia watched them, trapped on the tiny felucca.

'More money,' the boatman insisted. 'More.' He looked in disgust at the few coins in his hands. Rezia looked at him and held out her hands palms up.

'Your men,' the boatman, his face twisted, looked up at the retreating figures of Brian and Ali.

Teresa pulled herself together. 'I'll bring money from the boat,' she said, gesturing her intentions.

Reluctantly, he let them off. Teresa made towards her cabin but Rezia stopped her at reception. Quickly, she lifted an envelope from the silent desk and stuffed it with a wad of blank paper. From the deck, she threw it down, where it hit the water and slowly melted away. They waited in the shadows until the boatman, impotent with rage, had paddled off.

The two women looked at one another.

Each turned towards her own bed.

When Teresa didn't mention the evening, Brian looked relieved and also said nothing. The following day – their last – Ali was charming, Rezia impassive. They said their brief farewells and Teresa was already in the bus heading for Cairo, when one of the guides came running.

'A package for you, madam,' he held it out. 'Mrs Begum left it.'

Inside, the silver chain finished with three tiny blue sapphires was screwed up in a wad of tissue. Teresa bit her lip and shoved it into her pocket. Last night it had all made sense, the emptiness filled, the door to a new life opening. Daylight brought the panic, the risk of the unknown, the fear that she wasn't so different after all. And the door clanged shut again. She tried to smile as Brian arrived.

'You feeling alright, love?' he asked. 'You didn't eat anything at break-fast. Not like you.'

'Someone told me there's a hidden garden and a pool just over the other side of the Nile.' Teresa said, the first thing that entered her head.

'Yep,' said Brian, immediately distracted. He tapped his guidebook. 'Only we experts know it as the private residence of the descendants of the Aga Khan. His tomb is there. Closed to the public though.'

Teresa said nothing.

Brian hesitated. Then deliberately he turned back to the book, creasing the spine further. 'Right,' he said, *'…the mathematical genius of the pyramids of Cairo…'*

'Brian.' Teresa tossed a metaphorical coin in the air, where it spun, hovered, and landed on familiarity. 'Will you marry me?' she said.

Sushirexia

That Bitch

Victoria Murphy

—◆—

'The first fucking interview Martha's given since her husband left. A big fucking exclusive, and *she's* got it!'

'Jon, I'm sorry, there's nothing I can do,' said Tom Dixon, the showbiz editor. 'The Boss said, she got the interview, she should do it. I warned him, though. She won't get a bloody word out of Martha. He'll wish you'd done it instead.'

It didn't do much to improve the mood of his chief showbiz reporter.

'How?' he said, giving the bin a kick. 'How the fuck did she get it?'

It was indeed a mystery how Angela Thomas, eighteen years old and just two months into her job as trainee showbiz reporter at the Post, had managed to secure an interview with Martha Mason. Martha Mason was an actress, an ethereal red-head with creamy skin and long, glorious curls, just as able to convince on stage as seduce on screen. She was a star, a beautiful, talented, elusive star. In these days of celebrities appearing in the press for sneezing, Martha Mason only gave rare interviews and they were always to promote her work. At forty six she still had considerable appeal, so when her husband was spotted with an attractive, very young blonde, photographers and journalists were sent off in pursuit of a story.

'I got it!' said Angela Thomas to her dad and younger sister, Kayleigh, on the phone that evening. 'I got an interview with Martha Mason.'

'Oh, that's great love. I bet the Boss is chuffed.'

Angela's dad had worked with the editor of the Post when they were both training to be journalists on a provincial newspaper. Twenty years later, Mr Thomas was still at the Darlington Daily News, a single dad of two girls after his wife died of cancer when Kayleigh was three. His former colleague had moved down south, and now had a high profile job as Editor of a national newspaper. It was good of him to have given Ange her first taste of newsgathering.

'He said I'm to do it. Jon Power, you know, the chief reporter, he wanted to take it off me. He's furious about it.'

'You take no notice,' said her father. 'As long as the Boss is pleased, that's all you need to worry about.'

'Eh, Ange, yer lucky cow,' shouted her sister in the background. 'Gonna get me an autograph.'

Angela didn't mention that it had been easy to get the interview. All she'd done was write a polite letter, enclosing the questions she wanted to ask Miss Mason about her career. It was good fortune that Martha's agent was thinking it would be helpful for his client to do just one interview which would hopefully put a stop to all the requests. As to which journalist should do it, who better than a young, admiring trainee, who would no doubt write a sensitive feature? So a fortnight later, Angela presented herself at Martha's home in West London, wearing her new navy 'interview suit' and carrying the roomy faux leather bag she'd treated herself to when she got the job.

The actress felt a little sorry for the young woman, who looked so uncomfortable and in awe. She even asked for an autograph, which journalists usually considered 'uncool'. But at least she was familiar with Martha's work, which bolstered her recently dented ego. They were just discussing her latest movie, an account of a woman's broken engagement, when Martha was horrified to see tears running down the young journalist's face, forming two black rivulets as they merged with the non-waterproof mascara she'd so carefully applied that morning. Angela quickly wiped her eyes, streaking eye liner out towards her temples like a crazed Cleopatra. For all her success, Martha was a compassionate woman. She began pulling tissues out one at a time and handing them to the weeping girl.

'I'm sorry.' Angela sniffed. 'I split up with my fiancé a few weeks ago. I thought we'd get back together but I've just found out he's been seeing someone else, and it's been going on for months! A friend of mine rang me and said "You must want to kill that slapper?" I said "what?" and then it all came out. My friend's husband said that at a stag night ages ago, Martin got off with one of the girls who 'entertained' them. That's when it started. I can't believe I was so stupid not to have realised.'

'I can assure you, you're not alone,' said Martha, patting Angela's hand. 'The whole world knew about Fred before me. First I heard about it was when a journalist rang me up and asked me how I felt.'

'Oh, that's awful,' said Angela. 'But at least he couldn't deny it. Martin said my friend was making it all up because she didn't like him.'

'Well, actually he did deny it. A while before it all blew up, I'd had a feeling something wasn't right. I asked Fred if he was seeing someone and he gave me a really hard time for not trusting him, said I was being controlling. And when that journalist rang me, Fred made me feel a bitch for believing the press and not him. I ended up thinking I was going mad. It wasn't until their pictures were in all the papers that he had to admit everything, and then it all made sense. You know, I reckon women realise what their men are up to but we don't want to know, so we sort of shut it out.'

Angela nodded.

'Yes. When I look back now, there are so many times when it was obvious, but I didn't seem to take it in. I still don't understand what Martin sees in her though. My friend said she wears loads of make-up and short skirts, and has her tits hanging out - he hated all that.'

Martha laughed.

'Well he may still hate it. The trouble is he's thinking with something else right now. If he said it had all been a mistake, would you have him back?'

'No way,' said Angela.' I could never trust him again. Why, would you have Fred back?

'Oh no! Not after what he put me through, the bastard.'

'Do you know what I can't bear?' said Angela. 'It sounds really stupid, but it's the thought of him actually kissing her. It makes me feel sick.'

'I know exactly what you mean. That intimacy that you think only you and him have, caressing, touching. And then men say it didn't mean a thing!'

They both sat for a moment.

'Right, time for a cuppa. Tea or coffee?'

'Tea please,' said Angela. She looked up at Martha. 'Thank you.'

While Martha was in the kitchen, Angela looked around the room. Two huge squashy sofas, covered in grey velvet, faced each other. Books and magazines sat on a white coffee table. Several pieces of modern art hung on pale walls. There was no sight of the Baftas, no pictures of Martha meeting the Queen, and no pictures of Fred. Just a photograph of two smiling teenage girls in sunhats, their slender, suntanned arms around their mother.

Martha came in with two mugs and some biscuits.

'You should have something sweet if you've had a shock,' she said.

'I still can't believe it,' said Angela. 'If anyone had ever asked me if I thought he'd cheat, I'd have said, "never." I will never trust anyone again. If I was that sure about Martin and I was still wrong...'

'Oh, you will. You're young enough, at least. I won't live with anyone again. It's just me and the girls from now on.'

'Do you still have to see Fred, because of the girls?' asked Angela. 'I don't think I'd ever be able to do that.'

'No...well, Fred isn't their real father, though he's been like a dad to them. It's been tough on them. I'd find it impossible if they were younger and every bloody weekend I had to hand them over to him and TB.'

She smiled at Angela's quizzical face.

'TB – That Bitch. It's what me and the girls call her!'

Angela laughed.

'You know, I've spent days thinking up how to get back at Martin,' she said, looking embarrassed. 'I've even been looking up ways women have got their revenge. My favourite is from years ago, the girl who knew her boyfriend always came home late on a Thursday, so the next Thursday evening, she let herself in, took out all the light bulbs downstairs and littered the hallway with his beloved record collection. He broke them all himself as he walked in!'

The two women laughed.

'We've been a real couple of miseries haven't we?' said Martha, getting up.

'I'm really sorry for getting so emotional,' said Angela.

'Don't worry, I've enjoyed chatting,' said Martha.

'It's been really lovely to meet you. Thank you so much.'

The two women hugged and when Angela reached the pink wooden gate she turned and waved. She walked up to the main road, hailed a taxi and climbed into the back, giving the driver the address of her work. Then she opened her new bag and switched off her tape recorder. She didn't think she'd be a trainee for much longer.

Sushirexia

Soup

Sarah Ward

People love my soup, even if I say so myself. Every day there's more folk asking for a bowl. I put up an ad that says, *Get your five-a-day for £1.50!* Okay, maybe that's a slight exaggeration but my portions are generous. There's a lot come in here that wouldn't touch a vegetable on a plate, never mind a piece of fruit. I like to keep an eye on them. It's not just old ones and mums: there's workmen, home helps and then there's the ones who can't get a job because they're not well or because they're too fond of the bottle.

Minestrone's the best, it's a meal in itself, but the chicken's popular too. I always have a choice because you never know how people are feeling on a particular day. There's a woman who loved the chicken at first but then she found a bone and she's never taken it since. I said, Godsake, Sandra, that's proof it's real! but she wouldn't listen. Then I heard she takes anaphylactic reactions and that's how she's paranoid, so now I make a special French onion for her.

On Tuesdays the kids come in after school and they're straight to the counter with Gonny give us a poke of chips but I won't give them chips until I know they've had something proper; they can have chips after if they're still hungry. They moan on at me, Aw Marie, that's pure shite and all that, but I tell them, Somebody's got to look after you, and if it's not me, who will?

A few weeks ago wee Jamie-Lee started turning up at the back of five. She came to the counter and asked me, What can you get for twenty pence? I told her she's a rascal because she knows all I've got at that price are penny chews and plain biscuits, and I can see she's starving. I said, Jamie-Lee, you need to tell that mother of yours that if she canny feed you, at least she can give you the right money. But then I looked at her wee face and thought what a shame no-one bothers about her; now she comes in every night to get soup and a roll for nothing. She likes tomato best, same as all weans, but she'll eat whatever I put in front of her.

Apparently Mum's shacked up with a guy that doesn't like kids, so Jamie-Lee's started hanging about until ten o'clock when Tommy gives us both a lift home after he's locked up. Jamie-Lee's mum has a disability so she can't get out the house and she relies on this chancer to get her messages. I'll bet he's living there and not paying a penny. Jamie-Lee says sometimes they're up all night and she has to get herself ready for school in the morning. Even when she comes in at three in the afternoon he'll shout at her to F off and give them peace. When she told me that, I'd a mind to go straight to the social there and then because it's a disgrace, a wean getting treated like that. Then I thought I might make it worse, if he thinks she's been telling tales, god knows what she'd be in for.

Last night she was in as usual. I'd given her the leek and potato with a ham roll for protein, and a glass of milk. She finished it down to the last drop then went to play dominoes with Sandy and Jim.

Watch out, said Sandy, here comes the champ.

Jamie-Lee lined up her dominoes and propped a book behind them so no-one could see. She likes to take her time but she's good; it's not just the old guys letting her win. If one of them took so long they'd huff and puff, but they don't mind with Jamie-Lee because she's only a wee lassie. They were getting towards the end of the game when PC McNeill, the new community polis, turned up. He's taken to stopping in on his rounds. He's alright for a polis, although you never can trust them. They act nice but they've got eagle eyes and they like to see which of the young ones is hanging about.

Give me a cup of your pea and ham, Marie, he said, and went over for a chat with Tommy at the desk. Now I know for a fact that children under eight aren't allowed in here without a guardian, it's against the law, and Jamie-Lee's only just turned seven. So I leaned over to Sandy and said, Just kid on you're her granda for now, Sandy, and I'll give you a doughnut after. Aye okay, Marie, said Sandy, and gave me the wink.

When McNeill came back over he sat down at their table and said,

That's the best pea and ham I've tasted in a while, Marie.

Thanks very much, I said, and asked if he wanted a biscuit with his cuppa. He took a fruit Club.

I see you're recruiting the youngsters for dominoes, he said to Sandy. Jamie-Lee smiled at him like butter wouldn't melt.

Aye, this is my granddaughter, Jamie-Lee, said Sandy.

You getting her started early?

Sandy laughed. She beats us every time, doesn't she, Jim?

Four times out of five, said Jim.

Where d'you stay, Jamie-Lee?

Up the flats, she said.

McNeill looked at his watch. That's nearly nine now. I take it you've done your homework?

Aye, you have, haven't you? said Sandy.

Jamie-Lee nodded.

You shouldn't be late getting to your bed when you've got school in the morning.

I'll be straight up to my bed after this, said Jamie-Lee, quite the thing.

McNeill finished his tea and paid. Better be getting on, I'll see yous later, he said.

When he'd gone we all breathed a sigh of relief and I gave Sandy the last jam doughnut.

You'll need to be careful, Jamie-Lee, I said. I don't want you getting in bother with the police. Maybe you'll need to go up the road a bit earlier from now on.

She looked miserable so I went over and gave her a cuddle.

It's not that we don't want you here, honey, I said. I just worry about what your Ma's boyfriend'll say if a polis arrives up at the door with you.

He'd give me a doing, she said.

Exactly.

It's worse if I go up early but, she said, looking up at me like she was going to greet. I didn't have the heart to chase her.

Come and help me in the kitchen, I said. I need to make a batch of soup for tomorrow. Let's make tomato.

She cheered up at that and skipped after me into the kitchen.

Right, Jamie-Lee, I said. What's the key to a cracking tomato soup?

She shrugged. Dunno.

I opened the fridge and stuck a chilli on the counter.

Urgh.

Trust me; you won't even know it's there, but it makes the soup dead rich and tasty.

She helped me chop, except for the chilli in case it was too burny on her fingers then I pulled over a chair and she stood by the big pan, stirring. She stuck her wee nose over the edge and sniffed.

Smells beautiful, she said. I don't normally like tomatoes unless it's smooth like ketchup.

What is it with weans and real tomatoes, I said. Where d'you think ketchup comes from?

The soup took half an hour to make then while it simmered she sat on the counter and I showed her photos of my cakes. She chose the princess one for her next birthday.

You can have a party in here, if you like. Bring your friends.

Jamie-Lee bit her lip. My Ma'll not let me, she said. She's skint.

Don't worry about the money, I said, It'll be my treat. I always look after my pals. I gave her a squeeze. Right, honey. It's time you were in your bed.

We were waiting outside for Tommy to pull down the shutter when I heard the car pull up behind us.

Is that you done for the night? McNeill lowered the electric window of the police car.

That's us, I said, taking Jamie-Lee's hand and heading for Tommy's Astra.

I'm surprised Sandy didn't take the wee lassie up the road, he said.

He was in a hurry so I said I'd take her on my way home.

I'll take her, Marie, he said. I'm thinking on having a word with her folks anyway. Staying out till ten o'clock.

It's just a one-off, I said. Honestly, it's no trouble.

You shouldn't take that responsibility, Marie. It just encourages them. Come on, Jamie-Lee, he said, opening the passenger door.

Jamie-Lee looked up at me and kept a hold of my hand.

With all respect, I said, you'll make it worse for the wean by going up to her door.

I understand your concern but I can't see a child out herself at this time and do nothing about it. Sorry, Marie, I know you mean well. Hop in, he said to Jamie-Lee, patting the seat next to him.

By the time Tommy came out jangling the keys in his pocket I was watching McNeil's tail lights as the car turned into South Street and disappeared from view. It wasn't until then that I remembered Jamie-Lee's jacket over my arm.

I've never tailed a polis before, said Tommy. He's a terrible driver, dead nervous at the best of times. He crawled along South Street and parked in the shadows under the bridge round the corner from the flats. We waited ten minutes then Tommy said, It's him! We watched McNeil zip up his jacket and get into his car. He put on the light and wrote something in his notebook, then switched off the car light and pulled away into Dumbarton Road.

I'm going up, I said. If I'm not back in twenty, you better come after me.

Tommy sighed and got the paper out. I hope you know what you're doing, Marie. Sometimes you're best leaving people alone. You always think you can fix things.

I've let her down, I said. She's only a wean. I closed the car door and walked across the wide forecourt, pressed the buzzer and waited.

Who is it? The voice crackled over the intercom.

It's Marie from the community centre. I've got Jamie-Lee's jacket.

Leave it with the concierge, he said. Then there was a clatter and the intercom went dead. I buzzed again but there was no answer.

Damn. I went in to see the concierge. Can I take a wean's jacket up to 6/3?

He buzzed the flat. Stuart, it's Colin. There a woman here with the wean's jacket. Shall I send her up? He covered the handset.

He says he telt you to leave it at the desk.

I just wanted to give it to the wean myself.

She just wants to see the wean, he said into the phone.

He replaced the handset. It's too late, he said. She's just come in with a polis. I doubt she'll be too popular tonight. He shrugged. Sorry. He reached over for the jacket and put it under the counter.

At five o'clock today, Jamie-Lee didn't come. The tomato soup was nearly finished so I put aside a bowl, every time I passed it thinking about that big bastard in her mother's flat. Why did I not get in McNeill's car with her? I could've gone up to the door at least. I decided to make a batch of carrot and butterbean to take my mind off things. Chopping helps me relax. I sliced the onion extra thin and diced the carrot. I decided to use veggie stock because this batch was for the yoga class. There are loads of them on a Wednesday, and they appreciate something different from a cheese sandwich.

About six, Tommy calls me out to the counter and there she is, stood whistling a tune and looking the other way.

Jamie-Lee! You okay? Her eyes are red so I run round the front to give her a hug.

C'mere, I say.

She slaps a pound on the counter. Roll and sausage please, she says.

I've saved you some of the tomato we made.

She looks me in the eye. I don't like soup, she said. Especially not tomato.

Oh right. I'll bring your roll over.

She turns and makes her way to the farthest table by the window. She sits with her chin on her hand, watching folk coming in. I put a couple of sachets of ketchup by the side of her roll, and hide the pound under the napkin. When I take it over she won't turn to look at me.

I'm sorry about last night, Jamie-Lee, I say. I see you got your jacket.

She wraps her roll in the napkin and stands up. Stuart says I've not to come in here any more, she says, looking straight ahead. He says you canny even trust your pals not to grass you in. A dot of blood appears on her lip where she's bitten it.

You can trust me, Jamie-Lee, I say.

How can I? she blazes. You never even came with me! You made me go myself even when you know what he's like! Then she turns on her heel. As she steps out she puts up the hood of her anorak against the rain, which is falling in diagonals across the darkening street.

The yoga class is streaming out of the hall and forming a queue so I hurry over to the counter. I ladle bowl after bowl of the soup until the pan is empty then I go over to clear Jamie-Lee's plate and cup. The pound is still there. I wash and dry them by hand in the kitchen, and put them up on the shelf with the pound. The bowl of tomato soup has formed a skin on top so I sling it into the sink and watch while it swirls and breaks over the stainless steel, streaking the water until it runs clear.

Sushirexia

Sushirexia

Jackie Copleton

The old man winces when he stands up but he is determined to give me his seat. 'Here you go, love,' he says, indicating, with the Reader's Digest he holds in his liver-spotted fist, towards the empty chair. I dip my head in mute thanks and hope he doesn't interpret the gesture as an invitation to talk. A snotty toddler, sitting by my feet, stops playing with his plastic dumper truck and stares, transfixed. He alternates between pushing his toy truck around the carpet and testing the soft give of my suede sandals with tentative prods. I stiffen against his touch and concentrate on the poster of a cancerous tongue displayed above the head of the boy's mother, who is lost in a world of Heat. Dr Bunyan is only 10 minutes late for our appointment when he calls me into his office. I watch him rolling up his shirt sleeves with tight-lipped purposefulness. He looks like a plumber who is about to get to work on a kitchen pipe blocked with rotten food and congealed fat.

Thankfully we have gone past the stage of polite formalities. 'Usual procedure,' he says, pointing at the scales. I press my toes against the back of each sandal and kick them off. I do this not to lessen the load, but because I know Dr Bunyan finds my tiny, shrunken feet distasteful. It amuses me to see his nose wrinkle with displeasure. His hands flick weights back and forth along a sliding metal rule and we wait for the rule to settle. 'Another bad week, I see,' he says, raising chiding eyebrows when he sighs 'Another'.

'Too many bad weeks, Hazel,' he adds, peering over his glasses. He walks to the sink to wash his hands and talks with his back to me. 'I've made an appointment for you to see Sally Mathers. Sally is a psychologist, a good one, too. Not a quack, certainly not. Lots of experience with this condition. It's time we tackled the issues properly, dissected what's up, really, with Hazel. What's making Hazel this way?' Dr Bunyan turns and smiles, his beatific smile, the one where his lips disappear and his eyes don't focus, as if he's doing a big shit. This is how I like to imagine him during these monologues when he refers to me in the third person. I like to imagine him squatting on the toilet earnestly focused on his morning evacuations. 'To understand the motivation, the compulsion,' Dr Bunyan continues, sitting down and removing his glasses to check for smears. 'The root, Hazel, the root of this behaviour.' Dr Bunyan has been threatening this mind stuff for weeks now, banging on about cognitive behavioural therapy and rewiring my brain and getting to the bottom of my problem. He stops talking, waits for me to say something. I say nothing and Dr Bunyan looks disappointed. He puts his glasses back on and crosses his hands, leans forward. 'You do understand the seriousness of all this, Hazel? You do know what will happen?' I nod. 'Before we go to Sally, let's try one more option.' I nod again. Together, Dr Bunyan and I have tried many options over the months we have been forced into this acquaintance. First came the liver diet option, next the heart surgery diet option, and then the only-eat-when-you're-hungry option, which we both agree, was a laughable failure. Dr Bunyan prints off sheets of paper, and the breeze from the window rustles the hairs on his knuckles when he hands the sheets to me. 'This is a new innovation from the States, high success rates. I want you to follow it. This is possible, Hazel. You can do it. Hazel has to believe in Hazel.' Dr Bunyan smiles, a satisfied smile; he has met, he is sure, his responsibilities. He looks at his watch. 'Start with the sushi plan. I hear it works wonders. Time is running out, Hazel.'

Time has been running out for a while now. My mum, especially, worries about time, and then worries, this worry is some kind of betrayal. 'You're still young, love, and you've got so much love to give,' my mum tells me, usually after one glass of white wine too many. 'You remind me so much of your father, so soft, no idea how good, how lovely you are.' Mum stops mid glug and shakes her head. 'Not that you need to change, dear. You're just fine as you are, just fine, but your health love, I don't know what I'd do.' And I'm thinking about my mum crying into her wine when I walk past the junkie man, who leans against the wall outside the GP surgery. He looks me up and down and says, 'You should be fucking ashamed of your-self.' White spittle sticks to the corners of his mouth, and his yellow face scrunches up like dry chamois leather as he bares his teeth like a dog. The junkie man steps in front of me, lowers his face closer to mine and says, 'You're horrible, fucking horrible.' The junkie man shakes his head and staggers up the surgery steps, shoulders hunched. And so I'm not sure if it's the memory of my weeping mum or my need to wipe the junkie man's spit from my face that makes me think: maybe the sushi plan will work.

I walk to the sushi restaurant because it's not far from the surgery and I'm worried I won't be able to afford raw fish and a taxi. I listen to my breath as I walk. It sounds like radio interference and tastes like pork crackling. Two boys jog past me and the smaller boy goes, 'Fuck sake,' laughing. And I know they are laughing at me, just as I know when I reach the restaurant that the passing driver tooting his horn is tooting at me.

I pull open the door and, inside, I see a carousel so small it must have come from a factory in Lilliput. Clear plastic domes placed on tiny plates jiggle along the metal belt. Inside the carousel, a man scratches the rim of his paper hat and runs the tip of a knife along a slab of quivering tuna. A Japanese girl appears at my side and screams, 'Irashairaisha,' and the girl screams it like an alarm bell, but then she smiles and I realise she's not shouting at me to leave. The girl indicates one of the stools next to the carousel and we look at the stool, and we look at one another, and the girl says, 'Booth is better?' I nod and do one of my half-smiles as if I'm sucking meat from my teeth. 'You eat here before?' I shake my head. 'Colour of plates is price of dish. Red most expensive. Take from here.' The girl points at the moving metal belt. She picks up a small jar of green paste. 'Wasabi,' the girls says. 'Not too much, bad for brain, hot.' The girl makes the sound of an explosion and laughs. 'Put little bit wasabi in soy sauce and ginger to clean mouth and this free water in tap. Okay?' And I look at the oblongs of pink, red and cream flesh wobbling their way towards me on the carousel and I think, 'Is Dr Bunyan taking the piss?'

The sushi plan tells me to eat every day for a week five small plates of raw fish and two plates of edamame beans, and drink two litres of water, and four bowls of miso soup, and two pots of green tea; and swim thirty lengths in a pool. The cuts of fish trundle past my nose but I can't make up my mind what to choose. The girl walks by and I point at three parcels of dark seaweed wrapped around fat orange balls, the size of peppercorns. 'What is it?' I ask.

The girl says, 'Fish eggs. Ikura, ik...u...ra,' and then the girl says, 'Oishi, delicious, super oishi,' and out of politeness I pick up the plate of roe and the girl smiles. Popping one of the seaweed parcels in my mouth, I'm surprised when I don't gag. Plump eggs pop against my teeth and the juice seeps over my tongue. I pour soy sauce into a small dish and mix a dollop of wasabi into it. I pick up a plate of tuna stacked on small mounds of rice and dip one of the sushi pieces in the sauce. The fish melts in my mouth and then it hits me, an explosion at the base of my head, synapses ablaze. 'Too much wasabi'. Drinking gulps of water, I rub the back of my neck. Dr Bunyan has told me that spicy food burns more calories.

The burning spreads up inside my head and now I'm worried it won't stop. Wiping tears from my eyes, through the blur I see a woman sit opposite my booth. She doesn't look at me and she's skinny, skinnier than the boys that laughed at me in the street, skinnier than the tiny waitress. The woman is wearing a tracksuit, one of those velour designer ones, and a giant red fire gem flashes on her wedding finger. She looks unhappy, or maybe angry. The woman doesn't turn to look at the waitress, and the waitress doesn't warn her about the wasabi. The woman leans forward and lifts two plates of salmon sashimi from the carousel. She opens up the wasabi pot and uses the tiny spoon to tip half the paste into her dish of soy sauce. The sauce turns from a watery brown to a sludge grey. The woman uses a chopstick to smear the sludge over the fish. She begins to eat and her cheeks bulge out like a spineless puffer fish. Her eyes water; she blinks twice and carries on eating.

No carbs. No lovely carbs. What's it like to be this no-carb woman with the breakable wrists and boy hips? I imagine her fiancé, bloated on success, her rich house, the woman's designer set of scales in the bathroom. Are these the rewards of the sushi plan? Right, this is it, I'm only going to eat what the woman eats; when the woman picks up a plate of thinly sliced salmon so do I. Together we eat 10 plates of salmon and two plates of tuna. The woman puts money on the counter, and when the waitress isn't looking she furtively take a dish of three small round cakes from the carousel. The woman picks up the sticky rice cakes and crams all three of them in her mouth. She looks straight ahead and chews. The woman stops chewing, gags and swallows. Carbs, I note triumphantly. To mark her carbohydrate intake I join her in a plate of cakes. Not once does the woman look at me, even though I'm the only other customer in the restaurant. The woman never smiles at the waitress when she leaves and she never pays for the cakes. I want to tell the waitress about the stolen dessert, but don't, and stand up to pay my bill. The waitress asks, 'Oishi?' and I reply, 'Yes, delicious,' and then I decide to bugger the cost and take a taxi to pick up my swimsuit from my home to swim my 30 lengths.

'Would you like to use the disabled changing rooms?' the receptionist asks me at the leisure centre. Not really, but how do you say no to that question? The sushi plan says 'daily swimming will vastly improve your chances of success on the program'. I mentally add 'me' to the end of 'program' when I read this. Standing next to the disabled toilet, I can't avoid my naked body in the full-length mirror. I turn away from my reflection and hold on to the plastic railing to pull up the swimsuit. It smells of musty drawers. My inner thighs hurt from walking, as if someone has rubbed sandpaper over the skin, and there is a hole in the seam of my swimsuit under my right arm. I joined the private leisure centre last year but this is my first visit. The last time I was here a man made me wear blue plastic bags over my shoes when he took me on a tour of the facilities. The man knelt down to help me put the bags over my tiny feet. I remember how close his head was to my crotch. My crotch ached and then the man stood up and walked me around the pool and I tried to stop the ache in my crotch from fading. That's not the worst thing I can confess.

Pushing against the door to the disabled changing room, I slowly walk across the wet tiles. Chlorine fills the air and the sun fogs behind frosted windows. Two men with wide chests, rugby players, sit in the hot tub, and a man floats on his back in the pool, jerking his thin legs like an overturned frog. The pool attendant has taken off his top to mop out the steam room. His back is covered in sweat and he wears blue bags over his trainers. When I walk past the hot tub, the rugby men laugh and I hear one of them say, 'Bet you twenty, if you…' and I have to turn and face them to lower myself down the steps into the water. The men pretend not to watch, but

I catch one of them smirking. The frog man heads towards me and I don't have time to move out of his way. 'Sorry pet, didn't see you there, I'm just getting out, give you some room.' Thirty, thirty lengths and then I can go home. Hazel can go home.

The cool water feels good against my sore thighs. I swim, breast stroke. I push forward and puff and push forward and puff. My toes scrape along the bottom of the shallow end but I can't lift them any higher. When I turn to do my second length someone walks towards the pool. It's the woman from the sushi restaurant. She pulls at her pale pink bikini top and corrugated rows of ribs protrude below her chest. How must it feel to have bones push against taut, polished skin? The woman passes me in the next lane but she doesn't look at me. Twenty-nine, twenty-nine lengths and then I can go home.

I've only got nine lengths to go when the pain starts. It's nothing too bad, just a mild throbbing down my left arm. But with only six lengths to go, the pain is stronger. Maybe I should stop. But it's only six, only six lengths and I'll have almost succeeded on the first day of the sushi plan. I keep swimming, puff my way to my twenty-seventh length, and the pain grows stronger. Maybe it's only indigestion. Or what if it's a heart attack? What happens if I die in this pool? Maybe the two rugby men will push my body to the side and the pool attendant will use the hoist for people in wheelchairs to drag me out. Or maybe firemen will lower a crane hook in through the roof, attach the hook to my swimsuit and yank me out. But what if the worn material won't take the strain and the straps snap and I plop back into the water, naked?

I've only got one length to go and I think I can make it even though I've swallowed water and my eyes sting from the chlorine. I keep swimming but my nose slips under the surface and then my eyes fill with water. I try to move my legs to stand up but my legs won't move. I try to move my arms but my arms won't move. I'm strangely calm when my head disappears. Through the haze of chlorine, I see my flesh wobble in the water, like the fish on the carousel, and I watch myself wobble and sink and wobble and sink to the bottom of the pool. I say, 'Help,' but under the water the word sounds like 'Guullpp,' and I know the woman in the next lane won't hear me.

It's how they say it is, foggy, then gentle darkness. And maybe this is it. Time has run out. The sushi plan has failed. But then, there's not so much a light as the motion of retching. My body convulsing, and gagging and then my innards seem to want to lurch from my body. Vomit. Pink pools of salmon and tuna and roe erupt over my chest. I wipe my mouth and stare at the pool attendant, crouching next to me. Beside him stand the two rugby men, Jacuzzi juice dripping from their bodies on to mine.

'You okay, hen?' the pool attendant asks. But I'm not listening. I'm looking at the pool, looking for the woman, wondering if she raised the alarm. No one's there. Then the smell, the vomit, hits my nostrils. I wipe the half-digested sushi and sashimi off my swimsuit which, in the glare from the sun through the frosted windows, looks as pink as the bikini on the woman who has disappeared from the pool. One shiny orange fish egg nestles against my wedding finger, large and smooth as the fire gem on the missing woman's bony hand. 'Can we help you, love?' the pool man asks, looking up to the rugby men who, sickened by the smell, step back.

And I take a step back too. 'I'm fine, I'm fine,' I say. I flick the fish egg off my hand and it tumbles down the pool's metal drain. No more sushi, no more Bunyan, no Sally Mathers, I'm fine. And tonight, sticky spare ribs to celebrate.

Sushirexia

Arc Lights

Carol Farrelly

—◆—

Veronica leaned back into the alcove and slipped her bare feet slow and careful out of her high heels. She liked to give the illusion of nylon. Let the audience imagine she had some smitten G. I. showering her with stockings and purple high heels. Let them make up their hokey stories. None of them had any nose for the truth. They would never put her with Frank, one hour's time, in the empty back seats. And wasn't that half the reason she had started this thing with him? To give herself a better story.

She half-closed her eyes, and pressed her palms against the wall's embroidered coolness. The cinema screen continued to flicker off to her right – silver then violet, blue then white – but its lights did not touch her in the alcove. Bogart's kiss, a slow violet glow, did not catch in her eyelashes. Bergman's smile, a throw of silver light, did not wisp through her hair.

Sometimes she needed this darkness. She needed to recline in her alcove beneath the plaster Juliet balcony, which had neither door nor stairs. Catch her breath. Imagine one hour ahead. Think of Frank. Escape the eyes – lustful, jealous, disapproving – that strayed from the screen to travel her hips or her breasts. It was always she they watched. Not the other girls. Never Phyllis Donoghue. One of the miserable little Jane Eyres of the world. How she had ever managed to lay her mucky hands on an usherette's uniform...

But even in her alcove, the audience reached Veronica. Smoke coiled anonymous across the aisle and tickled her throat; sweet wrappers glinted in nearby laps; scents burst up from one row then another like little puffs of perfume – rationings of apple then mint, chocolate then aniseed. And all the while the audience kept searching for her. They thought the beautiful edible darkness gave them that freedom. And, most of the time, she did not mind; but tonight she could not bear their eyes upon her.

She turned in and pressed her back against the darker wall. It was hard to think of Frank, to concentrate on only him, when the auditorium rustled so much life at her. Rows of heads fanned out before her. Mr Godwin, the grocer, sat in the nearest row, bald-headed, sucking a slug-like stick of liquorice. His curl-topped wife was next to him, all buttoned up in one of her boxy high-collared overcoats. Not that it was any kind of disguise. All those too easily stolen ounces of butter and sugar turned to fat. Three rows further back sat Dr. James Mann, only a few months out of the medical school, cufflinks gleaming like new shillings. She smiled. He was here two or three times a week now, ever since she'd quick-stepped with him down the dance hall. Tomorrow, perhaps, she would let him make his move. She would wander up the aisle, drop her torch by his seat, reach down, and flick the orange light up into their craning faces. They would both smile because they liked what they saw. But tonight she would be with Frank. They still had a little more story left.

Tilting her head, she stared back at Frank's projection booth. His beam of whirring light splayed out through the auditorium, spinning gold into the hair of all the people below. His silhouette peered through the small square of glass. It was almost time, perhaps, to change his reels. Two thousand foot spools, he had told her that first night. He had to watch for the cue marks, he explained: a small dark blotch in the corner of the screen that told him it was time to change reels. Or perhaps he peered out, trying to catch sight of her.

It still surprised Veronica – that they had noticed each other. They had spent their childhoods ignoring one another across their back-garden fences; each taught by their mothers that the children next door were not their kind. 'Did that Casey boy walk you home again last night?' her mother muttered almost every evening now over the steaming dinner plates. 'A projectionist?' 'The family's riddled with TB, you know. That'll be why he's not away fighting. Not fit...' Frank Casey, her mother insinuated, was not good enough for Veronica Palmer. And she was right, of course. Veronica knew. Frank knew too, even though he played the besotted fool sometimes and stared at her, all intense patience, as though he were waiting for her to turn and notice him when, god's sake, wasn't she already staring back into his blue eyes? An audience would sense it too, if they ever watched their story. From the first moment, they would anticipate the goodbye scene – its fading cigarette chill. Frank Casey, they would know, would never suit Veronica in the long-term: the long-term of houses and cradles and the shop-bought softness of babies' christening shawls. But for this moment, he was fine.

These scenes with Frank would always be her finest. She knew that already. The first night she brought a milky cocoa to his booth and he smiled at her and talked of arc lights. The electrodes inside – they move slowly apart, he said. They're not touching anymore but the current between them creates a blazing arc of light. They burn quick, though. You had to be careful the film didn't catch fire. Bogey and Bergman might blister into brown flames. She had laughed in delight. The second night, they kissed against the jangling locked doors. A few nights later, after everyone had left, they made a bed upon the red, tobacco-scented seats in the beautiful, edible darkness.

Most people, of course, would say he had taken advantage of her. And perhaps it was true. He had drawn out the hunger in her. But she was hardly some fool innocent. She knew how things went better than most of the folk in here, sucking on their flown-in dreams.

She flashed her torch onto her wristwatch. Only half an hour more.

Frank buttoned up his shirt while Veronica slid her bare feet into her high heels.

'We need to watch,' he sat back in the red seat and smiled. 'We'll get caught one night. Phyllis will come back to check the lights or the sirens will start...'

Veronica shrugged. 'That won't happen.'

'Always so sure, aren't you?' he tried to tease a curl of her hair, which was all unpinned now. She shook her head and stood up.

'No-one will catch us, Frank. We'll never do this again.'

She stared down at the carpet as she told him. Two flattened cigarette butts. A brown apple core. She didn't want to see how his face would change.

'What?'

'We always knew we'd have to end this one day. Didn't you say...?'

'What did I say?'

His voice had turned cold.

'Look, nobody's found us out yet, Frank. And we've had a great time. Haven't we, though? You've been great.'

'Great, eh?' he whispered.

His chair creaked as he leant forwards and picked up one of her kirby grips from the floor. He twirled it between his thumb and forefinger and then began to pull back one of the coppery legs.

'So, it's thanks for the memories, is it?' He looked up at her.

She straightened her skirt and brushed away a white thread. 'All the girls love you, Frank. You'll have yourself another sweetheart in a month's time. A girl like...'

'A girl like what, Veronica?'

A girl like Phyllis, she hoped. All bony arms and perfect cross-stitching. A girl who would know how to play second-best.

'And you'll have a man, will you? A man that's better suited? Is that it?'

Veronica began to put on her coat, not rushing at the buttons.

'Yes,' she nodded.

Frank was being more difficult than she had expected. Men should know not to prolong goodbye scenes. And he should know that better than most. The cue marks were up.

'People always stick to their own kind in the end,' she said, pushing her hands into her pockets. 'We can't change that.'

He laughed. 'You spout a few bitter truths and you think you sound wise? A few Casablanca lines? But you know? You just sound like your mother.'

Veronica's cheeks burned but she said nothing. She knew she would forgive him this cruelty later. Her mother had always been hateful to the Caseys, embarrassing them with a knock at their door and a bag of hand-me-down clothes in the morning then trotting past them on the high street the same afternoon. Why shouldn't Frank say it aloud, now of all times?

'I'm sorry, Vee,' he tried to grab for her hand. 'I didn't mean that. You're...'

She looked down into his face. He didn't look that much changed, not yet. The same eyes. The same maddening wisp of a smile.

'Of course you meant it,' she said. 'But I can't help how I am, can I? If it's in the blood...'

'You don't want to fight it?'

Veronica shook her head.

He blinked at her as though he had lost or gained focus. She wondered a moment if she would look in the mirror when she got home and see her own face changed. Her mother's quiet, slate-grey eyes staring back at her. Mirrors, though, told her a different story every other day. The trick was only to look, only to believe, on the good days.

'I'll think of you, Frank...' She reached out her hand towards his face.

He took her open hand and pressed the twisted kirby inside.

'I won't think of you at all,' he replied.

Veronica smiled. That was the spirit. Tell the customary lie.

She scooped up her handbag from the floor and clattered down the aisle towards the frosted streets outside.

He would never stop thinking of her. She glanced up at the clear night sky. He wouldn't be able to stop. Wouldn't they spend every night still bedded up next to one other? The walls between their two houses, the plasterboards between her bedroom and his, were newspaper-thin. Her stories would still print themselves on his wall. In the mornings, he would stand barefoot on his floorboards, wiping the sleep from his eyes, and the skirt she'd pull over her hips would brush against his calves. She would lift the stopper from her perfume bottle and he'd smell her apple-dabbed wrists. He would still hear the unclipping of her bra. 'Like ladybird's wings,' he'd told her one night. None of that would change. Not quite yet. They would share each other's bedrooms for at least a few weeks more, until she left, only a little hesitant, with the better-suited man.

Sushirexia

Whit Div Ye Want Me Tae Say?

Fiona Ashley

Ah only came in tae get ma smear test. Ah didnae want tae get a 'Well Woman' check fae onybody. Thon nurse is fair thraan, nae taakin no fir an answer. Next thing Ah ken, Ah'm oan the scales an she's tellin me ma BMI is ower thirty-five so Ah've tae come an spik tae you aboot ma lifestyle an ma food choices. Ah telt her there wis nae wye Ah wis spikin tae onybody aboot ma lifestyle an food choices, it wis naen o yer business, bit she started oan aboot the risk o developin type two diabetes in later life an the drain Ah wid be oan the National Health Service, nurses wastin their time taakin care o folk thit shoulda taen care o themsels, an did Ah ken there wis nae money fir the health service onymare? So here Ah am. Wha kint me likin sticky toffee puddin wis gaun tae be the final nail fir the NHS? Nae smilin? Fine then. Let's jist get this ower an done wie.

Ah started eatin whan Ah wis wee. Well, whit div ye want me tae say? Ah eat mair than Ah need tae? Ah'm nae feel, Ah ken thit Ah should be eatin fae the five main food groups, which Ah dae, an Ah ken Ah should be eatin five helpins o fruit an veg a day, which Ah dae, an Ah ken Ah should be exercisin fir thirty minutes aboot four times a wik, which Ah dinna. Ah'm nae the only ane. Ah bet thit if ye 'Well Womaned' ivery peer quine thit came in fir her smear test, ye wid be here spikin tae lassies thit like ice-cream an cake an mair puddin than's guid fir them, aa day, ivery day. That is whit yer daein, is it? That's whit wye Ah'm sittin here like a puddin masel.

Ah hinna aye bin this size ye ken, whan Ah wis at University Ah wis thin. Ye hid tae prioritise yer spendin then. Ah'm auld enough thit Ah goat a grant fae the government tae go tae the University. Jist as weel, cause ma Ma an Da werenae weel aff. Ah kin even mind foo much it wis, sixteen hundred pounds fir the year. Ah thocht Ah wis loaded. Ah seen realised it wisnae gaun tae go far though. By the time Ah hid payed fir books an fir rent, there wisnae much left tae divvy up intae food money, drinkin money, an drugs. Nae real drugs like heroin or onythin, jist some hash tae maak tea fae an a few Es whan Ah wis oot duncin. It disnae taak lang fir the weight tae faa aff ye whan ye owerspend oan yer drugs budget, Ah kin tell ye. Ma pal discovered the butcher doon the road selt whit he caaed 'pensioners' packs', a cling filmed mass o meat thit fell apart intae lorne saasages an mince an stuff like thon. It wis a life-saver fir us peer students. Ah loved University. Nae mither naggin at ye tae tidy up an dae yir studyin. Jist freedom. Ah hid pals an a lad an Ah wore size eight jeans. So Ah guess ye want tae ken whaur it aa wint wrang?

Ah goat ma degree an decided tae move back hame fir a joab. Couldnae afford tae buy somethin an tae tell ye the truth, Ah wis fed up wie pishy wee student flats. It's aa richt whan yer a student yersel bit nae ance yer lookin fir a joab. Ah wis lucky, goat a joab wie Peters an Strudy, the big accountants up past the fire station. They taen me oan as a graduate trainee an this guy caaed Tony wis ma boss. He wis a looker an he kint it. Aa the lassies in the accounts department dressed up tae try an catch his eyne. Ah run up ma only credit card tae buy suits, tae maak a guid impression. Ah certainly did that. Ah started sleepin wie Tony aifter aboot six months. Ah wish Ah could say thit it wis real love an he left his wife fir me, bit of course it wisnae an he didnae.

Ma wint nuts whan Ah telt her Ah handed in ma notice. She couldnae understand whit Ah wis daein, throwin awaa the chunce o steady money. A joab fir life she caaed it. Thon wis like the holy grail tae ma Ma. Ma Da's a fine bloke bit he couldnae keep a joab an wis aye jist workin fir agencies, casual labourin, thon kind o bloke. Ma wis affronted at haein sic a useless man, an whan she could finally haud her heid up in kirk an blaw aboot her cliver dochter, Ah hid goan an ruined aathin. Ah didnae tell her aboot the abortion, Ah mean, handin in ma notice hid bin trauma enough fir her.

Aifter that Ah goat a joab in the office at Robertson's factory, accounts bit nae graduate work or onythin. It did mean Ah could pit doon a deposit fir a flat though, nae posh suits needed at Robertson's. Fair leaves ye wie money in yer haund whan ye can buy yer claes fae Asda, even if yer buying a size twelve. That wis whan Ah met Craig. Craig wis couthy. Ah met him at Lacy's nightclub. Ah wis there wie a group o quines fae Robertson's an we wir a wee bit worse fir wear Ah must admit. Ah wis duncin an Ah seen this loon waatchin. Ah showed aff a wee bit, Ah suppose, an whan we wint tae the bar, he came ower an asked if Ah wanted tae go an get a kebab. Well, whit lassie can refuse sic an offer? We wint oot fir a few months afore he moved in wie me, it didnae maak sense tae keep payein rent fir his flat whan we wir aye thegither. Ma wis delighted thit Ah hid met Craig bit she nagged me tae get a ring oan ma finger. Nae laddie likes left overs, sae maak sure this ain bides. She his a wye wie words ma Ma.

We hid a laugh tae start wie. He worked fir the council, in the parks department, workin oot whit needed daein in the different parks an whan tae send men oot fir repairs, plantin flooers, that kind o thing. Ah niver thocht thon wis a real joab. Ah mean, ye dinna go tae the careers wifie at school an say ye want tae be responsible fir the flooers oan the roundabout on Mackie Drive, dae ye? Craig liked his joab though, didnae want tae go ony further in the council, hid nae aspirations fir becomin Heid o Parks or onything like that. Ah didnae mind at first, liked thit he wis relaxed an content wie himsel.

Ah cannae really say whan we stopped gaun oot an started haein Chinese takeaway as a treat oan a Friday nicht an mibbe an Indian oan a Saeturday. It jist kind o happened. We wir baith tired by the wikend, naen o us could be bothered cookin. Ma weight wint richt up. Ah pretended Ah didnae care an he pretended he didnae notice. Tae tell ye the truth, Ah think Craig liked me bein big. It wis like he hid got haud o me an didnae hae tae worry aboot keepin me, cause let's face it, wha would Ah hae run aff wie at thon size?

We muddled along, nae really gaun onywie an nae really as happy as we used tae be. He gaed me an engagement ring an Ah said aye, we wid get mairried. He wanted a bairn an Ah said okay. Ah ken it sounds bad, bit there wis nae spark onymare. Ah didnae feel thon churnin in yer belly whan ye ken he's gaun tae be hame in ten minutes, checkin yer watch an whan he comes in the door, kissin an kissin cause ye canna stop. Ah didnae dress fir him, didnae even dress fir masel. Ah didnae like lookin at masel in the mirror so gaun tae buy claes wis nae fun. Ah suppose haein a bairn wis ma wye o nae haein tae lose weight. Ye canna diet whan yer pregnant, can ye? He telt ma Ma we wir tryin fir a bairn an she wis delighted. Telt me thit Craig an me wir jist like her an ma Da. That wis whan Ah realised whit Ah wis daein. Ah telt Craig it wis aff an he moved oot. Ma didnae spik tae me fir four months.

Ye widda liked me back then, Ah wis thin again. Nithin like nerves an fear tae pit ye aff yer food. Ah kint leavin Craig wis the richt thing tae dae, bit Ah still missed him. Ah wis feart thit Ah wis riskin losin a fine enough bloke fir somethin thit micht niver show up. Ma wis oan at me tae spik tae Craig, sort it aa oot. Ah nearly did, bit then Ah taen a tumble tae masel, Ah wis only twenty-seven, this didnae hae tae be ma last chunce tae dae somethin wie ma life. Listen tae me, foo dramatic is that? Ah jined a gym an started gaun tae classes. Oh Ah wis gaun fir it, spinnin, weight trainin, Ah wis daein the works. Ah goat back doon tae a size twelve an started gaun oot wie ma pals again. It felt rare. Ah felt like Ah wis young an free. Ah wint hame wie different blokes ivery wikend, nae attachment, nae expectations, nae wantin onythin fae them. Dinna worry, Ah wis canny. A quine can get caught oot ance bit she disnae maak that mistake again. Ah even pushed fir promotion at Robertson's, an Ah goat it. Ah hid ma ane place, a guid joab, pals, Ah hid the lot. Ah even thocht aboot taakin a year aff an travellin. That widda bin rare, richt enough, bit Ah niver goat roon tae it, probably niver really hid the guts tae dae it if Ah'm honest wie ye.

Ma thirtieth wis great. Me an ma pals wint oot fir an Italian meal at thon posh place oan Back Wynd. The food wis gorgeous. Ah hid bruschetta an Pollo Roma an tiramisu an funcy coffee, an the quines hid goat me a chocolate cake fir ma birthday an the waiters brocht it oot an aa sung happy birthday tae me. Ah wis affronted bit it wis great fun. That wis whit sparked ma interest in cookin. Ah signed up fir a course in Italian cuisine at the college, jist a wee nicht class, bit it wis great fun. Ah learned Ah wis actually a nae bad cook. Ah stick tae the recipes though, nae sure aboot deviatin or maakin up ma ain dishes, bit Ah can cook maist stuff. Nae mair takeaways noo. Ah micht eat ower much, bit it's decent food Ah'm eating. Ye hiv tae taste as ye go along, hiv tae try new things. Ah love bakin, cakes an puddins especially. Ma custard is jist delicious, if Ah say so masel. Ye should try maakin yer ain, it taaks a bit o time bit Ah swear, ye winna buy the packet stuff again.

Ah met Catriona at the cookin. She jist hid somethin aboot her, Ah canna explain whit it wis, bit Ah wanted her tae like me. Ah started lookin forward tae the class, jist so Ah could be wie her. Ah even bocht new claes, nae fae Asda this time, an wore perfume. Ah wis gettin ready ane nicht fir class, whan Ah realised whit Ah wis daein, Ah wis tryin tae attract her. Ah swear tae God, ma bleed run cauld. Ah hid niver felt like that aboot a lassie afore, Ah mean, Ah hid worked ma wye roon maist o the eligible blokes in the toon. It sounds daft, bit ma first thocht wis, whit will ma Ma think? Ah nearly didnae go that nicht. Ah wis feart, feart aboot whaur Ah wis in danger o gaun, bit Ah wis mair feart that she wouldnae feel the same aboot me. Foo affronted wid Ah be then? Ah neednae hae worried. She wis lookin fir me coming in, she tried tae say she wisnae, later oan whan we wint fir a drink, bit Ah kint she wis. Whan Ah kissed her, it felt mare richt than ony kiss fae afore, nae Tony nor Craig, nae onybody. Ah suppose thon wis why Ah kint it wis the richt thing tae dae.

Ah'm proud o masel fir sittin here theday an tellin you aboot me an Catriona. It's taen me a lang time tae be able tae tell folk. Tellin Ma wis the hardest. She didnae get it, telt me she felt sick an she wid niver accept it, her quine couldnae be a pervert like thon. Ah did try, fir the first couple o years, asking Ma roon fir coffee an maakin sure Catriona wisnae gaun tae come hame, bit it upset me. Ma couldnae accept thit Ah wis happy. She kept tellin me aboot Craig an his new wife an their wee bairn, bonny wee thing, a loon, caaed Gavin. Ah sent a card whan Ma telt me, Ah wis chuffed fir Craig, nae jealous, that's fir sure. Tae be honest, Ah wis affronted at ma Ma. Ye niver see the worst o yer mither, dae ye? Yer trained tae only see the guid bits. Ah hid tae face up tae the fact thit Ma wisnae affa bright, couldnae see thit whit wis important wis me an foo Ah wis feelin, nae whit the wifies at kirk thocht aboot it. Ah stopped phonin her an she didnae phone me, she wis huffin cause Ah wis supposed tae be the ane maakin aa the runnin. It suited me fine. We hinna spoken noo fir ower a year.

Ye see, whit naebody seems tae get is Catriona loves me. She loves ma thighs the maist, especially thon saft bits on the inside. She touches me there an, weel, whit Ah'm tryin tae say is thit Ah dinna care whit size ma thighs are cause she disnae care. Ma weight gings up an doon, dependin oan whit Ah'm daein. Ah aye lose ma boobs whan Ah lose ony weight. Typical, is it nae? The ane place ye dinna want tae get ony smaaer is the first place the weight comes aff. Catriona loves ma boobs. Am Ah embarrassin ye? Ah can stop if ye like. Ah jist thocht it wis important tae tell ye whit Ah feel aboot ma weight. Ah love me cause she loves me, an that's it.

Ah ken that's nae whit ye want tae hear. Ah ken ye hiv bin taakin wee notes as Ah've bin spikin. Nae doobt ye noted doon ma relationship wie Tony an the abortion. Ah reckon ye've goat comfort eatin doon there anaa. Craig wis the man fir me an Ah pushed him awaa. Noo he's goat the bairn Ah goat rid o. Wrang again. Ah'm delighted fir Craig, he's nae a bad bloke, an he's goat whit he wanted, it jist wisnae whit Ah wanted. Then Ah think ye've goat somethin doon aboot ma Ma. Ivery quine his issues wie her Ma, bit Ah'm the ane wha broke aff fae her an Ah didnae turn tae food fir the love thit ma Mither shoulda gaen me.

Ah choose whit tae eat an whit tae leave. Ah understand aboot healthy eatin an aboot gettin enough fruit an veg. Ah dinna drink much onymare an Ah've niver smoked. Ah've goat a great joab an Ah'm in a rare relationship. Of course Ah hae regrets, bit wha hisnae? So, ye see, Ah'm nae eatin ma pain, Ah'm jist enjoying ma food.

Author
Biographies

Juana Adcock

Juana was born in Mexico in 1982. She writes poetry and prose in English, Spanish and Spanglish, and works as a freelance translator. In 2006-7 she was awarded a creative writing fellowship by the Centro de Escritores de Nuevo León. She has collaborated in several music projects in Mexico and in Scotland and is very interested in projects combining music and spoken word. She is currently studying the MLitt in Creative Writing at Glasgow University.

Fiona Ashley

Writes mostly about women because they are complex and fascinating creatures, and mostly in Scots because she loves its unique vocabulary and subtle tones. In her first novel and short story collection, she tried to show the humour and compassion that Scots like to hide from the rest of the world, through different characters interacting and how they reveal their personalities to each other. She finds people intriguing and an endless source of inspiration for her writing. She is currently living and writing in the North-East of Scotland with her partner and two children.

Elinor Brown

Elinor's short stories have been published in anthologies by Freight (*Let's Pretend*), Pulp Faction (*Allnighter*) and Egmont Press (*Love from Dad, Would you Believe It?*). Her first novel is a psychological drama set in Sardinia. She has also written a collection of fairytales. In 2010 she was short-listed for the Sceptre prize. Elinor is co-editor of the *Brown Williams Journal*. For more information, visit www.elinorbrown.com

Nikki Cameron

Born in Forres but has spent most of the last twenty five years living on the Isle of Bute. She is now based in Glasgow where she teaches creative writing. She also works with children and adults using story-telling and expressive writing as therapeutic tools.

Jackie Copleton

Having studied English literature at Cambridge University, she moved to Japan to teach. On her return to Britain, she worked as a newspaper sub-editor based in Glasgow and London. She left London in 2008 to begin her MLitt at Glasgow University and is currently writing her first novel.

Frances Corr

Frances started writing in a community group in Glasgow's Year of Culture 1990. This led to writing a play for The Lone Rangers which toured community venues round Glasgow. She went on to write 'The Price of Eggs' for the Ramshorn Theatre Company, and 'Options' for Dogsbodies in 1994. A short drama documentary for Schools Television followed on the subject of dyslexia. In 1999 she wrote 'Glasgow's Fallen Women' which was performed at the Citizen's Theatre. In 2000 she was part of a group of writers who wrote '24 Hours' for 7:84. She also paints for her sanity.

Jill Creighton

Jill lives and works in Glasgow. Currently, she is studying, part-time, at The University of Glasgow, where she is half-way through the MLitt in Creative Writing. Thanks to her trusty laptop, Jill writes most days. She combines studying and writing with a career in Public Relations. Over the last year, Jill's short story Ten Minutes has been published at www.from-glasgowtosaturn.com (May 2009) and she has set up The Reading Party, a series of private and public gatherings, where fellow Creative Writing students read their work aloud. Jill is working on her first novel, a quirky whodunit set in Glasgow.

Carol Farrelly

Carol currently lives and works in Edinburgh. She has a DPhil on Hardy's novels. (Her love for Hardy survives...) She has lived in Bologna, London, Brighton and Oxford. Bologna, London and her hometown of Glasgow are the places she misses. She has several short stories published or forthcoming in literary magazines such as *Stand*, *Markings*, *Litro*, *Random Acts of Writing* and the *Willseden New Short Stories 3* anthology. Her work has been shortlisted for both the Asham Award and the Willesden Herald Short Story Prize.

Anne Hamilton

After several non-fiction publications, Anne completed her first full length work in 2006. A travel memoir of Bangladesh, with a strong narrative voice, this book found a literary agent, inspired the setting up of an international charity, and still seeks a publisher. Anne has had modest success in a number of writing competitions, including the long-list of the Fish Prize and second prize in a University of Edinburgh annual award. She is now embarking on a PhD in Creative Writing at Glasgow University, and is working on a novel.

Ulrich Hansen

Originally from Denmark, Ulrich currently lives and works in Glasgow. His writing has appeared in anthologies, literary journals and online. Together with a Mexican and an American writer he is co-writing an OuLiPoean novel. Apart from literary collaborations he has also worked together with Mari Lagerquist and Robertina Sebjanic on installations and most recently a video project. His latest piece is a contribution to a project that the Swedish artist Thomas Dahl will take to a forthcoming performance festival in Paris. Ulrich is a member of Shift and is currently writing his first novel. Ulrich is the recipient of the 2010 Curtis Brown prize for the Best Fiction Writer.

Vicki Husband

Vicki has published poetry and short fiction in: *The North*, *Mslexia* and *Aesthetica* magazines, *New Writing Scotland 25 & 27*, *Present Poets* anthology, and on *LauraHird.com* website. Vicki was a runner-up in the Edwin Morgan International Poetry Competition 2008. She works as an Occupational Therapist for the NHS.

Elisabeth Ingram

Received a *Dewar Arts Award* in 2009 which funded her postgraduate study at Glasgow University. During her studies she co-edited Glasgow University's *From Glasgow to Saturn*, and founded *The Glasgow Student Short Story Prize*, with the aim of supporting and promoting other new writers. Her first published story '*Green Line*' appeared in 2009 anthology '*In the Event of Fire – New Writing Scotland No. 27*'. She previously studied English Literature at Oxford University, and is currently working on writing a collection of stories.

Joyce Ito

Joyce is forty six and a (mostly) enthusiastic mother of two teenage girls: a scientist to trade and wordsmith by inclination. A gruesome bout of illness in 2005 (a lymphoma) gave her the time to start scribbling. She kept a diary recording the science behind her illness and treatment as well as the often black comedy of family life during treatment; some of it was serialised in a national newspaper; a short story about losing her hair was published in *Riptide*. She now writes fiction and is working on a first novel.

John Jennett

Son of a famous brain surgeon, John Jennett trained in music, going on to become a successful hotelier then sailing skipper. Shortlisted for the *Fish One Page Prize*, he was runner up in the prestigious 2009 National Gallery literary competition. In March 2010 John was awarded the Sceptre prize for new writing. *Gutter Magazine* selected John's fiction for its showcase launch, whilst his poetry has been published in the UK and Ireland. John studied with bestselling novelists Suzanne Berne and Niall Williams then Glasgow University writers under Professor Michael Schmidt. John says that he writes under an "inescapable influence" from the physical and cultural landscape of his native Scottish Highlands and Islands.

Arthur Ker

was raised in Argyll, studied design at Glasgow School of Art, and worked as a design lecturer in further education for twenty-five years. He has had short stories and poems published in literary magazines including *Words*, *Cencrastus*, *Northwords*, *The Eildon Tree*, *From Glasgow to Saturn* and *Poetry Life*. He has been short-listed and awarded highly commended in several national writing competitions. His first novel was short-listed for, but unfortunately didn't win, The Dundee Book Prize (£6,000 + publication by Polygon). The novel is currently undergoing yet another edit, the last hopefully.

Kirsty Logan

Kirsty is a writer (kirstylogan.com), editor (fracturedwest.com), teacher, grad student, and general layabout. She likes red wine, retold fairy-tales, and sticking pins in maps. She dreams of one day being published by Virago, Alyson Books, or in one of those orange Penguins. She lives in the south side with her girlfriend.

Neil Mackay

Neil is a multi-award winning investigative journalist, non-fiction author and film-maker. Originally from Northern Ireland, he lives in Glasgow with his partner and two children and is working on his first novel, a darkly comic study of childhood violence set in Ulster at the height of the Troubles. His journalism has been described by acclaimed writer and broadcaster John Pilger as 'the stuff of newspaper legend', and his television documentary work has been Bafta-nominated. His journalism covers crime, extremism, terrorism and intelligence, as well as issues such as child-poverty, social exclusion, homelessness and addiction.

Harry McDonald

Lives in Glasgow with his wife and two daughters. He has recently completed the final year in the MLitt course in Creative Writing at Glasgow University. He has previously had fiction and poetry published in literary magazines and anthologies, both in print and online; including poetry in the current edition of NWS 2009. He is happiest writing short stories under the influence of the three wise men: Hemingway, Joyce and Maupassant, but also enjoys working with other forms of writing, such as poetry and novel writing. He is currently working on a screenplay for a World War 1 musical.

Julie McDowall
Julie is 28 and was born in Rutherglen. She studied History at Glasgow University. She is working on a novel set in Blackpool and London during the Second World War.

Linda Duncan McLaughlin
Linda lives and works mostly in Glasgow. She has been a professional actor for 16 years and first started writing seriously with the aim of producing starring parts for herself. Over the past couple of years, however, she's found that there's a lot of fun to be had in fiction and poetry, and is enjoying exploring these avenues, and gaining First Prize in The Glasgow Student Short Story Prize competition of 2009. She was awarded one of the first bursaries on *The Fielding Programme Hothouse* at Cove Park, and now intends to spend as much time as possible in staring at beautiful scenery and thinking about – and perhaps even producing – good writing.

Duncan Muir
Duncan grew up on an old farm in the Hebrides where he spent much of his childhood riding horses on the beach and terrorising small furry animals. He writes poetry and short stories and has lived in Glasgow on and off for the last nine years.

Victoria Murphy
Victoria worked as a staff feature writer on women's magazines, winning two major awards (PPA & IPC). Writing about a huge variety of subjects, her interviews ranged from Prime Ministers to pop stars. She left London to undertake her MLitt in Women's Studies at Trinity College, Dublin, also freelancing for the Irish Times and writing the (authorised) biography of a senior Irish politician, published by Basement Press. Victoria returned to London to help set up a new magazine but gave up her career due to

illness. She now lives in Glasgow with her husband and children and concentrates on writing fiction.

Mark Russell

Mark has had poetry and prose published in West Coast Magazine, Rebel Inc. and Fromglasgowtosaturn. His plays have been performed by The Playwrights' Studio, Scotland, at Glasgow's West End festival, and by Edinburgh-based Siege Perilous. He supports Bristol City Football Club.

Alison Ryan

Alison has studied and worked in the area of social policy for the past fifteen years. She manages a voluntary organisation which supports women who have experienced domestic abuse. She writes as a feminist and her writing is informed by issues of inequality, both class and gender. She is also interested in gender identity and often explores this in her writing. Alison is currently working on her first novel, which she started three years ago when she took up evening classes in creative writing. Alison is studying for the MLitt in Creative Writing, part-time at Glasgow University, and lectures at Strathclyde University on the Modern Novel.

Genevieve Schrier

Genevieve is an American fiction writer who is currently working on both a short story collection and a first novel. In addition to penning fiction, she is a freelance journalist, focusing on travel, pop culture, and fashion at both the national and local level back in the U.S. She likes and is influenced by airplanes, airports, cooking, and sports, and is constantly on the lookout for projects that combine these elements. While she'll continue to live in Glasgow after the completion of the MLitt, her dog unfortunately will remain stateside.

Martin Shannon

Born in Paisley in 1965, Martin Shannon has worked in journalism and public relations since passing unnoticed through classrooms and cloisters to kitchens at parties. His unshakable belief in literature offers him hope for salvation or, at the very least, a means of getting even. His short stories have been published in a variety of literary and popular magazines and The Guardian newspaper described his debut novel *The Tin Man* (11:9) as 'an uncommonly authentic voice that suggests an engaging new talent.' In 2010, he made the shortlist for the Sceptre prize.

Rob A. Smith

Born in Chesterfield, Rob headed south to study Zoology at Oxford University, followed by postgraduate research in Cell Biology at Southampton University. Nearly thirty years ago, he overshot Derbyshire by coming to work in Glasgow, where he has lived ever since. He has published many scientific articles from his day job, but only recently has he started to indulge a secret ambition to write creatively. He is currently studying part time on the Glasgow University MLitt course. He enjoys writing short stories: his characters are often depressed and/or suicidal, reflecting his cheerful and optimistic view of life.

Kathrine Sowerby

Kathrine has frequently exhibited her written work in a visual art context and has produced editions of hand bound books including *Weakly Reading (a revolution)*, *An Argument about Discovery*, and *Too Full for Sound*. Her 15 page poem *Unnecessarily Emphatic* was adapted for theatre and performed at Columbia University, New York. Kathrine lives in Glasgow with her partner and three children. She is currently working on her first novel.

William Stevenson

William grew up in Glasgow, Scotland. He studied at Glasgow Caledonian University and now works begrudgingly in Edinburgh. He enjoys reading, cinema, and playing tennis and squash in his free time. His writing to date has been mainly Haruki Murakami-inspired short stories and one long novel about the pitfalls of cloning Vincent Van Gogh. *The Inferior Cave* is his first published work. He is currently working on his first 'proper' novel, a story about six dead horses and an angry middle-aged woman known only as 'The Sheriff'.

Jose C. Velazquez

Jose was born in Masaya, Nicaragua, a small city in the shadow of a very active volcano. As it is with Latin America, a revolution broke out and his family emmigrated to the United States. He grew up in the suburbs of Washington, D.C. and has lived in the District, Los Angeles, Miami and now Glasgow. He enjoys eating, drinking, reading, writing and images projected from rectangular screens of all sizes. He is completing an MLitt at the University of Glasgow and should start the PhD in Literature with a focus in creative writing in the fall.

Sarah Ward

Sarah writes short stories and is currently working on a novel set during Stanley Spencer's time in Port Glasgow. During the day she manages a community centre. She lives in Glasgow with her family.

J.L. Williams

JL was born in New Jersey and studied at Wellesley College with the poet Frank Bidart. She has been published in *The Wolf*, *Poetry Salzburg Review*, *Poetry Wales*, *Fulcrum* and *Stand* and was awarded the Edwin Morgan Travel Bursary 2009 from the Scottish Arts Trust to write a collection of poetry inspired by Ovid's *Metamorphoses* on the Aeolian Isles which can be found at http://jlwpoetry.googlepages.com